Praise for *The Jewel of the North*

"A dazzling display of raucous American history and the seamless blending of perfectly drawn vignettes of some of the most colorful figures of the period into a tale of high adventure and mystery. London is the perfect two-fisted literary hero. King pulls it all together in a tale full of back alleys, bawdy encounters, and violent twists in the style of a turn-of-the-nineteenth-century adventure. May this be the first of many Jack London tales from the masterful Peter King."   —Stuart M. Kaminsky

"A jewel of a book. Cleverly plotted and written with a rare combination of gusto and suspense, this one will keep you reading and guessing to the end. Surely King has led a previous life among the hard cases and colorful characters of post–Gold Rush San Francisco's Barbary Coast. . . . London himself would heartily approve, and probably not change a word."   —John Lutz

"Aficionados of the historical mystery will be delighted with *The Jewel of the North*. The sense of decadent, turn-of-the-century San Francisco and its gold rush fever is as thick as a Pacific fogbank."   —Les Standiford

"[An] engaging mystery that seems to leave out none of the raucous places or eccentric personages familiar in the city at that time."   —*January Magazine*

continued . . .

"King hasn't lost his cutting edge or his wry humor. . . . Jack London is surely an inspired choice for a sleuth."
—*Booknews* from The Poisoned Pen

"The hard-living, hard-drinking Jack London makes an excellent detective and Peter King brings him fully to life. . . . Pure entertainment. Not only are we treated to a cunningly deceptive mystery, but the cast of characters reads like a Who's Who of the time." —*Romantic Times* (Top Pick)

Praise for Peter King's previous mysteries

"King's novels are filled with cliff-hanger endings and near-death adventures. . . . A fun read."
—*Ventura County Star* (CA)

"An appealing detective series. . . . [King] keeps the well-spiced plot bubbling along."
—*People* (Beach Book of the Week)

"[An] engaging hero."
—*Alfred Hitchcock's Mystery Magazine*

"Fast, fun, delightful characters." —*Library Journal*

DEAD MAN'S COAST

A JACK LONDON MYSTERY

BY
PETER KING

A SIGNET BOOK

SIGNET
Published by New American Library, a division of
Penguin Putnam Inc., 375 Hudson Street,
New York, New York 10014, U.S.A.
Penguin Books Ltd, 80 Strand,
Longon WC2R 0RL, England
Penguin Books Australia Ltd, Ringwood,
Victoria, Australia
Penguin Books Canada Ltd, 10 Alcorn Avenue,
Toronto, Ontario, Canada M4V 3B2
Penguin Books (N.Z.) Ltd, 182–190 Wairau Road,
Auckland 10, New Zealand

Penguin Books Ltd, Registered Offices:
Harmondsworth, Middlesex, England

First published by Signet, an imprint of New American Library,
a division of Penguin Putnam Inc.

First Printing, May 2002
10 9 8 7 6 5 4 3 2 1

PUBLISHER'S NOTE
This is a work of fiction. Names, characters, places, and incidents either are the
product of the author's imagination or are used fictitiously, and any resemblance to
actual persons, living or dead, business establishments, events, or locales is entirely
coincidental.

Chapter 1

The ghostly white fog writhed over San Francisco Bay like a snake. It crept along alleys and up hills, leaving only the tops of buildings exposed, while on the ground pedestrians cursed, cable cars clanged incessantly and even horses drawing vehicles trod uncertainly.

The fog was thickest along the waterfront, where the dark bulks of freighters etched splotchy black stains against the fogbanks that heaved and shifted over the water. The shadows hid two furtive figures and the fog cloaked them further.

One was a big, heavyset man in a police uniform. He had long arms and a powerful chest. He wrapped his arms around his chest and hugged himself in an effort to stave off the damp fog that was chilling his bones.

The other was twenty years younger, with unruly brown hair that forced its way out from the seaman's cap jammed tightly on his head. His old seaman's jacket was buttoned firmly and he resisted the urge to stamp his feet to sustain circulation.

It was a nasty night for a stakeout, Jack London was thinking. Nobody could see him and Officer Healey, but then they could not see much either. How had he gotten himself into this? he asked silently. He thought back to the previous day.

Jack had walked up to the bar at the Grasshopper Saloon, where the barkeep, Mickey, promptly placed a glass of beer in front of him and said, "Grady wants to see you."

Jack had known Sergeant Grady for many years. At the age of fifteen, Jack had earned for himself the title of Prince of the Oyster Pirates. Older and more experienced men had yielded the title to him, for Jack had the daring and imagination of youth coupled with natural physical ability, a rare understanding of boats and the ocean, and a friendly disposition that prevented the kind of jealousy that often leads to betrayal. Jack's seamanship was second to none on the California coast, and he and his boat earned as much as two hundred dollars on a good night, robbing the oyster beds.

It had been the sergeant's unhappy task to catch the elusive young Jack London, and the policeman had been at the end of his tether and facing demotion when he'd had his inspiration. He sought out Jack and offered him a job on the California Fish Patrol. His job would be to catch the oyster pirates who were causing such havoc in San Francisco Bay.

Jack had a hard time keeping himself from laughing. Surely Grady knew—yes, of course he did. This was a last desperate try to regain authority over the choppy waters of the bay and the pirates who plagued them.

No one ever knew exactly what Grady said. He never told and neither did Jack—despite the fact that Jack continued to write the stories that he hoped would one day make him famous. The story of how he was recruited would have made a great plot but it never appeared in print. Nevertheless, the unthinkable happened—the two-hundred-dollar-a-night pirate changed his profession to that of a five-dollar-a-week law enforcement officer.

Grady had received Jack cordially when he responded to the message left at the bar of the Grasshopper. "How's life, young fellow? Selling a lot of stories?" He was a gruff, serious man and one of the few honest cops on the Barbary Coast. His light manner now meant he wanted something.

"Not quite enough," Jack told him.

"Like to help us out? Won't be much but it'll buy you a few meals."

"Always ready to help the law," said Jack, although at the moment he was more interested in the money.

"We've had a tip that there's somebody important coming ashore tomorrow night. West end of the Embarcadero, we think."

Jack nodded. Past the docked ships was a stretch of coast that was popular with smugglers, risky because it was so convenient and therefore much used, but a favorite because it was close to the sanctuary of the city. On a foggy night the odds would be in favor of the smuggler, regardless of how many men the police might deploy.

"You say somebody. It's not a cargo, then?"

"We think it's a person," said Grady. Jack wondered if he was unwilling to say more or if that was the extent of his information. Grady's answer made a difference in how an interception might be planned. In Jack's smuggling days, a man coming ashore along that stretch from a small boat would be hampered by a net heavy with oysters and would be more likely to beach farther west.

"Gonna put you with Healey," Grady told him. Jack nodded. Healey was another of San Francisco's many Irish cops and Jack knew him to be a sound, reliable man.

"One man?" he queried.

"Might be one, might be two," Grady said cautiously.

"Important, you say?"

Grady waved a hand uncertainly. "Can't tell you any names 'cause I don't know 'em. Maybe somebody up there knows but I don't. I do know that there'll be hell to pay if we don't catch him."

And it doesn't seem likely that we will, Jack was thinking as he stood there tonight, recalling Grady's words and trying to stop a shiver. The fog was getting thicker and no wind had yet risen to disperse it. He and Officer Healey had stood there for nearly three hours now and the cold was getting more biting.

A sound came from the shifting white wall near them. Both men turned and a man called out, identifying himself. "It's Bristow!" He emerged, a tall, energetic man in a heavy overcoat. Captain Bristow was an efficient if not too popular officer, and Jack reflected that the mysterious quarry must be really important to merit so many men to catch him.

Bristow joined them, his breath coming out in pale wisps. "We've been misled," he told them harshly. "This was a decoy. A shipload of Chinese is coming in at Destiny Cove."

"That's ten miles up the coast," Jack said. Bristow nodded curtly. He had not been in favor of hiring a former oyster pirate to help them but he had been overruled.

"You two better stay here another couple of hours and keep your eyes open. The rest of us are going up to Destiny Cove. We may still be in time to catch them."

Bristow disappeared back into the fog and Jack and Healey looked at one another. "Guess we can talk at least," said Grady. They chatted for a while, mainly about shared acquaintances on both sides of the law.

The forthcoming election was a subject of much controversy, and Jack's socialist convictions made him an ardent debater on the issues. Healey held to opposing political beliefs. They reached a point of heated disagreement, then both laughed. "You'll see how wrong you are at next week's polls," promised Healey. He slapped his hands together. "How about a stroll?" he proposed. "Orders said to stay here but they didn't say not to move around."

They walked cautiously among the ropes and bollards on the waterfront. At the end of the docks, paths led up among the rocky crags. The water lapped softly, muffled by the fog. "Better go back," said Healey. "We'll give our orders another half hour, then call it a night."

They had turned to saunter back when Jack raised a hand

in warning. Healey opened his mouth to speak but held his tongue. Jack tapped his ear and they both listened intently. Only the occasional splash of the water broke through the clammy fog. Jack shrugged in apology for mistakenly thinking that he had heard—then his head jerked around. Healey heard it too this time: a scrape of boots on the sand around the rocks.

There was no cover. Healey pointed to the bay. Jack nodded and they crept silently in that direction. A black shape loomed high above them, the bow end of a big freighter. They might not be seen here, because whoever was coming over the rocks would be heading the other way, toward the city.

It was oppressively quiet. The two men stood motionless. Time seemed unending, and Healey was just about to speak when footsteps could be heard along the dock. They waited. Slowly, the footsteps came nearer.

A gentle breeze rippled across the bay. It was the first stirring of air the whole night, and it came just in time to peel away some of the fog and reveal two figures in dark clothes. They saw Healey and Jack at the same moment.

"Let's get 'em, Jack!" Healey called out.

The two figures were slow to react and were quickly overtaken. Healey grabbed the nearest, who tried to squirm away, but Healey held on to his overcoat. Jack went for the other, who was more agile and not averse to a fight. He swung a punch at Jack, who swayed and took it on the shoulder. In turn, he jabbed a fist viciously and heard a gasp of pain.

His opponent pulled away but Jack moved after him. The man turned and looped a blow at Jack's head. It missed his ear but made his head ring. He took a blow to the body, then retaliated with a rapid one-two. Over the other's shoulder, he could see Healey and his man locked in a close struggle. Wrong tactics to use against Healey, Jack thought fleetingly; the officer's long arms would squeeze the breath out of him.

His own adversary came back with a firm right-hander that sent a stab of pain through Jack's lower ribs. A left followed, aimed at his chin, but Jack blocked it. The man grunted as Jack punched viciously, speed and power making up for lack of accuracy as he tried to get in as many blows as he could. The grunts grew louder; then the man moved in, trying to get inside Jack's punches.

A yell from the other two told of Healey's bear hug taking its toll. The man was almost as big as Healey but not as beefy in build. Jack pushed his man away as they came face-to-face. He was about to unleash a devastating left when, without warning, the other kicked out. A boot caught him on the kneecap and he groaned as a fiery pain spread. The man turned, jabbed Healey in the back with a kidney punch, gasped out some words, and the two intruders ran, stumbling, and vanished in the fog.

Jack tried to follow them but his knee was in agony, and he was forced to give up and return to Healey, who was doubled over, breathing heavily. He straightened with difficulty, his face contorted with pain. Gradually he recovered and was able to speak.

"A fine pair we are," he gasped. "If we hadn't been outnumbered . . ."

Jack chuckled despite his knee, which felt three times its normal size. "Is that what you'll put in your report? Five of them, each as big as a house?"

Healey gurgled a laugh. As both returned to normal, Healey asked, "Did you get a look at your man?"

"I didn't recognize him," Jack said, "but I'd know him again."

"Good," Healey said. "We'll arrange a few lineups for you tomorrow. Maybe you'll spot him."

Healey blew out a lungful of damp air and breathed in another as if it were the sweetest he had ever tasted.

"What about you?" asked Jack.

"Never set eyes on my man before." Healey's words

were slow and Jack looked at him as the other added, "But I know his name."

"How do you know that?"

"Because I've been staring at his face for days."

"What do you mean?" asked Jack, bewildered.

"His face is on a wanted poster in precinct headquarters."

"You're sure?"

"Positive. He's Lou Kandel, the finest safecracker in the country—although that's not why he's wanted so badly."

"Go on," urged Jack. "Why is that?"

"It's because he escaped from San Quentin last week. He was awaiting the death penalty for killing a guard who interrupted him while he was pulling his latest job."

"So now he's here," Jack said. The pain in his knee was easing up and the slight limp would be gone by morning. Healey was back to his hale and hearty self. Scuffles in the dangerous Barbary Coast section were common and the sergeant was no stranger to violent resistance.

They walked through the fog and into the nearest alley. The heat from the buildings had thinned the air and visibility was better. It was enough to reveal a man watching them from a doorway just a few yards away.

Corpulent and squat-looking, like a large toad, he held a bone-handled blackthorn walking stick in front of him. A broad-brimmed hat was pulled down over his forehead, making his face difficult to see. A tweed suit and vest made him look even fatter and a gold watch chain was draped across his chest. A droopy gray mustache straggled wide and gold-rimmed spectacles glinted in the dim light.

He might have been just standing there but Jack had an uncanny feeling that he was watching them. He did not look away as Jack and Healey stared at him. His appearance was intimidating, and even motionless he gave the impression of being threatening.

Another man, spare and lively, appeared out of the fog and came directly to Jack and Healey. "Does one of you

gentlemen have a light?" he asked, taking a large black stogie from a jacket pocket and confronting them.

Both said no, and the man nodded as if he'd expected the
answer. He stepped aside, gave them a polite nod and
walked off.

Jack and Officer Healey looked at the doorway. The man
who had been standing there was gone. Healey frowned.
Then he went and tried the door. It was locked.

Chapter 2

Jack began his writing the next day after the big brass alarm clock had woken him promptly at five o'clock, as it did every morning. He tried to write a thousand words a day, but were they always the words he wanted?

After his sale of "To the Man on Trail" to *Overland Monthly*, Jack had been exultant that his writing career was launched, but it was not to be that easy and rejection slips followed in every mail.

His most recent success had been a story that he had originally called "Northland Incident" but which had been renamed "The White Silence." It was the tale of the Malemute Kid and his sidekick, Mason, struggling to survive across two hundred miles of ice and snow with only six days' food for themselves and none for the dogs. Jack was especially pleased with his descriptions of the elements, hostile to man and his intrusion into the natural world. It had helped Jack's career tremendously when it had appeared in the *Overland Monthly*, and it had caused the *San Francisco Chronicle* to be unusually complimentary in its review.

Jack was still elated over this success, especially after the story had been rejected by *Godey's Magazine*. He had learned a good lesson there: Don't despair; keep on sending in submissions.

That had been some time ago though. Submissions since then had been returned with infuriating frequency, and it was only the recurrent reminder to himself that he had sold and therefore could sell again that kept him going. It was with a sense of desperation that he forced himself to continue.

He wanted to call the one he was working on now "An Odyssey of the North," for it would again draw on his experiences in the frozen wastes of the Yukon. It seemed to be coming along, he felt, as the afternoon drew on. Another few days . . . At least he had the couple of dollars that Grady had paid him for the vigil last night, so he would not be forced to an extreme remedy for poverty.

When he caught himself yawning for the third time he decided he had written enough. He was hungry too, having eaten nothing since a sparse breakfast. This was his regular routine, for he could eat free at the bars on the Barbary Coast and he made that his evening meal.

His first stop was Belinda's Melodeon. In reality a music hall, it offered entertainment that was occasionally ambitious but other times coarse and vulgar. There was no dancing, and an admission fee of twenty-five cents was charged. Lottie Crabtree, Eddie Foy and James A. Hearne had all appeared there. Drugging and robbery on the premises were forbidden and gambling was not permitted in the saloon area, but private rooms were available upstairs for any purpose desired by the person paying for them. It was rumored that big-stakes poker games were held.

Right now, there was a hiatus between shows, so the admission fee was waived. Posters outside announced that the next series of shows would start in a few days.

Jack ordered a beer. It was not too busy and only a couple of prospectors stood at the bar, arguing over where to return in Alaska to make a real fortune. Jack listened to them in amusement. He decided not to pass along his own experience in the Yukon, from where he had returned with only four dollars and fifty cents' worth of gold in his pocket.

He chatted with the bartender; then one of the waiter girls he knew came over, bored with not enough tables yet filled to make much money in tips. After talking to her, he was about to drink up and leave when the swing doors opened and Sergeant Grady came in.

"Tried a couple of places," Grady said, joining him at the bar. "Said you might be here."

Jack motioned to the bartender to bring Grady a beer. "Looking for me?" he asked. "Another job?"

Grady waited until the beer came. He drank half of it, then looked into the glass as he put it down. "Got bad news," he said heavily.

Jack waited.

"Healey's dead," Grady said in a flat tone.

"Dead? But he was fine last night. What—?"

Grady put a hand on Jack's arm. "I know, lad. He finished his shift last night after he left you. Came in this afternoon, and an hour later he was supposed to link up with a man from the Twelfth Precinct. This officer went looking for him, found him in an alley off Sacramento Street, dead."

Jack finished his beer and ordered another. "How?"

"Garroted." It was a common murder method on the Barbary Coast.

"Any idea why?" asked Jack, still stunned by the news.

"That's what the captain thought I should ask you."

"Did Healey file a report when he came in last night?" Jack asked.

"Sure. Reported seeing a man he was sure was Lou Kandel. I guess you were with him at the time."

"That's right. Only I didn't know who this Kandel was. Healey said he recognized him from seeing his face on the wanted posters at the station."

"Well, it's causing a panic down there, I can tell you. We don't like officers being killed."

"Nor do I," said Jack.

"You saw him," Grady said urgently. "This Kandel."

"You think he killed Healey? Why? Because he recognized him?"

"Captain's theory is that Kandel killed Healey before he could identify him—or so he thought. Healey had a great memory for faces but Kandel wouldn't know that. He must have hoped he could get Healey before he could spread the word about Kandel being in town."

"Did Healey say anything about the other man?"

"The one who was with Kandel?"

"No. Later on, we saw a man in a doorway. He was watching us; then he disappeared."

"Did Healey know him?"

"He didn't say anything," Jack said.

"What makes you think he had anything to do with this?"

"Just a gut feeling. Nasty-looking fellow."

Jack described him but Grady shook his head. "Can't think of any villains who look like that." Grady finished his beer and waved for another. "Anyway, the captain wants to talk to you."

"Me?" said Jack. "Why? Wants to hire me again?"

"He doesn't tell me much," Grady said and sighed. "Might be something like that. This is going to blow up big. We're gonna need all the help we can get."

"All right," Jack said. "When?"

"Like right now," said Grady. "Soon as I empty this."

He drank most of the beer in a couple of huge gulps.

Pausing for breath, he said to Jack, "I'm sure you must be thinking what I'm thinking."

"I am," Jack agreed. "If Kandel didn't want Healey to identify him, he won't want me to either."

"Right." Grady was eyeing the young man appraisingly. "I didn't want to scare you but you've been around enough. Just be careful."

Jack grinned his appreciation of the other's concern. "Thanks, Grady. Now—you want to be my bodyguard as far as the station?"

Jack found himself facing Captain John Morley in the small room at the precinct station. Morley was a compact man with a competent air. His face was not remarkable but the eyes were steady and the chin firm. He looked more like a bank manager, Jack thought. The two were not acquainted, though Jack had heard Morley's name. He was said to be hard but fair and he got results. He seemed to have some special standing in the San Francisco police force, only nobody outside the force knew what it was.

It was quickly apparent that Morley knew a lot more about Jack than Jack knew about him. "So your days on the Fish Patrol are over and now you're a writer, eh? And I hear that you were helpful to us in a private capacity during that affair of those music hall girls who were murdered."

Jack nodded. He had been contacted by Ted Townrow, a former classmate at the University of California at Berkeley who was now a top aide to the mayor of San Francisco, Hiram T. Nelson. The mayor had asked Jack to be an undercover agent on that occasion and Jack had played an important role in the recovery of a load of bullion hijacked on its way from the Alaskan goldfields.

He waited for the captain to move on to the subject of the murder of Officer Healey.

"We want to ask that you join us temporarily as a volunteer in another matter." He paused, waiting for Jack's reaction. Jack tried to look encouraging but was unwilling to commit until he knew more.

"The Barbary Coast is having a famous visitor," Morley went on. "That visitor's life will be in danger. We in the police will be doing all we can. Leave will be canceled and all auxiliaries and specials will be called in, but we still need a few more qualified men. I would like you to be one of them."

Jack tried not to show his surprise. Morley took Jack's reaction for hesitation for a different reason. "It won't require too much of a change from your present life. I believe that you spend time in the bars and the music halls on the Coast—ah, gathering material for your stories. That is where you can make your biggest contribution to our effort.

Gossip, information, hints, suspicions—any of these may make a huge difference. We will pay you five dollars a day, and if you need money for payment to informers, that can be arranged."

Jack was balancing his surprise against his curiosity. Who was this famous visitor? Could it be Teddy Roosevelt? No, he had just been in San Francisco. A foreign dignitary, such as the emperor of Japan?

Morley showed no sign of being aware of Jack's interest in the identity of the visitor. "I hope you'll agree to help us," he said. "I'm told you know the Barbary Coast as well as any man in this state. You've faced peril many times—at sea and up there in the frozen North, as well as here in what our newspapers describe as the most dangerous city in the world. Well, there may be some risk, but gathering information to protect our visitor may help save her life."

Her! Jack could contain himself no longer. "I think I can help," he said cautiously, "but I'd like to know who it is I'm protecting. I mean, it makes a difference."

"Of course," said Morley. "The name will be all over the city tomorrow anyway—you'll see it on every billboard. It's Belle Conquest."

Names had been flashing through Jack's mind. Lillie Langtry, Sarah Bernhardt, Lillian Russell—but Belle Conquest! The greatest star of the American stage. Belle of Broadway they called her, while at the same time she was known as the Wickedest Woman in the World.

Morley smiled thinly at Jack's involuntary reaction. "Yes, and she's coming here."

"Has her life been threatened?" Jack asked. "You seem to be mustering a lot of men just to guard one woman."

"No, her life hasn't been threatened," Morley said. "But one of her possessions is threatened, we believe. The Rajah's Ruby."

"Isn't that the stone some Indian prince gave her?"

Jack was kept up to date on the gossip of the theater world by Flo, one of his current girlfriends.

"It's more than just a stone," Morley said, a little stiffly. "It's the largest and most valuable stone ever found."

"And you think someone is going to steal it?" Jack felt deflated. All this over a shiny bauble!

"It has caused dozens of deaths in the past and probably another here," Morley observed.

"Who?" Jack shook his head. "Surely you don't mean Officer Healey?"

"Have you heard of Glass?" Morley asked quietly.

"Glass? I know what it is."

"It's also a name. Glass is the most powerful man among the criminal element in San Francisco."

"I've never heard of him."

"Few have," said Morley. "We know he exists and we know he has been behind some of the biggest crimes in this city, but nobody has seen him. Nobody knows who he is."

"What makes you think he wants the Rajah's Ruby?"

"Fragments of information we've picked up here and there," Morley said.

"So why is Officer Healey's death connected?"

"We think that Lou Kandel's breakout from San Quentin was masterminded by Glass. A month ago, Soapy Groves, an explosives expert, was broken out of Q in a similar manner. With Kandel the finest safecracker in the business, the two of them should be able to steal anything."

Jack grunted. They sounded like a dangerous duo. Jack knew that the nickname "Soapy" was given to explosives experts of top caliber. The name came from "soap," the slang term for nitroglycerin.

This was a development that promised a new wave of crime would sweep through Jack's beloved San Francisco. Already the city teamed with crooks, gunmen, killers, thieves, bandits, muggers, pickpockets, burglars—if the situation deteriorated as Morley was suggesting, martial law might have to be declared. It would be the end of San Francisco's bid to become one of the truly great cities.

"I'll do what I can," Jack promised.

"Good man," Morley said, the first sign of heartiness he had shown. "I had hoped you would. Do you know a bar called the Plucked Chicken on Fraser Street?"

"I'm not a regular patron," said Jack, "but I know it."

"You learn anything, go there and tell the bartender you're looking for Niccolo. Have one drink and leave. Niccolo is one of our best undercover men—he'll get in touch with you and you can give him the information. He'll get it to us right away."

Jack nodded. "All right."

"Now, you may need another contact, in another part of the city. I have one in the Produce District, near the Embarcadero. It's a fish market, ask for Noah. It's an appropriate name, as you'll find out, and he has a beard to match."

Jack nodded his understanding again.

"You'll need to spend time at the Midway Plaisance," Morley went on.

Jack could hardly conceal his surprise. "Is that where Belle Conquest is going to appear?"

"Yes," Morley said and noticed Jack's quickening of interest. "Why?"

"I already spend time there," Jack explained. "There's a girl, Flo, she teaches dancing there. I see her a lot."

"That's what I heard," Morley said. "Little Egypt. That will make you less conspicuous, as you go to the Midway already. One other thing—other people are concerned about this situation. One or two of them may be hiring people of their own."

Jack knew of the rivalry between the politicians, the police, the port authorities, the army—all struggling for domination in a game where the stakes were usually high.

"Another point," said Morley. "Grady says you may be able to identify the man you fought while Healey was engaged with Kandel."

"I got a good look at him," Jack said. "I've never seen him before but I would certainly know him if I ran into him."

"Let's hope you don't—might be dangerous, especially if he spotted you first. Anyway, Grady is arranging for you to look at some sketches. He's picked out a likely lineup of suspects."

"I should be able to recognize him," agreed Jack. There was a knock at the door and Grady entered.

"Ah, Grady, got the sketches ready?"

Grady nodded and took Jack and Morley into another room lined with shelves. Sketches taken from the shelves had been laid out on a table. "Here's a few to start with," Grady said. "A few *gonophs,* but our man may not be one of them." Jack nodded, familiar with the Yiddish word commonly used to mean a thief. "He must be somebody in the criminal world of our fair city, may have worked his way up from a gonoph and now he's getting more important jobs."

Jack went through the sketches, Morley sitting opposite and watching him. Jack shook his head. None of them resembled the man he had fought. Grady brought another set with the same result. Half an hour later, Grady was breathing heavily with disappointment and Jack was finding that too many of the faces were beginning to look alike.

"Then there's these." Grady dropped another heap of sketches onto the table. "None of these have a record, but that just means we haven't been able to catch them in the act. They are all suspicious, though, for one reason or another."

The second face was just being tossed onto the pile to be returned when Jack frowned. "Wait a minute. . . ." He picked the sketch up again and placed a hand over it to obscure the beard and mustache.

"That him?" Grady asked, excited.

Jack held the sketch this way and that. He moved his hand. "Yes," he said slowly, "I'm pretty sure that's him. He's shaved it all off, but that's the man."

Morley turned the sketch over, eager to read the number. He read it out to Grady, who went to the file and looked up a moment later. "Manny Thurston. Well, his name hasn't shown up in quite a while."

"Do you have anything on him?" Jack asked, sinking into a chair, glad that it was over.

"He was a gambler when his name first came to our attention," Morley said. "He was caught cheating a few times. Sometimes he just smiled it away; others he shot his accusers. He always managed to plant a weapon on them so that he could claim self-defense. After that, he ran a protection racket, nothing big but a steady income: laundries, grocers, butchers. He used his money from that to buy gold from prospectors, paying better than the going rate—right, Sergeant?"

Grady nodded emphatically. "You've got him to a tee, Captain."

"You mean he went legitimate?" asked Jack in surprise.

"Not Manny. We found several prospectors' bodies, dead, pockets emptied, and we were able to trace them back as Manny's customers."

"He bought their gold, had them followed and mugged. Got his money back."

"That's right," said Morley. "We couldn't prove anything though."

"And since then?"

"His name has come up but never anything definite tied to it," Grady added.

"He's probably gone higher in the ranks and made his way into bigger crimes," Morley said.

"Such as bringing criminals like Lou Kandel into San Francisco?" Jack suggested.

"It sounds like the kind of progress a man like Thurston would make," Morley agreed. "Particularly as we haven't run across him for some time."

Grady wagged a warning finger at Jack. "Thurston may have gone up in the ranks, but remember that he's killed a few men in his time. He can be dangerous."

The captain got to his feet. "You can go out the back—

and it's better if you aren't seen here for a while." Jack went with him to the door and Morley turned, shook his hand firmly. "Needless to say, no one must know about this."

Grady conducted Jack through a labyrinth of passages and corridors. They finally emerged in an alley between two bars. The iron door clanged behind him like a cracked bell, with an echoing ring of finality.

Chapter 3

The Midway Plaisance was nearly full by the time Jack arrived. He made his way through to the bar, ordered a beer and ate some fried shrimp from one of the large baskets set at intervals in front of the customers. He thought of asking for a whisky. He could afford it with his new wealth of five dollars a day, but he still had unpleasant memories of his battle with John Barleycorn, Jack's favorite name for drink.

The original Midway Plaisance had been a pavilion at the 1893 World's Fair in Chicago. There, just across the Illinois Central Railroad tracks from the main exposition grounds, was Sol Bloom's Egyptian Village.

The fair had taken ten thousand men three years to build. It was also known as the Columbian Exposition, because its opening was supposed to coincide with the four hundredth anniversary of Christopher Columbus's discovery of America in 1492. However, the enormity of the task of building it had been underestimated, and after the expenditure of thirty-two million dollars, it finally opened a year late in 1893.

The Barbary Coast's Midway Plaisance had a wide repertoire of entertainment that appealed to a vast range of tastes. It offered everything from risqué sketches and revealing dances to lavish shows by the Shubert Brothers, to Ellen Terry as Portia and Enrico Caruso singing operatic arias. Jack looked around the huge auditorium. There were no seats, just tables, and the wide balcony that ran all the way around the inside walls was full too. It was a break between shows and the orchestra was playing a totally inappropriate Strauss waltz as a prelude to the display of female pulchritude and flashing limbs that was to follow.

The usual mix of cowboys, miners, sailors and merchants was there, Jack noted, studying the crowd. The con men and the cardsharps would be upstairs in the gambling rooms. The Plaisance was close to the higher end of the scale of establishments on the Barbary Coast. Complete nudity was rare on the stage and the members of the audience were not permitted to strip the pretty waiter girls, as they were known, as was the custom in many places. Drinks were not watered and the use of cantharides to inflame the passions was not practiced.

The waiter girls had a complete costume change every few weeks. This was unusual too, and tonight they wore very short purple silk jackets, tightly cinched at the waist and cut low on the breasts. Black silk stockings and high-heeled purple shoes completed the ensemble. The question of whether they wore any garments underneath was a frequent subject of argument. An occasional aroused customer determined to find out, but it was an inquisitiveness that was not encouraged.

Jack was well known at many of the bars, saloons and music halls on the Coast, and here he chatted with one of the bartenders, Andy, who had aspirations of making a fortune in gold prospecting in the Yukon. He had a near reverence for Jack, who had been there—which was true—and had done just that—which was not. Jack reached for a handful of pickled squid and called for another beer.

"Flo'll be out in a minute," Andy told him as he brought the foaming stein.

Flo was the name by which she was known in San Francisco. The public had known her as Little Egypt when, at the World's Fair, she had become an overnight sensation with her hoochy coochy dance. Until then, the cancan had been considered the ultimate in provocative dancing, but

Little Egypt set a new high, and before the fair was over, she had received tantalizing offers from all over the world.

She was a levelheaded girl, though, and knew how ephemeral fame could be. She turned down the offers to perform and instead began a career of training girls to dance. The Barbary Coast, with its five thousand entertainment establishments, was a natural magnet for her. Since coming here after periods in New York and Chicago, she and Jack had formed a close relationship. Jack was reaching for more fried shrimp when a hand squeezed his arm.

Flo was only medium height but she had the most exquisite figure Jack had ever seen, with a slim waist, full breasts and long shapely legs. She wore a long dress in a silvery-gray color, and although it was not tight-fitting, it accentuated her curves with every movement of her lithe body. "I have a table in the corner," she said quietly, her large dark eyes shining in a delicate, heart-shaped face.

They chatted for a few moments; then Flo drummed long slender fingers on the tabletop. "I have some news for you," she said, mischievously stopping there.

"A new show?" guessed Jack.

Her eyes widened just slightly.

"Why, yes, it is as a matter of fact. It's the star of the show who's the big surprise though."

Jack pretended to ponder. "Let me guess. . . ."

"I'll bet you can't," Flo said with a confident smile.

"Let me see," Jack said. "Not Lillian Russell. Can't be Tetrazzini. Sarah Bernhardt can't be coming back so soon—it can only be one person. It's Belle Conquest!"

Flo's lips parted in amazement; then she sat back and regarded him with an accusing stare. "Jack London! You knew!"

"I'm a good guesser."

"No, you're not. You're a terrible guesser. You knew!"

Jack chuckled. It was hard to deceive Flo, and he had all but given up trying.

"You knew—I can tell!" She banged a small fist on the table. "Who told you?"

"I'm sworn to secrecy," Jack said.

"Nonsense," said Flo scornfully. "You can tell *me*!"

Jack gave her a highly abbreviated and understated version of his conversation with Police Captain Morley.

"So you're up to your investigating tricks again," Flo said. "You nearly got killed last time."

"Just passing on information this time. Anything I hear that might help. That's all, no risk."

"Hmm," Flo said, studying his face suspiciously. "You don't know how to avoid risks."

"The police will have extra men out by the dozen. They don't need me. It's just that I might hear something here or there."

Flo did not look convinced, but the excitement of the visit of the fabled entertainer was too much for her. "You know the story of the Rajah's Ruby? I read all about it."

Jack knew that Flo was avidly interested in the personalities of show business despite the fact that she could have been one of them with no difficulty. She read all she could lay her hands on, and she was as adoring as a young schoolgirl. She went on in a rush of words.

"The ruby was mined on the Kistna River in India. It was put into the forehead of a statue in a temple and a priest stole it but was caught and tortured to death. A Belgian trader got hold of it years later and sold it for enough money to buy himself an island and build a huge house. The man he sold it to was killed in a duel and the trader was torn to pieces by his own guard dogs.

"King Louis the Sixteenth bought it and gave it to Marie Antoinette. They were both executed on the guillotine. One of their jailers got the stone but was stabbed to death, and then for some years the ruby disappeared. A jeweler in Paris finally put it on sale and it was bought by a Russian nobleman, who gave it to Catherine the Great of Russia. The nobleman was murdered and Catherine died of apoplexy."

Jack smiled into Flo's big, wide eyes. "Do I hear something about a curse coming up next?"

"Don't make fun of me, Jack. This is serious history I'm telling you."

"All right, Flo. Go on."

"The Sultan of Turkey got it then. He gave it to his bride. After the wedding night, she stabbed him and then herself."

"Is that a warning to me not to get married?" Jack asked.

Flo scowled and continued. "It appeared next in the possession of a banker in Berlin. He committed suicide when his bank failed. Others owned it for a short time, but all of them sold it when they had some misfortune or their heirs sold it when the owners died or were killed—as most of them were."

"It's an extraordinary story," admitted Jack. "These things fascinate you, don't they?"

"Yes, they do." She eyed him impishly. "I suppose you're more fascinated by Belle Conquest, the ruby's new owner."

"Some rajah in India gave it to her, didn't he?"

"Not just *some* rajah: the Rajah of Rajitstan, the richest man in the world." Flo leaned forward. "That's what the police are concerned about, isn't it? The ruby! They expect an attempt to steal it."

"I prefer to think of being a bodyguard to Belle Conquest," Jack said. "Now *that* is a body to guard."

"And you said no risk." Flo shook her head. "You won't be safe from her. From what I've heard, she eats writers for breakfast."

"Do you know as much about her as you do about her ruby?"

"Probably," said Flo. "The Belle of Broadway, they call her. Blonde, beautiful and buxom, according to one headline. She loves to be quoted. 'Sex is good for my health,' she once said, 'and, boy, am I healthy!' She's the biggest earner in show business. The *New York Times* wrote, 'Belle

Conquest *is* entertainment.' She packs them in wherever she goes."

"When does she wear the ruby?" Jack asked.

"At every show."

Jack frowned. "That's asking for trouble. Here especially."

"You're only gathering information, remember? Don't go looking for danger."

"It's an easy job," Jack assured her. "Which reminds me—I need to move on. Got one or two more places to visit tonight."

She leaned across the table and gave him a kiss. "I'd tell you to be careful but I know you never are."

"Of course I am," Jack protested. "That's why I've lived so long."

He pushed his way between the tightly packed tables and out the door. The street was busy as always. A group of sailors was staggering and trying to sing, a couple of cowpunchers in tall Stetsons went by and a party of college boys was arguing over which place to enter and the delights to be found inside each.

When the attack came, it was completely unexpected.

Chapter 4

Jack had turned onto Claremont Street, a narrow street off Montgomery. If he had thought about it, he would have gone on to Harper, which was wider and busier. Claremont was poorly lit and passersby were only shapes in the darkness.

The first man came at him across the street. Initially pursuing a diagonal path, he turned abruptly and ran at Jack. His thoughts still on Flo, Jack was taken by surprise. Instinctively, he backed up, only to find another man behind him.

Jack twisted away to get his back to the wall. The two came at him from different angles. His eyes adjusting to the darkness, he could see that both were Chinese. One had a long knife but the other seemed to be unarmed. Then Jack noticed the unnatural way he was holding his hands, and he knew that between those hands the other had a garrote, the thin piano wire invisible in the gloom.

Jack maneuvered to keep the garroter in front of him. He knew that if the man got behind him, he would be dead in seconds. Both were wary, both were silent. These were not back-alley thugs but professional killers. Whites called them highbinders, but they rarely ventured out of Chinatown. Each had the usual broad-brimmed black slouch hat, pulled well down over the eyes, and wore loose cotton shirts.

The knife man came at Jack in a sudden but controlled rush. Jack jerked away at the last second and clamped a hand on the man's wrist. They strained for supremacy and the Chinaman, quickly finding that Jack was stronger, concentrated on keeping his grip on the knife. He glanced over his shoulder, waiting for his partner to make his move.

Out of the corner of his eye, Jack could see the second man creeping up behind him. He let him get close. When the man made his final rush, Jack tightened his grip on the first man's wrist and threw all his body weight into swinging the knife man into the path of the other.

They collided. Both cursed. Then, like the professionals they were, they instantly pulled apart and rushed at Jack again. He caught a glimpse of the face of the knife man as a shaft of light came from an opened window. It was not a face he could recognize, but one just like a thousand others in San Francisco's Chinatown. Jack paid more attention to the knife than the garrote—it carried the more immediate threat. He spread his hands, fists tightly clenched, ready.

The two closed in. Jack had been in dozens of fights, on ships, on shore, in prison, in hobo camps, and he knew all the essentials of hand-to-hand combat. One of the more important rules was to take the initiative whenever possible. This was one of those occasions. He took two fast steps forward and swung a looping left hook into the side of the knife man's face.

Taken unawares, the man stumbled and almost fell, but the garroter, without hesitation, leaped at Jack. Keeping him at arm's length so the man could not loop his wire over his head, Jack jabbed a left and a right, speed more vital than accuracy. The first hit home on the throat and the second on the corner of the jaw. Jack was about to follow up his advantage when the knife man changed his stumble into a full-length dive. He threw himself toward Jack and grabbed his ankle.

Off-balance as he was about to throw another punch, Jack tried to pull loose. It was a mistake. The Chinaman jerked harder and Jack fell. He tried to roll into his shoulder, but he did not have preparation and he hit the ground hard. His breath came out in a swoosh. He tried to wriggle away out of reach but was aware of the figure looming over him. A voice came from nearby.

"Well now, what have we here? Two against one? Don't seem hardly fair, do it? 'Specially when the two's armed and the one ain't."

A tall figure loomed closer. He wore a high-crowned Stetson hat that gave him extra height. The Chinamen paused, uncertain of their next move. The garroter backed away, looking to see if anyone else was near and no doubt deciding whether to ignore the intruder. The knife man was getting to his feet. He let out a snarl at being interrupted but evidently had no intention of abandoning his assignment. As soon as he was upright, he jabbed at Jack with the knife.

Jack tried to kick at the knife hand but did not kick high enough. Still, he grazed the man's arm enough to make the knife snap upward, and Jack jumped inside the knife arm, grabbed it and twisted. Hot, garlicky breath came at him as the Chinaman grunted with effort. Jack made use of his superior strength, exerting all the pressure he could muster, forcing the other's grip on the knife to loosen.

The sleeve of the loose shirt had pulled up in the struggle and Jack saw, even in the dim light, a colored tattoo on the Chinaman's wrist. Then, just as the knife clattered to the ground, Jack felt the second man at his back and had a fleeting glimpse of arms swinging over his head with the deadly garrote.

The clicking sound was loud in the otherwise empty alley. Each of the three combatants recognized it instantly. It was the cocking of a revolver. A second's delay was all Jack needed. He pushed his hands up in front of his face just as the black wire swung invisibly over his head. It pulled his wrists back but achieved its purpose of protecting his throat.

"I was goin' to fire a warning shot," said a languid Western voice. "But seems like you fellers might take no notice. The next man that moves gets a bullet in the head."

Jack and the two Chinamen froze in a bizarre tableau.

"Now, very slowly, all of you step apart."

Jack was just wondering if the two understood English when they both did as they were bid. In a low voice, one muttered something to the other, who answered briefly. When they were all well separated, the two Chinamen abruptly ran off in opposite directions. The six-shooter clicked again as its holder released the hammer. He came forward into Jack's full view for the first time.

Wearing Western garb, he was just as tall as Jack had originally thought. He was holstering the pistol as he came up to Jack. "Maybe it ain't Christian of me," he drawled, "but anytime I see two Chinee fighting one white man, I know whose side I'm on. I ain't gonna ask no questions."

"Jack London," Jack introduced himself and held out a hand. "Thanks for saving my life."

"Hank Barstow—my pleasure, sah."

"You look like a lawman," Jack said.

"Former deputy sheriff, Carson City."

"Thought so," said Jack. "May I have the pleasure of buying you a drink?"

They had three drinks in the nearest bar; then Hank Barstow left to meet an old acquaintance. Jack went at once to a Chinese restaurant on the next block, a place owned by one of Jack's shipmates from earlier days.

Steamy smells assailed Jack's nostrils as he entered. The tables were close together and covered with white napery. The walls were decorated with paintings of the Great Wall, dark green forests and a wide, sweeping river. His former shipmate, Jing Yo, was a tubby, round-faced man with a perpetual smile. He assigned his duties to another man and conducted Jack to a table, where a waiter appeared immediately with a pot of tea and two elegantly decorated cups. He set them on the table and left. Yo beamed.

"Jack, my friend, what can I do for you?"

Jack grinned. "How do you know I want something, Yo?"

"It's after midnight, you don't like Chinese food and you show signs of having been in a fight. Am I not right? Is there not something I can do for you?"

"All right, Yo. Do you have a pencil?"

On the paper tablecloth, Jack sketched what looked like a tapering tower, a half dozen stories high. On one side, he drew a knife and on the other side a hatchet. Jing Yo's beam faded as Jack described his encounter.

"This is not good, Jack." His voice was low.

"What does this mean?" Jack asked.

"These are *boo how doy*. It means in Chinese fighting men. They are trained assassins. You are lucky to be alive. They are under the direct control of a tong. They receive a good salary and get a large bonus for every man they kill." Yo looked at Jack over the teapot as he poured. "You must have done something very big for this. *Boo how doy* do not usually attack white men. They are used for wars between tongs."

"One carried a knife and the other a garrote," Jack said.

"They also use hatchets and bludgeons. One of their names in Chinese is Hatchetmen—that is why they show a hatchet on their emblem. It is their practice to leave the weapon at the side of the person they kill."

"I am glad I wasn't responsible for them losing either of their weapons tonight," Jack said wryly.

"*Boo how doy* are very dangerous men," Yo said with a reproving shake of his head. "They are subject to strict discipline and spend many hours a day in training. They obey at all times and without question the orders they are given. I recommend that you stay away from these men."

"I hope you'll recommend to them that they stay away from me. I know I was lucky today."

Jing Yo's eyes still held a glint of alarm. "The ranks of the *boo how doy* have provided many renowned killers— some have killed more than your white gangsters. Hong Ah

Kay is one such name. He was a scholar and a poet but an assassin of great skill. On one occasion, in a fight in a cellar, single-handed against seven foes from another tong, he split their skulls with seven blows. Ye Toy was another. The name means Girl Face in English. He could look like a woman, which was a great help in his profession. It was his custom, after he had murdered his victim, to straighten the dead man's clothes and comb his hair, make him look respectable."

Jack repressed a shudder. These were formidable enemies to have made.

"I can't tell you why they want to kill me," Jack told his friend, "but you can be sure I am not doing anything illegal."

Yo brought back his customary beam. "I do not think that for a moment."

"Which tong is this?"

Yo hesitated, then said, "The Suey Chun."

"What do you know about them?" Jack noticed that Yo's hesitation was longer this time. "I wouldn't ask you these questions if my life were not being threatened," he told Yo.

"They are very powerful. They receive assignments from the Six Companies."

Jack knew that the Six Companies owned most of the businesses in Chinatown. Yo went on to explain.

"You are thinking that the Six Companies do not engage in bad things. They do not break laws. They are very careful. This is true. I do not understand why they should want to kill you." He shook his head. "The Six Companies do not usually order the tong to kill white men. Very bad. This, they do not do."

"So the Suey Chun tong gets its orders from the Six Companies," Jack said. "Who would pass on such orders?"

Yo poured more tea. Jack noticed that both of their cups were still half full. Yo was stalling.

"Just a name," Jack urged. "No one will know who told me."

Yo still hesitated, glanced quickly around the restaurant, then leaned across the table and said in a low voice, "How Chew Fat."

Jack knew a few names in Chinatown but that was not one of them. "He is a very powerful man?"

Yo nodded vigorously. "Very powerful."

"Where can I find him?"

A look of alarm crossed Yo's countenance. "I hope you do not intend—"

"Just ask him a few questions, that's all." Jack showed his friendliest grin.

Yo sighed resignedly. "You are a very determined young man—but you are my friend. Ask along the Lane of the Golden Chrysanthemum. Anyone will direct you, though you may not be permitted to see him. Your way may be blocked. But do not go tonight. Daytime is better."

"Thanks, Yo." Jack drained his teacup. "I'll be back and show you I can eat Chinese food. Can you cook something special for me?"

"I will." Yo beamed. "Meanwhile, be careful. San Francisco is a dangerous place."

"So I've heard," Jack said and gave Yo a jaunty wave as he left.

Chapter 5

The trip to Chinatown was an exhilarating feature of the long, steep descent toward the bay. The wheels of the cable car rattled approaching the narrow, level strip of Dupont Street as the gripman used two hands to pull the brake handle and bring the shivering car to a stop. Jack jumped off and walked through the gateway of Chinatown.

It was a brisk, cool morning with a hint of rain, but a weak sun bled through and much of the sky was light blue. Dupont Street was cobblestoned and cluttered with rambling buildings, many of them three stories. The numerous balconies were strung with giant lanterns and massive signs, freshly lettered and painted. The rooftops were a forest of pagoda towers, some flying the dragon pennant of China.

Chinatown was a small area, picturesque in the extreme, and Jack loved to visit it. The streets were packed with street peddlers and sidewalk merchants. Bicycles, pushcarts, small wagons, rickshaws and portable stands were everywhere. Colored bunting attracted the attention of eager buyers to displays of candies, nuts, fruit and cakes. Bulletins several feet high and covered with news of importance served in place of newspapers, which few could afford. The delicate Chinese calligraphy, with its intricate whorls and flowing curves, added to the exotic picture.

Jack went along Dupont Street, called the Lane of the Golden Chrysanthemum by the Chinese, past cigar shops, shoe shops and displays of powders, tablets and wrapped scrolls of paper containing miraculous cures. Embroidery, bronze statues, delicately carved wood, ivory and coral items and fragile blue-and-white plates and dishes from Canton filled storefronts. Smells of incense and sandalwood in a dozen varieties perfumed the air, and the shrill cries of vendors rang out.

Jack came to a shop selling fruit and flowers with slender pillars in front. He went in and asked for How Chew Fat. He was greeted with a blank stare and a suggestion that he try the store farther along. It was even larger and had food and provisions of all kinds, even bottles of whisky.

An elderly Chinese with a long pigtail addressed Jack in excellent English, inquiring how he could help him.

"I'm sorry," Jack said. "I don't want to buy anything. I am looking for How Chew Fat."

"What matter does it concern?" the Chinaman asked politely.

"I can't tell you that," Jack said. "But he will want to see me."

The Chinaman scrutinized him for a moment, then turned and called out in Chinese. A young girl with a pale oval face came trotting out, hands hidden in her sleeves. She bowed gravely to Jack and the Chinaman spoke rapidly to her.

"She will conduct you," he said, turning to Jack.

The girl hurried out into the street and Jack followed after her. Farther along, she turned into a Chinese laundry, where the hot, damp air was suffocating. Dozens of women massaged soaking wet clothes like lumps of dough. Jack and the girl went through another room, then another. A flight of rickety stairs led down. Jack had to take long strides to keep up with the pattering feet of the girl.

They hurried along narrow corridors, some with dirt floors, and Jack was soon hopelessly confused. They descended another long flight of stairs, and Jack recalled hearing that most of Chinatown went six floors underground. When they came to a storage room filled with boxes and crates, the girl knocked at a large iron door. A slit opened, then closed with a snap. After a moment, the door squeaked. The girl stood aside, motioned for Jack to go in, then turned and pattered back the way they had come. Jack went through the iron door.

It was another world inside the big room. Silken drapes in bright colors covered the walls with spaces only for oil paintings, all depicting scenes presumably of China. Expensive old rugs covered the floor and the pieces of furniture must have been hand-carved centuries ago from some dark hardwood. A couple of bronze urns stood on a large sideboard and a long low table was inset with silver. On it were a silver tray and several small statues in jade. An aroma suggested flowers but was stronger and less familiar. Candles of different colors burned all around the room, their flames changing color slowly.

Only one person was in the room but Jack did not doubt that other eyes were watching from hidden places. His heart beat was faster than normal, and he walked forward a few paces, slowly, keeping his hands well away from his sides. His palms were sweaty. He deepened his breathing.

"Come." The voice was high and squeaky. A jeweled hand flashed, indicating a chair. It was the only one in the room other than the elaborate thronelike affair with wide wooden arms that the other man occupied. Jack sat and observed him.

He wore Mandarin-style clothes in a slightly shiny material, a long coat in royal blue with a high black collar and cuffs on the long sleeves, and wide trousers in a lighter blue. Gold-colored sandals had winking blue stones in their tips.

The rest of him was a sight that caused Jack increasing dismay. He was of that indeterminate age which, in Orientals, seemed to indicate a suspension of aging. If he had to guess, Jack would estimate the man to be in his mid-forties. He had a round, fat face with protruding eyes that dripped tears, which he periodically wiped away with a lace handkerchief. He rubbed his nose from time to time with the handkerchief too. His thick lips were pink and bulging. Jack waited for him to speak.

"I am How Chew Fat." The words were chopped. "You want see me. What is your name and why you here?"

Jack took a breath. "My name is Jack London. I live here in San Francisco. Two of your men tried to kill me last night and I hoped you could tell me why."

"My men? What you mean, my men?"

"They had the tattoos of the Suey Chun."

"How you know the tattoo?"

"A Chinese friend told me."

The bulging eyes surveyed him skeptically. "You have Chinese friends?"

"I have many," Jack said.

"I am not member of a tong. Not Suey Chun, not any tong."

"Perhaps not, but you are an important man in the Six Companies. If you need someone killed, you can arrange for a *boo how doy* to do it."

The Chinese was silent. His eyes flickered and he moistened his blubbery lips. "What you know of *boo how doy?*"

"I know they are professional assassins."

"Who tell you this? Chinese friends?"

Jack knew he was approaching slippery ground. Officer Healey had been murdered—garroted—because he had been able to identify Lou Kandel, the killer who had escaped from San Quentin. Or so Captain Morley believed. Jack had a slight twinge of doubt as to what the captain had not told him. But there was the possibility that he could learn something of the threat to Belle Conquest and her priceless ruby if he could find out why Chinese assassins wanted to kill him. There was no way anyone could know that Officer Healey had confided in Jack the identity of the man who had come ashore in the fog. Jack's fear that he was taking a risk in coming here increased but he kept his voice steady.

"I have many Chinese friends," Jack repeated. "I have no animosity toward Chinese people. I saved the life of a Chinaman and another saved my life. I just want to know why the Suey Chun tong wants me dead."

The other's stare was blank though his lips kept moving slowly. Then he spoke in that high voice. It was in Chinese. He spoke fast and for two or three minutes. Jack had no idea what he was saying but thought better of interrupting to say so.

The room fell quiet except for the sputter of a candle. For whose benefit had that monologue been?

"What you do?" The question came suddenly and Jack jumped.

"I'm a writer."

"What you write?"

Jack told him—of his Yukon experiences and how he had made use of man's battle against the elements in the icy north. He told of his years at sea, on whalers and sealers, and of his short time as a railroad hobo. How Chew Fat listened impassively. On two or three occasions, Jack wondered if he should stop, for he had not intended his answer to be this long. Yet the other said nothing, and Jack hoped that the more he explained, the better his chances of winning the other's confidence.

Finally he stopped, deciding that was enough.

"You adventurous man," How Chew Fat said.

Jack nodded.

"What you look for?"

Jack wasn't sure what the question meant and he had no intention of referring to his job gathering information for the police.

When Jack didn't answer, How Chew Fat spoke again. "What you want? What you look for in life?"

The question surprised Jack. He had not expected a semi-philosophical query like that. He composed his thoughts. "I want to live life, not just to pass through it. I want to experience, I want to know joy, to know pain, to know fear. I want excitement but I also want knowledge."

How Chew Fat's face still showed no reaction. Jack wondered if he understood. He did not speak English well, so maybe he did not understand it well either.

The silence was an uneasy one. The Chinaman raised his left hand and rapped twice on the heavy wooden arm of the thronelike chair. A curtain parted in the wall on one side and a small Chinaman entered. He wore the traditional clothing seen in Chinatown: a long white shift with blue pants, black slippers and a small blue cap. He did not look at Jack, but rather walked with short steps to How Chew Fat. He stopped in front of him and to one side, bowed, and in a high singsong voice, talked in Chinese.

How Chew Fat seemed to be listening but gave little visible sign of it. When the other finished, he fired a question and the other answered. How Chew Fat rapped twice on the chair arm, and the man bowed and left.

Jack waited. The bulging eyes appeared to be looking right past him. Jack felt the hair rising on the back of his neck but firmly resisted the impulse to turn his head.

The squeaky voice said, "The Six Companies not make arrangements kill you. Nor anyone else. Many months since that happen. Suey Chun tong not carry out executions some time."

His tone indicated that was all, as far as he was concerned. Jack was not satisfied and did not intend to leave until he learned more. It was time to push his luck.

"The men who tried to kill me were professional assassins. They were not robbers. I am sure of that. Who does that kind of work besides the tong?"

Inquiries into the operations of the tong were not welcome and could be dangerous, Jack knew. Some of his Chinese friends steadfastly refused even to mention the tong in conversations, especially those with white men.

Jack was prepared for a glimmer of anger, but this Oriental was far more inscrutable than any Jack had encountered. Jack thought the other man was not going to answer, but when the pause had reached its limit, How Chew Fat dabbed his eyes with the silk handkerchief and said, "Can tell you this. Two men of Suey Chun tong commit crime not permitted in Chinese community. They throw out. Is known that these men now work for white man."

Was he telling the truth? Jack wondered. Or was he shuffling the blame? Jack's experience of the Chinese people led him to believe that it was the truth. They were not usually deceitful. "Some white man in particular?" Jack asked and waited for a scathing reply.

How Chew Fat fell into another of those silences that might indicate loss of interest. Then he spoke just one word, and Jack felt a sudden chill in his stomach.

"Glass."

The bulging eyes were on him. Was their owner assessing Jack's reaction?

"This mean something to you?" asked the high voice.

Jack's first instinct was to deny it, but a more measured consideration outweighed that. This How Chew Fat might not be very intelligent. Perhaps he was some kind of a puppet deliberately set up so as to reveal nothing to a white man who came asking questions. But behind the curtains could be others who controlled the destiny of tens of thousands in Chinatown. They might not be as easily hoodwinked. A leavening of the truth would be more prudent, and Jack decided to stay very close to the truth without revealing any sources.

"I have heard the name," he said. "He's a master criminal who has many other criminals working for him. He is very active on the Barbary Coast. Nobody admits to having seen him or has any idea who he is. He seems to work in many areas." Jack refrained from overdoing it. Even this had a few embellishments, but it was basically what he understood.

The Chinaman's eyes did not leave Jack's face. He wiped away some spittle from his lips, then rapped twice on the arm of the chair. The young girl came in silently and stood beside Jack. How Chew Fat waved a hand and the girl smiled a tiny smile and led the way out.

Chapter 6

A dance rehearsal was in progress on the stage of the Midway Plaisance when Jack arrived. It was a high-kicking number and Jack watched as Flo coaxed, bullied and cajoled the girls of the chorus to kick that little bit higher. Then she worked on their movements, for their coordination was ragged and lacked timing.

Jack leaned against the bar, and the bartender, Andy, who knew his habits, brought him a beer and a bowl of pickled squid left over from the night before. The girls were moving better now, keeping in line and holding their spacing. At last, Flo was satisfied and the girls sank to the stage, groaning and perspiring. Flo had seen Jack, so she came over to him. She wore a one-piece dancer's costume that would have merited a full-scale attack by the San Francisco Committee on Morals had they seen it.

Andy brought her a glass of water, which was all she drank during the day. She gave Jack a kiss on the cheek and took a grateful gulp of water. "It isn't me you've come to see, I know. She's here though, your Belle."

"I really came to see you, Flo, but since she's here, I might as well . . ."

Flo gave him a playful punch in the ribs. She noticed Jack's involuntary wince. "Have you been fighting again?" she asked accusingly.

"Just a skirmish," Jack said. "This fellow said the show at the Bella Union was the best in town. I said the best was at the Midway Plaisance. You wouldn't want me to let any man get away with that, would you?"

Flo smiled. It was one of her most beguiling characteristics, wholly natural and sincere. "You don't show any scars or bruises at least. After all, I want you to be at your best when you meet La Belle."

"What's your impression of her?" Jack asked.

"She's come here direct from Daly's Sixty-third Street Theater, where the show she was in, *A Woman of Pleasure,* broke all box office records. She says she expects to do the same here. She's bold and brassy and yet she still manages to be very feminine. She's surprisingly polite for such a big star. She's sexy and knows it and does everything to promote that image. Yet at the same time, she is friendly to everybody, none of that hoity-toity attitude that so many of them have."

"You could have been just as big a star," said Jack.

Flo cocked her head to one side. It was another charming gesture she had. "I doubt it." She smiled, but Jack knew how modest she was about her own accomplishments.

"Still," Flo went on, "you can judge for yourself. She's coming out here right now. She wants me to put on a chorus number just before she does her act."

One of the waiters ran across the floor to secure the front door and make sure no one could get in, while another was scuttling backstage to check the rear doors. Voices came from the rear of the stage and then the great star herself walked out, arguing strongly with a dark-haired, mustached man, whom Jack supposed to be her manager.

Belle Conquest wore a big black droopy picture hat and a summer print dress that Jack thought must have been designed to fit every inch of her body. Over it she wore a tiny scarlet jacket. She had masses of light blond hair and sulky green eyes that held an inner light and seemed to Jack to be just for him. Her body was an exaggeration—a large bosom, an unbelievably slim waist and hips that swayed as she walked. She was little more than medium height but

she had a compelling air that made her seem tall. Jack had
never seen anyone quite like her, even after all his years on
the Barbary Coast.

She broke off the argument with her manager and swaggered up to Jack. She stood close to him, appraising him.
When she spoke, her voice throbbed huskily.

"Are you one of my leading men?"

She had a brash, hard-boiled quality that Jack thought
was strictly her stage image. Yet Jack sensed, underlying it
and well hidden, a quietness about her, a reserve that was in
complete contrast.

Jack moistened his dry tongue.

"What's your name, sugar?"

"Jack London."

She nodded, approving his six feet of height, his strong
physique, the mass of curly brown hair and the bright blue
eyes.

"Are you going to be in my show? I need a few good-
looking young men like you."

Her manager had gone to talk to Flo and there was no
one within earshot. Jack lowered his voice nevertheless.

"I'm really here concerning your ruby. I—"

Her lips curled invitingly. "My, my, you want to see my
ruby, do you? You're a forward young fellow, aren't you?"

"A mutual friend, called Morley, told me about it."

The bantering attitude disappeared, though Belle Conquest remained just as regal and womanly. Her voice was
low and confidential when she replied, "Oh, you're one of
the empress's guards, are you? You're going to protect my
crown jewel."

"Yes, your majesty," Jack said.

Belle laughed. "Very good. I'll be relying on you."

"It would help if I knew where you keep it," Jack said.

"Oh, you'll find out in good time," she assured him with
another of those suggestive smiles. The dark-haired, mustached man came hurrying over. She introduced him as
Louis Lahearne, her manager, and though she gave him

Jack's name, she made no mention of his role. Lahearne gave Jack the briefest of nods.

Turning from both of them, Belle waved commandingly to Flo. "How is that number coming?" she asked sharply. Under Flo's expert coaching, the number was soon up to even Belle's very demanding standards.

Belle went to harangue the orchestra leader. "You're coming in too late on that chorus!" she stormed, and Jack and Flo exchanged a grin.

"Maybe we can find somewhere quieter than this," Flo said softly.

Her dressing room was quieter—at first. Then the gentle moans and gasps began. Flo tightened her grip around Jack's neck. "Stop thinking about Belle!" she whispered.

"Who is Belle?" murmured Jack.

Jack had already worked on his manuscript for "An Odyssey of the North" after rising from bed. He had trained himself to sleep only five hours a night, and this enabled him to write for three hours or so before a normal day began. Now it was close to noon, and with his hunger assuaged by a large bowl of pickled squid, he went back to his room and immersed himself in the howling winds and the freezing cold of an Alaskan winter.

Plots were the bane of Jack's writing. He found great difficulty in constructing them and was never satisfied with them. Settings and backgrounds were his strong points and he concentrated on those, endeavoring to help the reader to believe that he was actually there and experiencing the hardships and perils of the Yukon.

He was seldom fully satisfied with his characters either, though he modeled them on some of the many people he had run into in his adventurous and excitement-packed life. Also a voracious reader of philosophy, he had recently been reading Friedrich Nietzsche. He had become completely enthralled by the German's theory of the *Ubermensch*, the superman.

For the first time in his writing, Jack saw an opportunity
to introduce such a character into one of his stories. He
would be a Swede called Axel Gunderson. He would be
seven feet tall, with eyes of the lightest blue and hair the
color of ripe corn. He would weigh three hundred pounds
and have a massive jaw and rugged brow. Was he overdoing this character? Jack wondered. No, by gosh, if Gunderson was to be a superman, he would be a true superman.
Jack needed to give Gunderson a wife—now that would be
a real challenge—but one character at a time. He concentrated on fleshing out this Norse giant.

As always, night was falling before he realized that time
had slipped away from him. Still, there was no point in
being on the Barbary Coast too early, and in fact, when
Jack arrived there, the number of people on Kearny Street
was still short of the thronging mass that would fill it in a
few hours.

The Eureka Music Hall, just north of Pacific Street, was
famous for its shows, but many came to see its magnificent
bar. Built by Brunswick of Chicago, it was sixty feet long
and made of the noblest wood of all—Circassian walnut.
The whorled pattern was unique and the rich, deep red-gold
wood wore like iron. It took several bartenders to keep
thirst at bay, but the most renowned of them was Charlie
Breen. He knew the bar like the back of his hand and personally polished it every day. His knowledge of its shiny
surface was such that he never moved from his spot at the
beer pump. He would fill a mug of beer at the call from one
of the other bartenders, who named the customer. Then
Charlie would shoot the mug along the bar to stop precisely
at its destination. He never missed and never spilled a drop.
Others tried to emulate him but he remained the master of
his art.

The mirror behind the bar was almost as long, and under
it bottles, glinting red, yellow, green, brown and blue, contained every imaginable liquor. Kerosene lamps that burned
in clusters of four were dimmed when a show started. Tall

brass spittoons stood at intervals near the brass rail. Jack took up a position at a safe distance between two of them and called for a beer. It came whizzing down the bar to stop within inches of his hand. "Bit closer next time, Charlie," Jack called out. "I had to reach for that one."

Charlie Breen gave him a wave and the owner, Lemuel Tullamore, came down the bar to stop before Jack. Jack found Lem a good source of information, though he did not care for him personally. Jack knew that he watered drinks, and Flo had told him about girls that Lem had treated badly. The music hall owner wore a shiny brown waistcoat and brown pants that did not match. The pants were held up by red-and-white-striped suspenders. He had a lined face and a pugnacious expression that showed surprise now.

"Haven't seen you for a long time," Lem greeted him.

"Oh, I've been around," Jack said. "Time I came in here again though. Still quiet, huh?"

"Yeah, well, it's early. Be crowded in a couple of hours," said Lem. "Next week, you won't be able to fight your way in."

"Who's coming?" Jack knew that the Eureka was famous for its shows, which ran the gamut from nudity to plays such as *The Union Spy*.

"Eulalia Paradino's gonna be here."

Jack had to think for a moment. Then he had it. The famous spiritualist who could conjure up the ghosts of the dead. "She's coming here?" he asked incredulously. "Putting her séances on the stage?"

"She sure is," said Lem proudly. He turned away to order a bartender to take care of a customer requesting Tennessee rye whisky, and Jack was left to contemplate yet another new star turn coming to the Barbary Coast. The music hall and saloon owners were constantly trying to outdo each other and every conceivable novelty was explored. Jack knew that Eulalia Paradino was immensely popular back east, but he had not known that she was now putting her "act" on the stage. Must cost a lot of money to bring her,

Jack thought. He would have to come and see it, and he realized that many others would be similarly curious.

Here was an innovative form of entertainment. The spiritualism business was full of phonies and only a handful were real mediums. Eulalia was by far the most celebrated. She had been imitated by many stage magicians but her reputation remained unblemished. She maintained firmly that she used no tricks and that anything that happened during one of the séances was absolutely genuine. She claimed to be truly in touch with the dead.

She would be a great crowd puller, thought Jack. The Barbary Coast crowds believed they had seen everything, but bringing back people from the dead was surely something new and extraordinary. The Eureka would be packed. Jack had a fleeting thought about the fast guns in the audiences. How would they feel about facing the spirits of the men they had gunned down? Cowboys were a superstitious bunch. And what about judges who had ordered men hanged? Would they feel any trepidation at having those men come before them again?

The ramifications were intriguing, and though Jack did not see any immediate way in which he could use this in a story, it appealed to his imagination—although niggling, unpleasant memories began to surface.

As a boy, he had been forced to participate in séances conducted by his mother and the man he believed to be his father—William H. Chaney, known as the Professor. It had meant nothing to Jack at first. It was like playing children's games, but from time to time he would feel chilly fingers playing up his spine and he would hear strange sounds. Misty shapes would appear—were they imagined or were they something else?

After growing up, he had become a pragmatist, a realist, and the supernatural had no part in his life. Now some of those childhood images came back, unbidden. Could Eulalia Paradino really enter the world beyond the grave? And what might she bring back with her?

Chapter 7

Jack resumed his patrol of the Barbary Coast. After dodging two drunks weaving a zigzag path down the middle of Montgomery Street, he went into the Orpheum—"A Place to Satisfy Allcomers," according to the large board outside.

The Orpheum put on music hall and girlie shows, allowed gambling and sold beer and whisky at reasonable prices. Its clientele was as varied as its offerings in entertainment. Even art lovers were catered to with large oil paintings on the walls, all depicting men and women in negligible clothing but with unmistakable desires. Upstairs rooms were always in demand, and the more they were used, the fewer the number of pretty waiter girls downstairs.

Jack ordered a beer at the bar, then on second thought called for a whisky with it. The talk of spirits being brought to the Eureka required the application of spirits of a different kind to banish the unnerving thoughts.

A poker game was getting heated and voices were rising. One of the players wore a "gambler's vest," a garment like a waistcoat. Another had a belt with a worn holster that held a pearl-handled Colt. Jack watched for a while, ready to duck behind the bar if bullets started to fly, but one of the other players flung down his cards in disgust and a shout of glee went up from the others. The crisis was over—until the next game.

Jack looked around the smoke-filled room but could see no one he knew. He had just downed the whisky and was reaching for his beer when the door opened with a crash.

Heads turned even from some of the gambling tables and conversations quieted as several women strode in. All were severely dressed from neck to ankle in black alpaca with high white collars, white bibs, black bonnets with strings under the chin and high-buttoned black boots.

All looked purposeful. They moved to different quarters of the Orpheum as if working in unison to some pre-arranged plan. Surely not a holdup! Jack thought. No. Preposterous. Reaching an apparently agreed position, each stood with arms crossed. They appeared determined but content to wait. From all around the room, eyes were upon them, curious. Jack had a sudden flash of what was about to come.

One of the women detached herself from the others and moved to the center of the floor. She would have looked like a boxer had she been a man. She was beetle-browed with a crooked nose and a bashed-in face. She stood at least six feet tall and was buxom and muscular. The sound level went down still further with even the higher stakes poker games interrupted.

The head bartender appeared to be temporarily in charge of the Orpheum. He was a tall, almost bald man with a limp, which was probably a legacy of an Indian war. He came uncertainly from behind the bar. "I'm sorry, madam," he said, addressing the formidable-looking woman in the middle of the room, "but we don't serve ladies."

"Serve!" the woman shouted. "We don't want serving! Serve us indeed! You don't think any of us would drink the hellish poison you've got here, do you?"

She clapped her hands loudly. The doors crashed open again and two more women dressed in the same attire came in.

Both were young and good-looking despite the severity of their dress. They were also tall and strong and probably had developed their muscles and strength plowing fields, hammering fences and mending roofs. Each carried four or five axes in her arms. Jack's suspicions were confirmed just before the woman introduced herself.

"I'm Carrie Nation," the woman said, and her voice was more strident. "I've just come from Kansas, where my Anti-Saloon League has put more than two hundred gin mills like this out of business." Abruptly, she threw out an arm and pointed dramatically to one wall. "What are all those naked women doing there?"

Jack thought that the answer to that was blatantly obvious, but the unfortunate bartender was able to stammer only, "Why, they're just pictures, ma'am."

"You are a rummy and a purveyor of flesh! You should be behind prison bars instead of behind a saloon bar. Here's what I think of your pictures!"

She snatched an ax from one of the two recently arrived girls, strode over to the nearest painting and drove the ax into it. The canvas split and the ax bit into the wall behind it. She wrenched it loose and slashed at the frame until the splintered wood pieces littered the floor. The entire room was silent as a tomb. Carrie Nation walked to the bar, put two hands on the ax handle and flung it with all her considerable strength. Gasps of awe arose from the watchers as the huge mirror shattered and shards of glass tinkled onto glasses and bottles.

"That there mirror cost a thousand dollars!" gasped the bartender. Before the sounds had died away, the two girls had dispensed their axes to the others.

No one else moved as the girls and women of the Anti-Saloon League smashed everything in sight. Bottles of liquor gushed their contents onto the floor and glasses were smashed. Men scrambled to safety as card tables were chopped apart. Some dived to the floor to retrieve coins and notes, then yelled in fear when their avarice put them in range of the gleaming blades of those swinging axes.

The place was quickly in shambles, glass and shattered wood everywhere, the smell of whisky, good and bad, filling the air and the figures of these black-clad avengers stalking the room looking for anything still intact.

Carrie Nation planned and carried out her moves better than the U.S. Army, thought Jack. He remained at the bar, considering it the safest place, though his mug of beer had been one of the first casualties and it was not the time to order another. That daunting figure clapped her hands again and the sounds of destruction died away.

"There, you destroyers of men's souls! You rum-soaked allies of Satan!" she shouted. "That'll keep your murder mill from corrupting any more of these poor, weak men!"

Her ladies were filing out of the saloon in an orderly manner, axes on their shoulders. Carrie Nation was the last to go. She paused at the door to shout, "Glory to God! Goodwill to all men!" The door slammed behind her. The saloon was silent once again but it was a dazed hush.

Jack decided it was time to go. In a few minutes, the air would be thick with curses and imprecations, with blasphemy and profanity such as had not been heard for a long time—even in that acre of iniquity, the Barbary Coast.

Outside, a few curious onlookers were watching the line of black-garbed women marching off down the street. There was little disruption of life outside the unfortunate Orpheum, though, and people walked on past, unaware of the devastation inside. Jack crossed the street to select a place to drink an uninterrupted beer. A horse clopped by, pulling a wagon with a heavy sheet over it that no doubt concealed some illicit cargo under it. Stepping aside to let it go by, he noticed a man standing in a doorway.

Jack remembered the night of the stakeout at the docks and the fight with the two men coming ashore; then he recalled they had seen a man in a doorway watching them afterward. This was the same toadlike man. His eyes were unmistakably on Jack.

The same broad-brimmed black hat was pulled down to cover his face and he wore the same tweed suit and vest. A straggly gray mustache covered the lower part of his face, and above it was a glitter of gold—a pair of spectacles. Jack had just enough time to see the bone-handled black-thorn walking stick in front of him. He seemed to be leaning heavily on it. Jack started forward to confront the man when a hand took his arm, lightly but firmly.

Jack turned to see a slim man of about his own age with a face clean-shaven except for a tiny trim mustache. He wore an expensive-looking suit and a Derby hat, both out of place on the Barbary Coast. He was holding a big black stogie. "I wonder if you could oblige me with a light?" he asked.

Jack realized it was the same man who had asked him and Officer Healey for a light. He shook his head. "I don't smoke." He turned back to look at the doorway. The man had gone. Jack tried to find him on the sidewalk but he was nowhere in sight. He looked back at the man who wanted a light. He too had disappeared, melting into the crowd.

Almost opposite the Orpheum was the Tower, a music hall and saloon of repute and a close rival of the Eureka. It had originally been called the Eiffel Tower, but because no one knew how to pronounce "Eiffel," people called it Ethel, until that name was dropped and it became known only as the Tower. The owner of the Tower was Jim Laidlaw, who had made a fortune in silver in Butte, Montana. He was at the bar when Jack went in, and he greeted the writer in friendly fashion, even though Jack was only an occasional customer.

A resolute Westerner, Jim Laidlaw wore cowboy clothes. His shirt was dark blue with pearl buttons and his Levi's had never seen the saddle of a horse. The wide leather belt held two pearl-handled, nickel-plated six-shooters in shiny holsters. Some said they had never been fired, but the names of old-timers on the Coast were sometimes invoked as being witnesses to a real troublemaker being taken out feet-first. Jack suspected that this story was not true, but it helped to maintain order in the Tower.

"Hear there's been a spot of excitement over at the Orpheum," Jim said. There was a glint of amusement in his eye at the thought of a rival saloon being smashed up by women.

"Carrie Nation and her Anti-Saloon League," said Jack. "I was in there."

"You weren't helping those, er, ladies, were you?"

"No. They broke my beer glass before I could get a drink out of it though," Jack said.

"Soon take care of that," said Jim with the thickest Western drawl that side of the Rocky Mountains. He waved to the bartender, who promptly took care of Jack's thirst, which was still active from the pickled squid at lunch.

"Where were they headed?" Jim asked. "Not this way, I hope."

"Looked like they were going toward Pacific."

"Good," Laidlaw said, hitching up his belt. "Means I won't have to shoot any of 'em."

"Thought you were too softhearted a man to shoot a lady," Jack said.

"What! Probably shot just as many of 'em as men."

Jack looked suitably surprised at the statement, even though he knew Laidlaw's reputation for exaggeration. "Maybe that's why they went in a different direction," Jack suggested. "Your reputation scared them off."

A piano struck up with "There'll Be a Hot Time in the Old Town Tonight," and one by one other instruments joined it.

"Stayin' for the show?" Laidlaw asked.

"Believe I might," Jack said. "Got some talent coming on?"

"Cole and Johnson," Laidlaw said proudly. "Top o' the bill." Jack knew who they were. Bob Cole and Billy Johnson had been a great hit in New York with a string of songs that had become popular, their latest being "The Wedding of the Chinee and the Coon."

"Next week's when you want to be here though," Laidlaw told him enthusiastically. "Minstrel Man Eddie Leonard is topping the bill."

"You did well to get him," Jack said. "Be a big drawing card."

"He sure will, and that ain't all. On the same bill we got this new magician guy."

"That's a new act for you, Jim."

"Martin Beck got him for me," Laidlaw told him proudly, and Jack whistled softly. He did not think that a magic act would last long with the tough, demanding Barbary Coast audiences, but Beck was the biggest impressario in the music hall scene and he presumably knew what he was doing. Laidlaw was saying something else but the orchestra surged into its loudest phase and the girls came out onstage. Conversation was impossible after that.

Chapter 8

The turgid stretch of water between Pier 3 and Pier 4 in San Francisco harbor was reserved for vessels coming from the Far East. It was common for those piers to be idle for a day or two each week, but now, on this gray and unpromising morning, the dockworkers were on strike, and the only activity consisted of a hundred or so onlookers, a makeshift tent, a crane and a poster board that stood on an easel. It stated—

POSITIVELY

The only Conjuror in the World that Escapes Out of all Handcuffs, Leg Shackles, Insane Belts and Strait-Jackets, after being STRIPPED STARK NAKED, mouth sealed up and thoroughly searched from head to foot, proving he carries no KEYS, SPRINGS, WIRES or other concealed accessories . . .

Under management of Martin Beck, Chicago.

A banner was strung between two poles and flapped in the lazy breezes off the bay.

"HARRY HOUDINI—MASTER ESCAPE ARTIST," it proclaimed in large letters.

Jack approached the crowd waiting impatiently to be entertained free of charge. He had seen the name Houdini in the trade newspapers that Flo read avidly and knew that

Houdini had changed his magic act to promote himself as an "escapologist." He had been popular in the Midwest and Jack had read in the *Chronicle* that morning of this free demonstration, obviously intended to boost attendance at Jim Laidlaw's Tower.

A couple of cameramen were setting up their awkward-looking tripods and some newspapermen Jack recognized were making bets with one another. Two men stood apart, talking. Jack's gaze went back to them a second time. One of them—a stout, red-faced man with heavy jowls and gold pince-nez glasses—he knew from photographs in the newspapers. He was the famous impressario Martin Beck. The man with him was well known to Jack, and each referred to the other as a friend, though their definitions of the term differed widely.

Ambrose Bierce was a critic, a cynic, a writer of distinction. He was currently editor of the prestigious *San Francisco Examiner,* hired by the son of the great William Randolph Hearst. Sturdy in build, he had fair hair, thick and luxuriant, and heavy eyebrows that made him look younger than his sixty years.

The friendship between Bierce and Jack was a strange one. Bierce considered Jack to be his protégé and frequently claimed that Jack's talents emerged only because of his expert nurturing. On his side, Jack did not recall one occasion when Bierce had been encouraging or congratulatory. Still, it was sometimes helpful to be considered a friend of Bierce, who was a prominent figure on the San Francisco scene.

Bierce caught sight of Jack and waved him over. He introduced him to Martin Beck, a short, stocky, bustling man who nodded affably and shook his hand. Bierce knew everybody, so Jack was not surprised to hear him say, "Martin assures me that this is going to be a spectacular show today."

Beck gave Jack a slight smile. "You know that's got to be true. It would take a big event like this to get Ambrose out of his office. You usually send reporters, don't you, Ambrose?"

"There's one of them here," Bierce said with a careless wave of his hand, "but this event is a little special."

"I've heard great stories about Houdini," Jack said, "but what's so special about today?"

His last words were drowned out as a figure emerged from one of the tents. Small but heavily muscled, he had a large head with a lot of bushy hair and a broad, strong face. He had a firm stride and carried himself with an air of supreme confidence. He was barefoot and wore a one-piece, tight-fitting swimsuit.

A ripple of applause came from the crowd and Houdini held up his hands in acknowledgment. Martin Beck went forward and joined him. Beck turned to the crowd. In clipped words, he announced that "the World's Greatest Escapologist" would perform a feat without equal. He invited two people from the audience to come forward and examine Houdini to be certain that he had no keys, wires or instruments of any kind concealed on his person. They did so, and there were titters of laughter as one insisted on looking inside Houdini's mouth and down his throat. The other, not to be outdone, peered in his ears and ran fingers through his hair.

Four uniformed policemen came forward, and each snapped a pair of handcuffs on Houdini's wrists, one at a time. A set of irons joined with a steel chain was clamped around his ankles. Another steel chain was padlocked after being looped to pull wrists and ankles close together. Beck waved in the direction of the tents and a man came out carrying a large burlap bag and a blindfold. He tied the blindfold tightly around Houdini's head, then helped him into the bag. A few gasps arose from the crowd as the bag was tied tightly at the neck.

Four men came out now with a formidably sized metal-bound sea chest. Martin Beck stepped forward and asked the members of the audience to inspect it. Several did, including, Jack noted, a couple of seamen. All pronounced it genuine after finding nothing unusual about it. The burlap sack with Houdini in it was lifted inside the chest and the lid slammed shut. Chains were brought forward and wrapped around the chest. Murmurs from the crowd were getting louder now and Jack found himself wondering how any man could possibly escape from all these restrictions. Padlocks clicked shut and keys ground in locks.

Martin Beck waved an imperious arm. Creaks and groans could be heard as the dock crane lowered its chain and hook and swung it toward the sea chest. A shout came from the tents and the four men who had brought the sea chest came staggering out with a wooden crate. One of the men engaged the hook under the chains around the sea chest, then waved to the crane operator. The sea chest swung into the air and was lowered inside the crate. The four men swarmed over it, hammering the lid in place. Then, with the voices of the crowd getting louder and louder, they put more chains around the crate.

All the men left. Martin Beck stood alone, the perfect showman, pointing with one straight arm at the crate with its human contents and allowing the moment to be stretched to its limit. The murmuring of the crowd subsided uneasily. A flock of seabirds came low in ragged unison, their harsh squawks like a paean to the man hidden from sight. Then the hook of the crane came down. Beck pushed it under the chain, waved once, and the crate floated up into the air, swung out and disappeared beneath the gently lapping gray water of the bay. Bubbles arose.

A woman cried out in fear. There was some nervous laughter. Jack felt his own frame tense. A man's life was at risk down there under the water. It became so quiet that the splash of the waves at the pier columns could be heard. The bubbles became less frequent, then stopped completely. A ship's horn, far out, hooted twice.

"It's been nearly ten minutes," Jack said to Bierce.

"A man can last about three minutes without air," Bierce said in his brisk, matter-of-fact voice.

Jack shook his head. "I don't see how he can do it—survive, I mean, let alone get out of all those chains and manacles. It's not human."

"Houdini has made some remarkable escapes," said Bierce, apparently unworried.

Minutes passed. The crowd stirred nervously but no one left. Martin Beck, still standing out in front of the crowd, took out a large pocket watch and consulted it with a frown.

"Martin's a great showman." Bierce smiled. "He's thinking of retiring from show business—did you know that?"

"Martin Beck?"

"No. Houdini."

"He is? His career's just beginning, isn't it? He's just becoming well known."

"Not fast enough and not well known enough. He hasn't been able to get bookings in New York or Philadelphia, in fact anywhere back east."

"With Beck behind him, surely he will?" Jack said.

"No, he can't. Beck doesn't manage any of the big theaters back there."

"Jim Laidlaw told me that Eddie Leonard, the Minstrel Man, is top of the bill at the Tower," said Jack. "Jim did well to get Houdini also."

Bierce seemed to be staring at something far out over the bay. "Yes, didn't he?" he murmured.

Something in that purring tone made Jack look at him sharply. "What are you up to, Ambrose?"

The grayness of the morning was yielding reluctantly to patches of weak blue. Bierce was still staring out there, but Jack knew he was not studying cloud formations.

"'Up to?' My goodness, Jack, you are a suspicious young fellow."

"I know you too well, Ambrose. You have something up your sleeve. Want to tell me about it?"

"I'm a newspaper editor, my boy. People tell me things."

"So do I—when I know what it is you're after. I gave you the story on the murder of those music hall girls, didn't I?"

"Hmm," said Bierce. "Does this mean you're on another of those investigations of yours?"

I should have known, thought Jack ruefully. Ambrose is a wily bird. No one else would have made that connection.

"If I am," he said carefully, "what I learn might help you."

Bierce nodded slowly. "True." He ceased his examination of the horizon. "Laidlaw is in financial trouble. He'd like to sell the Tower but can't find a buyer. He is heavily in debt to people who don't tolerate debtors."

"So where has he raised the money to bring two acts like Eddie Leonard and Harry Houdini?"

"Precisely," said Bierce. "Taking that thought a little further, the people who have that kind of money don't help out ailing music hall owners—"

"Then who. . . ?"

"I haven't finished," Bierce said in his most urbane manner. "They don't help out ailing music hall owners unless they have some very good reason."

Jack was trying to see where Bierce was leading him. The *Examiner* editor went on. "To answer that puzzle, let's ask another question. Is there any other unusual or strange event or combination of events that might fit in with this hypothesis?"

Jack frowned, concentrating. From the crowd, a man called out anxiously, "Bring him up! Bring him up!" Women's voices echoed the cry. Martin Beck waved his hands in placation, assuring them not to worry. "Harry Houdini is the world's greatest escapologist. He knows what he's doing." The cries subsided. A couple more photographers arrived and started to set up their tripods after some friendly banter with their competitors.

"I'll give you a clue," said Bierce. "One of the reasons

Houdini is thinking of retiring from his present line of entertaining is that he feels he has a mission."

"I read a piece about that," Jack said.

"It wasn't in my paper," Bierce said. "It must have been in one of those unreliable rags that you read."

"It would have been in your paper if you had thought it was news," Jack replied. "Yes, Houdini has a detestation of spiritualists, doesn't he? Wants to expose them all as fakers—" He broke off and Bierce regarded him with an amused expression.

"Go on," Bierce urged.

"Houdini is appearing at the Tower," Jack continued slowly, putting his thoughts together as he went, "and on the same street—in fact, almost opposite—is the Eureka Music Hall, where the world's greatest spiritualist, Eulalia Paradino, is appearing at the same time."

He examined Bierce's face and was rewarded with the expression of amusement turning into one of Bierce's wicked smiles. It made him look like an actor playing Mephistopheles, Jack thought.

"Exactly," Bierce said. "Quite a coincidence, isn't it?"

"What you're telling me, Ambrose, is that it is *not* a coincidence."

"I'd like to know," said Bierce, and the smile disappeared as the serious newspaper editor emerged. "But wouldn't this suggest the strong possibility of a confrontation? Houdini is a fiery sort of fellow. When he gets a cause like this, he won't let go. Being almost across the street from a spiritualist who maintains that she can genuinely raise people from the dead will surely irritate him beyond his tolerance limit."

"Good for the music hall business," said Jack. "Both the Eureka and the Tower will be crowded every show. Just what Jim Laidlaw needs if he's short of money. I don't know about the Eureka, but the owner won't be too unhappy at full houses every show."

"Then there's Belle Conquest," Bierce continued, and

Jack tried not to let any reaction show in his face. "She's coming to the Midway Plaisance—have you heard about that?"

"It's all over town," Jack said. "Nothing unusual there though surely? We often get a half dozen headliners here on the Coast at one time. We've had Lillie Langtry, Luisa Tetrazzini, Lillian Russell, Eddie Foy—dozens of others."

"Possibly," Bierce purred, "possibly. But here we have an event that we've never seen before. Not only does the Belle of Broadway, the number-one female performer in the country, come here, but she brings a companion with her."

"Companion?"

"The world's most precious stone—the Rajah's Ruby."

Jack nodded solemnly. "Yes, I heard that. You think some of our less-law-abiding gentry here on the Coast will find that jewel irresistible?"

Bierce raised one eyebrow. It was something he could do very effectively. "Wouldn't you, if you were not law-abiding?"

"Speaking of law-abiding," Jack said, "does the name Glass mean anything to you?"

"It does," Bierce said after a pause, "but up to now it's been little more than a name. If you learn any more, I'd be interested."

The cries from the crowd had begun again. There was an undertone of anger now—anger at Martin Beck for allowing a fellow human being to drown, sealed inside a sea chest and a packing crate. Beck looked at his watch, probably unnecessarily, then out at the waters of the bay. He appeared to consider, then snapped shut the cover of the watch and returned it to his pocket. "Twenty minutes," he called to the crowd. He paused. "Bring him up!"

Cries of approval and sporadic clapping greeted the announcement. Beck waved to the crane man, who pulled levers and released handles. The chain rattled as it began to rise from the water, at last revealing the packing crate. A small cheer went up. The crate broke clear of the surface, water streaming from it. The crowd went quiet as the crane swung its cargo to stop in front of them. Mechanisms ground and crunched again as the crate descended slowly to settle on the spot where it had been loaded.

Four men came from the tent. Padlocks were opened and chains pulled aside; then the men used crowbars and levers to pry the crate lid free. Water still ran onto the dock surface as they worked. Martin Beck had gone to stand near the crate. He waved to the crane man, and one of the four reached inside as the hook disappeared from sight within the crate. The sea chest swung into the air, turning very slowly, and another cheer ran around the crowd.

The four men went to work again, opening locks and unfastening chains. The crowd was pressing forward in eager anticipation. The lid of the chest was lifted open and one of the men pulled out the burlap sack. He lifted it, then dropped it on the ground and stamped on it.

It was empty.

There was a moment of silence; then incredulous shouts went up, although the accompanying applause was tinged with disbelief. Martin Beck stepped forward, waved his arms for quiet. The crowd waited. He regarded them, not moving.

"My friends," he said loudly, "I give you—Harry Houdini!" He pointed dramatically at the tent. Jack turned to it, as did everyone else. The flap opened and Houdini stepped out, soaking wet.

Again there was silence; then the crowd went wild. They surged around the magician, who stood there, accepting their adulation, with his chin out and arms crossed.

Chapter 9

They adjourned to Louie's Crab House, one of Bierce's favorite eating spots. Beck was in an ebullient mood, jubilant over the complete mystification of everyone concerning Houdini's miraculous escape. Even Ambrose Bierce, cynic and disbeliever in nearly everything, failed to suggest how the escape had been effected. He had asked Houdini outright and received only a polite smile and the reply, "I'll answer any other questions, Mr. Bierce."

It was Houdini's intense personal charisma that impressed Jack the most. He almost glowed with an inner strength, a hidden power, although as they talked, Jack began to realize that the magician's secret was not only in his belief in himself—which at times bordered on egotism. It came from hours upon hours of study and practice, time spent working with locksmiths, with safe builders—"and safecrackers," Harry had added with a smile—in prison cells, in straitjackets, in asylums. All of this experience had built a base of knowledge that contributed enormously to his self-assurance.

"He just had a great week in Chicago. Didn't you, Harry?" prompted Martin Beck.

"Tell us about that," added Bierce, always on the lookout for material. Before Bierce's appointment as editor of the *San Francisco Examiner,* the previous editor had published an article on Houdini, denouncing him as a trickster. Bierce had been quick to distance himself from that attitude.

"I was at the Central Police Station in Chicago," Harry

said. He had a high-pitched voice that almost reached a squeak at times. It was strangely incongruous with his forceful physical appearance. "I was searched for hidden picks and keys by the jail keeper and four detectives. They put me in a cell that had two locks. One was an ordinary cell lock with a keyhole. It was different from the usual keyhole, though, because it was covered with a large steel flap. This flap was so large, in fact, that it extended to the outer frame of the cell, where it was padlocked in place—far out of the prisoner's reach."

"They take no chances on criminals escaping in Chicago," Beck said and chuckled.

"Go on, Harry," urged Bierce.

"The jail keeper and the four detectives strip-searched me. Then they checked the cell and made sure there was nothing concealed in it. They left. Three minutes later, I walked into the office of the chief of detectives."

"Incredible," breathed Jack. "But then I'm still trying to work out how you got out of that burlap bag, the sea chest and the packing crate."

"So how did you get out of the jail cell, Harry?" asked Bierce.

"I had to open that remote padlock first, swing the flap aside to expose the keyhole, then open the door lock."

"Yes but—" and Bierce himself joined in the laughter of Jack and Martin Beck.

"In less than three minutes," Beck reminded them.

"Nearly one minute of which I spent finding the office of the chief of detectives," said Houdini. "One man I asked sent me the wrong way. I learned later he was a burglar, not a detective."

"Had you been in the police station prior to this?" Bierce asked.

"No," Houdini said. "I was firm on that point. I wanted no help in the way of concealed tools."

"He repeated this escape a week later in Kansas City, Missouri," Beck said proudly.

"One thing my readers are going to be interested in, Harry," said Bierce, "is your fierce opposition to spiritualism. There's some talk that you want to give up the stage and devote the rest of your life to proving that spiritualist acts, séances, predictions and manifestations are all conjuring tricks. What can I tell my readers on that?"

Before Harry could answer, Martin Beck quickly intervened, clearly unwilling to see his investment in Harry's stage future compromised. "Harry hasn't made up his mind on that yet. But I'll let him tell you himself what his views on spiritualism are."

Houdini left no doubt in the minds of all present about that issue. His light blue eyes began to blaze with passion and his already high voice climbed higher.

"Mediums, palm readers, astrologers, crystal ball gazers, lucky charm sellers, clairvoyants, fortune-tellers—they're frauds, every last one of them. They are swindlers who practice the most contemptible form of deception. They take advantage of other people's misfortune. They make money out of the deaths of loved ones, relatives, parents. They think nothing of robbing older persons of their life savings. Cardsharps and second-story burglars are upright citizens compared to these people!"

There was a silence at the table. It was an opportune moment for the waiter to arrive with the crab soup Martin Beck had ordered, assuring them that it was the best soup west of Philadelphia. They had started on the soup when Ambrose Bierce brought up the subject that Jack had been expecting ever since Bierce had asked for Houdini's views on spiritualism—views with which Bierce was already well acquainted.

"I understand that at the Eureka Music Hall—which is across Pacific Street from the Tower, where you are performing, incidentally—a performer will be putting séances on the stage. Er, Jack, could you pass me another piece of that excellent sourdough bread?"

Jack felt like laughing in admiration at Bierce's audacity

in bringing up this confrontation so adroitly. Bierce carefully avoided Jack's eye as he reached for a piece of bread
from the offered basket.

Martin Beck was concentrating on eating his soup, leaving Houdini on his own to handle that question, so neatly
implied.

"Eulalia Paradino is a performer whose act I have not
seen." Houdini's answer was precise and noncommittal.
Jack did not expect Bierce to let go—nor did he.

"This will be an excellent opportunity for you to do so
then," Bierce told the escapologist with a pleasant beam.

You're doing your puppet-master act again, Ambrose,
Jack thought. You want to drop the starving fox in the middle of the chicken coop. Jack believed he caught a look
pass between Beck and Houdini. He knew he was right
when Houdini said in a neutral tone, "I shall be very busy
rehearsing my act. I want my first appearance here in San
Francisco to be one of my finest."

"And you are both invited to attend the performance on
opening night," said Beck.

"Please come to any of the rehearsals too," added Houdini. "I want you both to see that I have nothing to hide."

Bierce and Jack accepted without hesitation. Houdini finished his soup, then turned to Jack. "Mr. Bierce said you
are a writer? Are you the Jack London who wrote those
pieces on socialism?"

"Yes, I am," said Jack.

"I found them very illuminating," Houdini said. "I am
not sure that I agree with all of your points, but you made
them very well. Tell me, although sharing the wealth is a
very Christian notion, it is also Utopian. How do you propose . . ."

Beck engaged the waiter in a discussion of the next
course and Bierce tried not to listen to Houdini and Jack
talking about socialism, a doctrine he detested with every
fiber of his body.

Houdini was a good listener and he and Jack debated socialism without becoming heated—a rare thing for Jack, for he found that many people hated it without knowing much about it. Houdini asked Jack if he did other writing and Jack told him of his experiences at sea and in the snowy Yukon and how he was attempting to convert those experiences into words.

All four enjoyed the grilled fish that followed, and when they separated at the end of the meal, Beck and Houdini repeated their invitations to come and see the show.

Jack had no opportunity to talk to Bierce afterward, because the editor immediately took a cab back to his office. Still thinking over the conversation, he caught a cable car and then walked the next block to the Midway Plaisance. He was able to have a few quick words with Flo and reinforce his reason for being there.

"We're onstage in a few minutes," Flo told him. "The number is coming along well but this Conquest woman is a stickler for perfection."

"So are you," Jack told her. "You never put on a number until you are absolutely satisfied with it."

"Yes, well," said Flo with a sniff, "it's different when someone else is asking for that perfection."

"Especially when it's another woman," Jack said and grinned.

"Not just another woman—"

"And even more especially when that woman is Belle Conquest."

Flo made a face at him. "I have to go get the girls."

It was midafternoon. The cleaners were at work on the floors, the assistant bartenders were bringing up bottles and polishing the bar and the waiter girls were straightening chairs and tables. The few windows were open to air out the place from the previous night. Altogether the place had a forlorn look as it awaited the crowds, the music and the excitement that would bring it to life in a few hours.

Jack strolled along the bar, nodding to the waiters and

some of the waiter girls. A musician came in with a violin in a case. All was normal enough out there. Jack walked past the stage and through the door that led backstage. It was kept open now but would be locked later when the lure of the girls would prove too much for the hotbloods among the audience.

The girls were coming out of the dressing rooms dressed in tight, virginal-white bodices that failed to contain full breasts and short, frilly crimson skirts that revealed black silk stockings and high-heeled black shoes. They carried tiny parasols of red, white and black. Jack smiled at several of them whom he knew. They passed him and went up onto the stage. Jack walked along the corridor, which was quiet and empty. Suddenly, he heard a gasping from somewhere ahead.

It was a woman's voice, full of anguish. Jack hurried forward. A door banged and Belle Conquest appeared. She was wrapped in a shiny black robe trimmed with black fur at the neck and wrists. She saw Jack and came running to him, heels clicking on the wood floor.

"Oh, Jack, thank God you're here!" She grabbed his hands. He looked into her face. Whatever the cause of her grief, it made her look older despite the makeup.

Before Jack could speak, she pulled him with her down the corridor. "In here!" she said in an unsteady voice and opened a door. It was one of the rooms for the use of any of the waiter girls who wanted to entertain a man in private. The walls were hung with soft purple curtains and the room was lit with a large chandelier and fitted with antique furnishings. A bed was the main feature and above the quilted headboard was a large mirror. There were also a white sofa and a white armchair, and in the middle of the room was a small table, used for intimate dinners.

Two chairs were placed at it. One was empty but the other was occupied by a tall young man with long golden hair. He wore a white shirt with pearl-buttoned sleeves and a blue-and-gray waistcoat. A black hole in the middle of the waistcoat had blood around it.

Jack examined him, though he had no doubt of the result. The man was dead. A sob came from behind him.

"Do you know this man?" Jack asked Belle Conquest.

She nodded, whimpered, then gained control of herself. "Rollo, Rollo Masters. He's one of my bodyguards."

Belle's "bodyguards" were something of a joke at the Midway Plaisance, Flo had told Jack. She had four of them—all young, handsome, virile men. They played minor roles in many of her sketches but their principal job was to service Belle's sexual desires, which were numerous.

Jack looked at the table. It held two empty whisky glasses, but otherwise all that was there were playing cards. A stack was in the middle of the table and a hand of cards lay facedown in front of each chair. "I—I didn't know he was a gambler," Belle said in a weak voice.

"How long has he been your bodyguard?" Jack asked.

"Nearly a year."

"Did he drink?"

Belle looked surprised at the question, then said, "Only now and then." She wiped an eye. Her normal resilience was returning fast. "Did he suffer?"

"I'm sure he didn't," said Jack.

"Poor Rollo." Her voice was firm but the emotion was strong. "He died defending me."

Jack doubted the veracity of that statement, but said, "You'd better call the police. I'll stay here and make sure no one touches the body."

She stood regarding the dead young man and Jack expected more tears but she remained dry-eyed. She shook her head very slightly and went out.

Jack studied the table, the position of the chairs and the dead body. His eyes came back to the cards on the table. He turned the two hands over, one at a time, looking at each of the cards carefully.

He examined the floor near each chair but there was

nothing. There was no sign that either card player had smoked. Jack sniffed the glasses—bar whisky, both of them.

He turned the empty chair around so that he was not facing the corpse, and awaited the police.

Chapter 10

The name of Belle Conquest brought the police in double quick time. A lieutenant named O'Bannion—a slow-spoken man with a soft Irish brogue—was accompanied by a uniformed officer. Jack knew neither of them. He was not introduced to the third detective. It was John Morley.

O'Bannion went about the task of searching the room and asking questions about Rollo while Morley just stood around, eyes probing. He did not look at or acknowledge Jack, but after the two detectives had exchanged quiet words, Morley caught Jack's eye and motioned him outside. O'Bannion told the uniformed man to collect the other three bodyguards, as he wanted to interview them right away.

Out in the corridor, Morley took Jack into an empty dressing room. "What can you tell me?" he asked without preamble. Jack related the event of finding the body.

"These so-called bodyguards," Morley said. "Are the rumors I've heard about them true?"

"If you've heard that they don't do much bodyguarding, then those rumors are true," Jack said. "She keeps them around for her personal pleasure."

"There must be a strong rivalry among them for the lady's favors."

"I'm sure there is," Jack agreed, "but I doubt if one of the other three killed Rollo."

"Do you know them?"

"No, but take another look at the cards on the table. Oh, I

know that it looks like Rollo was cheating and that's why he was shot, but I suspect that's what we're supposed to think. You see, neither hand has anything in it. There's no motive there. Of course, they could have been arguing over something else—"

"Such as Belle Conquest," said Morley.

"Yes, but I don't think so. When your colleague has interviewed the other three, I'll bet he'll agree that none of them looks like a killer."

"That bullet wound—there's surprisingly little blood around it," Morley said.

"What does that mean?"

"We'll find out." Morley regarded Jack shrewdly. "What do you think about a motive if it was not a gambling feud?"

"I think it's a warning from someone who intends to steal the ruby. It's a message to Belle Conquest that she could be killed as easily as Rollo was."

Morley nodded. "Telling her not to hold on to the ruby— it's not worth another life. Frightening her so as to make the theft easier."

"She'll be afraid to hire a replacement," Jack said. "Could be a plant and then she'd be in even more danger from someone close to her. For whatever use these fellows are as bodyguards, there's one less of them now."

"We'll see what O'Bannion comes up with after he's interviewed everybody here," said Morley.

"Most of the staff were out front getting ready for tonight. They'll be able to alibi each other—a lot of them anyway. My guess is that Rollo had been dead about fifteen minutes when Belle found him and called me. The blood had stopped seeping but hadn't fully dried on his waistcoat."

"Plenty of time for anyone to get away. Any outsiders here?"

"I haven't seen any. A beer or whisky salesman comes in during the afternoon sometimes but I haven't seen any today."

"Good work," Morley said. "Keep your eyes open. Anything else?"

"Well, it probably has nothing to do with the ruby, but for what it's worth, I was attacked by two Chinese assassins. I suspect they may have been directed by Glass, but I can't get any lead on him." He went on to tell Morley of the meeting with Harry Houdini, Martin Beck and Ambrose Bierce. "A conflict between Houdini and this spiritualist woman seems inevitable. People's tempers get inflamed—there could be fights and people hurt. Some of your people should be alerted so that they can be prepared."

Morley looked somber. "I'll alert the higher-ups." A thought struck him. "This Houdini—I've read about him recently."

"He's been getting a lot of publicity," Jack agreed.

"He escaped from a safe in Baltimore."

"Did he? I didn't see that report."

Morley rubbed his chin thoughtfully. "If he can open safes from the inside, can he also open them from the outside?"

Jack considered. "Maybe it's easier from the inside. Thieves are always on the outside, aren't they?"

"Just a thought," Morley said. "I seem to recall that he has not been doing too well lately. Thinking about going to Europe, thinking about retiring. . . ."

"You've read a lot about him."

Morley shrugged. "I like to keep up with all these visitors to our city. Especially ones who have a financial motive."

"How about Belle Conquest?" asked Jack. "Have you kept up with her enough to know where she keeps the Rajah's Ruby? In a safe?"

"She won't tell us where she keeps it. Says it's safer that way. She's a fool if she keeps it anywhere else though."

"You could put pressure on the banks and storage vaults to tell you if she's made a deposit there recently, couldn't you?"

Morley didn't appear optimistic about the chances of any results from the suggestion. Jack guessed that the banks in San Francisco were sufficiently powerful that they could refuse to give out any information to the police about their customers.

They talked for several more minutes, then left separately. Jack sought out Belle Conquest. She was talking to her mustached, slick-haired manager, Louis Lahearne. He was cool to Jack and excused himself, saying he was next on the list to talk to the police. Jack turned to Belle.

"This is a terrible thing for you."

"Poor Rollo." She was a little pale but composed, the professional coming out uppermost. "He was such a nice boy."

"How do the other three feel?"

"Nervous, of course, but they're all so loyal."

"I'll spend more time here in the future," Jack said.

"Do you know anything about this Paradino woman?" she asked.

"I don't know anything about her, no, except everybody says she is a genuine mystic."

"They say she can communicate with the dead. Do you think she could talk to Rollo? Ask him who killed him?"

Jack was taken aback at the question. "I really don't know much about spiritualism, but I was curious about her. I thought I'd like to see her act."

"Would you see it and tell me what you think?"

For a very brief time, the brassy babe from Brooklyn was just a lonely little girl with big eyes and a vulnerable expression. Jack found it easy to say, "Of course I will."

She squeezed his hand and hurried away.

Jack sought out Flo. She had been interviewed by the police along with everyone else, but because she had been rehearsing her girls at the time, her interview was short.

"Are we still in danger?" Flo asked anxiously.

"I doubt it," Jack said. "This isn't a casual killing. There's a purpose behind it. I don't believe you or any of your girls are threatened. Still, it would be a good idea if they avoided being alone, and you too."

"I'll tell them," said Flo. "Does this mean that Belle's other three bodyguards are in danger?"

"Maybe," Jack said. "What do you hear about them?"

"One or two of the girls have made eyes at them but they got no response. They seem to be fanatically loyal to Belle." Flo smiled. "Studs is what the girls call them."

"Think they'll stay, with Rollo being killed?"

"I doubt if any of them would leave her."

"All right," said Jack. "Now, Flo, if you or any of your girls have the chance to talk to these fellows, let me know what they say, would you? It might be helpful."

"Yes, I will," Flo promised, "and you—you be careful, will you?"

"Worried about me?" He held her close.

"Yes, you're reckless. No more fighting on the streets!"

"That wasn't my idea. After Rollo's death, though, you can bet I'll be careful." They kissed and Jack gave her a wave as he left. Flo shook her head. Asking Jack to be careful was like telling the tide to hold still.

The police had looked as though they intended to be around the Midway Plaisance for some time, so Jack felt he could safely leave. He walked across Pine and Pacific Streets to the Tower Music Hall. He had an odd suspicion about Houdini's appearance there. The man himself seemed to be an unlikely accomplice in any criminal plot, as did Martin Beck, but a web of coincidence was being woven around the appearance of Houdini at the Tower and Eulalia Paradino at the Eureka.

Jack did not like coincidences. The two performers were like sparks and tinder. The principals themselves might not be involved, but they might well be the dupes of others.

Preparations were under way at the Tower for the evening performance. Houdini was due to open tomorrow night, and again Jack was struck by that fact—Eulalia

Paradino was opening two nights later. He hoped Morley would heed his warning and have extra men on hand, but the San Francisco police department's record of preventing or handling riots was poor. They regarded most such events as fights between rival gangs and considered it better to let them decimate one another and reduce the criminal population of the city without police involvement. Jack conceded that the idea had merit, but too often innocent citizens suffered as well.

The Tower had one of the largest stages in the city and a vast area behind and underneath it for storage and trapdoors and other devices. The stage was empty at the moment. Jack nodded to a waiter he knew and went backstage.

He could not see Houdini, but various pieces of strange equipment stood around and men were working on many of them. A cloth-covered frame cabinet stood next to a table with a large cage full of white doves. A glass tank half full of water looked as if it were just big enough to accommodate a man, and Jack shuddered at the thought of being inside it when the lid was fitted on. He wandered on into the next room, which contained only one piece of equipment—a steel boiler.

Shiny and new-looking, it was about six feet long and three feet in diameter. Rows of neat rivet heads joined the curved steel panels. The end of the cylinder was open. Jack was peering into it when a hand clapped onto his shoulder. He turned to find Harry Houdini, wearing a set of dark blue overalls.

"Jack, my friend! Welcome! You are looking at my latest escape."

The magician was much more lively and ebullient because he was now in his native element, the world of astonishment and illusion.

Jack listened to him describe the performance he intended to present tomorrow night as the climax of his opening show. "Several people from the crowd will be invited to come onstage and examine the boiler and make sure the joints are all genuine. The only way this differs from a real boiler is this open end."

He showed Jack what he meant. The full diameter of the open end had a half dozen threads, and Houdini pointed to a threaded dome lying nearby. It had two handles on the outside. "They will put me inside and then thread the end into place. Those same people will stand around the boiler, and it will be resting on a stand to keep it off the ground— that way, there can be no suggestion of a trapdoor in the stage."

"What about air?" Jack asked. "Once that end dome is threaded on, there will be no way for air to enter."

"Precisely," said the magician with pardonable pride. "Once I have entered the boiler and the end is in place, there will be five minutes of air at the most."

"I have seen Indian fakirs who learned to control their breathing," said Jack. "Real experts are able to breathe only four or five times an hour."

"That is true," Houdini said. "I can do it too. But that will merely extend the time I can survive in there. Can those same Indian fakirs escape from this boiler?" He rapped his knuckles on the metal shell.

Jack walked around it. He studied the rivets and tapped the steel hull in places. He came back to Houdini. "Harry, there's something you're not telling me. It's absolutely impossible for any man to escape from this once the end is closed."

Houdini smiled. It was a smile of utter self-confidence. "Of course it is. Any man except me."

A man came hurrying over to Harry. "Captain Bean is here. He's brought the giants."

"Ah, yes," Houdini said. "Jack, would you excuse me just a few moments?"

He left and Jack walked around the boiler again. It was impossible—there was no other word for it. He checked the rivets, even trying to pull some loose, but they were all real. He had a thought—all he could really see were the heads of the rivets. Did they really go through the steel sheets and out the other side? It was the only explanation, surely.

Jack went to the open end of the boiler. It might pique the great magician if Jack found out how the trick was done, but he had been boastful of his prowess. Jack could not resist. He peered inside the interior of the boiler. There was just sufficient light.

Without warning, something crashed onto the back of his head. He fell sprawling inside the boiler and was vaguely aware of his feet being pushed in after him. Then he heard a metallic clatter, and darkness descended rapidly. He was just conscious enough to realize that the domed end of the boiler was being threaded into place.

Chapter 11

There was not a glimmer of light, only the intense, searing whiteness of the north. All was white: the snowy ground, the sky filled with snowflakes. Jack could not distinguish the least shape. He tried to turn his head but his neck hurt. He attempted to lift his right arm but it was underneath him and he did not have the strength to move.

He was cold, very cold, but he could not feel the bulky furs that were his only protection. He managed to move a hand and touched icy-cold metal. His brain could not understand that. Now the white was changing, turning black—everything was black. He moved his legs but they hit some invisible obstacle and would move no farther. He reached out an arm and gasped as his fingers hit something solid and hard.

It was coming back to him. He realized that the whiteness had been only a memory, a memory of terrible times in the past. So where was he? He moved his head again and winced at the pain. The pain at the back of his head, where he had been hit.

He had been reaching inside—inside where? Then it all flooded back: the boiler, the rivets, the blow on the back of the head and the descending darkness. His head ached and he found it was painful to move his limbs, but he forced himself. He fumbled around with his hands. The circular section of the boiler, the domed ends—that was his world. A tiny, cramped space. And that man, the magician, what was his name? Houdini, that was it. What had Houdini said about the air supply? Five minutes?

He fought down a rising panic. He had looked death in the face many times before. He had faced five Chinamen with knives, a crazed Polack with a club, a howling gale in the South Pacific with sixty-foot waves and a ship cracking apart. He had looked into the muzzles of pistols and rifles—he was not going to die trapped in a boiler.

Houdini had planned on escaping from this tiny prison, so there must be a way out. Jack would find it. What had been his own idea about the way Houdini planned his escape? The rivets—yes, the rivets. They must be false. He fumbled over the inner surface with his fingertips. He found a row of rivets but they were secure. He found another row and another. Finally, he was sure he had tried them all. Not one would move. He tried them all again with the same result.

He squirmed around to get to the end cap. It was firm. He pushed and twisted at the curved surface but could not get a grip. It remained unyielding. A cold fear formed at the pit of his stomach. He fought it down. Lying on his back, he hammered against the wall of the boiler with his boots. It sounded loud inside, but could the noise be heard outside? He tired, rested a few seconds, then hammered again.

Breathing was getting difficult—was that his exertion or the reduced amount of air inside the boiler? Yet what was the point in preserving air if he was going to die in there? He hammered again and kept it up until he sagged into silent exhaustion. He felt himself slipping off into a stupor.

He had no idea how long it was before a scraping sound awoke him. It took him time to orient himself; then abruptly light flooded in as the end dome was lifted away. It stayed suspended in midair and a startled face peered over it.

"Vot you doing in dere?" a voice with a heavy German accent asked. "No place to sleep," it said reprovingly. The dome clanged on the floor and hands helped Jack to clamber out. He staggered, and an old whiskered face looked into his. "You all right?"

Jack nodded, wincing as his neck protested. "Thanks for letting me out," he said. "I'm sure glad you heard me."

"Heard you? I not heard you. I see the end cap on—we always keep him off." He looked at Jack curiously. "How you fasten it from inside?"

Jack grinned ruefully. "Magician's trick. We never give away secrets." He rubbed the back of his head. There seemed to be no breaks in the skin or even any swelling.

The man looked unconvinced, or maybe he didn't understand English well enough.

"You friend Mr. Houdini?"

"Yes," said Jack. "He had to go take care of some visitor."

"Captain Bean, *ja.* Still talking to him."

"I'll wait for him in the other area," said Jack, thinking it would be safer there with several people around.

It was some minutes before Houdini reappeared, and by then Jack was returning to his customary self. His headache was nearly gone and the stiffness in his limbs was forgotten. The intervening time had given him the opportunity to reflect that someone here had deliberately sealed him into the boiler, knowing that in five minutes he could be dead. He had looked at the faces of the men working in the other area one by one but they all looked busy and harmless.

"Sorry to be so long," Houdini apologized. "Manage to amuse yourself looking around?"

"I certainly did," Jack answered. "That boiler escape baffles me though. It really looks impossible."

Houdini held out what looked like a large plate of thin steel. He was excited. Clearly, he was more fascinated with what must be a new trick. "Captain Charles Bean is the man I have just been talking to. He has invented many ingenious devices for the police to use as what they call restraints. He calls this his Bean Giant."

He held it out. There were two holes in the sheet, spaced well apart, and Jack could see that the sheet was actually in two pieces. They were joined by two keyholes, both small and well out of reach of the prisoner's fingers.

"Most handcuffs are joined by a chain, so they have play. These don't, and each hand is clamped out of reach of the other." He handed Jack two keys. "The two keyholes have different locks too. Here, put these on me."

Jack took the two parts of the Bean Giant and Houdini turned so that Jack could fetter him behind his back. Jack turned a key in each keyhole. Houdini turned to face him, a slight smile on his face. Jack was still dropping the second key into his pocket when Houdini brought his hands out in front of him, the Bean Giant handcuffs in one of them. Houdini's smile spread over his face.

Jack goggled in astonishment. "How—how did you . . . ?"

"That's what Captain Bean said a few minutes ago. He couldn't believe it, said he had fastened ten thousand prisoners in his time with those handcuffs. Not one had ever escaped."

Jack had seen performers on the stage before but none like Houdini. The man was beyond belief. He was looking at Jack with a smile of satisfaction at his baffled amazement.

Jack steered the conversation toward tomorrow's opening night. Finally, the magician excused himself, agreeing that he had much to do to get ready for that occasion. Jack left him, giving an assurance that he would be there to applaud.

Back in his room, Jack wondered fleetingly if his latest encounter had been any connection with the attack by the two Chinamen in the alley. While looking at the workers in Houdini's area, he had not seen any Oriental faces. If there was no connection, did it mean that there were two groups wanting to kill him? It was a scary thought. His aches and pains came back and he fell asleep from the mental as well as the physical exhaustion.

It was night when he awoke. He ate roast beef, cheese and bread, drank a lot of water and went back to sleep.

The next morning he felt better, except that his head was slightly fuzzy, but he ignored it and sat down to do his writing. He was nearing the climax now. Alex Gunderson—the seven-foot, three-hundred-pound Norse giant—was working out well as a memorable character and Jack wanted to finish this story and send it to the *Atlantic Monthly,* the most prestigious literary journal in the United States.

Another reason for finishing this story, albeit a less important one, was that he had suspended his reading temporarily. He seldom did that, because he believed that reading great writers taught him about writing. He was currently partway through *Silverado Squatters* by Robert Louis Stevenson, one of his favorite authors, and he was eager to get back to it.

When he stopped writing, he was close to the end of the story. He liked to stop at a place where he could easily pick up the next time, and he was sure that one more writing session would enable him to complete the story. Then would come the dreary chore of revising. He hated that but it had to be done. Jack liked to send in a manuscript that was as good as he could make it.

Jack headed out for the docks at the foot of Taylor and Leavenworth Streets. He liked to go there and think. Sometimes he could bask in the sunshine, and other days he could shiver as chilly breezes swept in across the bay. Today was still undecided between the two, though it was getting warmer.

Just a few months ago, the state of California had given the area to the fishermen who had boats. It was not merely a generous gesture—it could be a good source for revenue for the ever-hungry coffers of the city and state treasuries. The amount of seafood being consumed in San Francisco was rising rapidly, and surrounding regions and cities were demanding more and more. Ships were being rebuilt with large ice chambers for carrying fish along the coast, and the fishermen families of Aliotto, Sabella, DiMaggio and Castagnola were becoming known. With the city's support, they could expect to prosper.

Jack loved it there. He walked along the wharf, stepping over nets and past men repairing traps and lines. The sharp smell of salt and fish mingled with the smoke of oil burners. Once a sailor, always a sailor. Jack believed in that very firmly. The savor of the salt never goes away, and the sailor never grows so old that he does not care to go back for one more wrestling bout with wind and wave. The port of San Francisco was a constant source of fascination to Jack. He knew that it was the largest harbor in the world and that it could hold every ship afloat on all the seven seas.

The fishermen were the only ones working. Jack went on to the main harbor, where a few ships lay silent, unable to escape before the longshoremen's strike had laid a monstrous constraining hand over the entire area. Jack studied the few vessels at the piers. They appeared forlorn and forgotten. They belonged out in the open sea, cutting through the white waves, proudly carrying their cargoes to distant shores.

Jack had never seen the area like this. It reminded him of ghost towns in the Yukon, abandoned when the gold ran out. He must get a newspaper today, he thought, to see what the *San Francisco Examiner* was saying about progress in ending the strike, and especially what its explosive editor, Ambrose Bierce, was saying. Ambrose never pulled any punches and he could launch devastating attacks on any side in any argument.

Ahead was the Longshoremen's Hall. A few men were coming out. A union meeting must be ending. Because Jack was a fervent socialist, his sympathies were with the union, but he hated to see the great harbor silent and motionless. He hoped the two sides were close to an agreement.

Union members were pouring out of the hall now and Jack slipped in among the crowd. A man, lean and gaunt, was walking alongside him, and Jack asked him, "What did you think of the meeting?"

The man grunted and spat. "The bastards are not going to give an inch," he said in a gravelly voice, "but like the organizer said, we're not going to give in either."

So the strike would continue. Jack talked to the man further as they walked off the docks. The mood of the union was bitter and that of the harbor authorities adamant. It seemed that the shipowners had banded together to support the harbor authorities, so any chance of an early settlement looked bleak.

Jack was in a somber mood as he left the man and headed for the Midway Plaisance. If the strike lasted much longer, it would affect the establishments on the Barbary Coast and, in turn, all of San Francisco.

Chapter 12

At the music hall the atmosphere was lively and cheerful and Jack felt his spirits rising immediately. The piano player was thumping out the latest song by Paul Dresser, whose previous hit, "On the Banks of the Wabash," was still a popular number. Flo was rehearsing a half dozen girls in a twirling dance that apparently needed a lot of improvement. Backstage, a trumpet blared and a flute trilled in a near-musical accompaniment.

Near the stage stood Belle Conquest. She wore a tight-fitting dress in yellow and black that contained her ample breasts with difficulty. It was cinched tight at the waist with a black silk sash and she had a large black hat in one hand. She was arguing with the stage manager, who looked as if he were losing on every point. He tried to protest, then nodded, resigned. He left and Belle saw Jack and waved him over.

Jack darted a glance at Flo to see if she was looking in that direction, but she was engrossed in the dance formation of the chorus girls. He went over to Belle.

She greeted him with a full-lipped red smile and just the least flutter of long eyelashes. "Well, handsome, you've come back to see me, have you?" Her blond hair was freshly coiffed and a haze of heavily exotic perfume enveloped her.

"I came back to be sure your, er, property was safe," said Jack.

She planted one hand on her hip and adjusted her body provocatively. "It's safe enough," she told him.

"Where did you say you kept the stone?" Jack asked.

"I didn't say." Her voice was more of a drawl, though not with any pronounced Southern origin. "Got any ideas on a safe place?" she asked, and her smile held a hidden meaning. Before Jack could answer, she said, "I can see you do. Come on, let's go to my dressing room and we can talk about—well, about safety measures."

Swaying sensuously, she led the way without waiting for an answer. Jack followed and they went into a dressing room that had clearly been remodeled very recently. It was startlingly white. The floors, the rugs, the walls, the ceiling were all white. The large bed was white and so was the quilted headboard above it. The large mirror on the ceiling was framed in white, and the ornate lamps were white.

Belle said, "White is my favorite color. Everywhere I perform, they furnish a dressing room for me all in white. This is a nice one, don't you think?"

"Very nice," said Jack. He had known a number of women but never one quite like this. She had all the power and impact of a Union Pacific express.

She kicked off her shoes, sprawled on the bed and leaned back languorously against the padded headboard. "Sit down," she invited.

Jack looked for a chair. There were none. Belle smiled at his dilemma. "Chairs are only for sitting. Come over here." She patted the bed.

Jack joined her on the large bed. She patted it again. "Over here."

He was within range of that overpowering perfume now. There was something else too, something like magnetism. This was an extraordinary woman. She leaned closer. "I told you I needed another handsome young man in my act, didn't I?"

"I've never done any acting," Jack told her. He liked women but was more used to the ones he had to woo. He had never met one who was so overtly sensual and aggressive.

"You don't need to be able to act in my show." Belle edged closer. Their faces were only inches apart. "Just do what comes naturally."

Her hand crept around the back of his neck. She pulled him closer. "What's the matter?" she murmured. "Not afraid of me, are you?"

"Not of you, no, but one of your handsome young men has just been murdered."

The remark might have shattered the mood of any lesser woman, but Belle was as resistant as a stone wall. "Poor Rollo," she whispered. "Now that he's gone, can't you see that I'm in even more need of you?"

Their lips were just touching when a knock came at the door. Belle was prepared to ignore it but it came again, louder. A female voice called out, "Miss Conquest! Could we have you onstage?"

"Later!" Belle shouted, but the voice said, "Miss Conquest, there's a problem with your opening number. We may have to change it so that—"

"Change it?" cried Belle. Her eyes blazed. "You'll change nothing. I—wait a minute!" Forgetting Jack, she slid off the bed and ran to the door.

Jack listened to the sound of footsteps die away down the corridor. He had recognized the voice as Flo's. He quickly left the dressing room but had not gone far when a door opened ahead of him.

"Oh, Jack, there you are!" Flo's voice was like melting butter. "I didn't interrupt anything, did I?"

"Nothing to interrupt," said Jack.

"You're a little flushed."

Jack grinned. "La Belle was telling me that she had need of me. With Rollo gone, she doesn't feel safe."

Flo pouted. "Yes, I'm sure he was a very good bodyguard. Anyway," she went on, "I have greater need of you than she does." She drew him into her room and pulled him close. "Let me show you what I mean. . . ."

*   *   *

When he emerged, Jack made a tour of the backstage area. Nothing was unusual; all was quiet. Returning, he could hear voices raised in argument, and there was no difficulty in identifying the loudest as that of Belle Conquest. Jack avoided the stage and left by a side door.

His mind was buzzing with an idea. He was always alert to anything that might initiate or contribute to a story, and Belle Conquest had provided that stimulus. He had to work hard at building characters, especially women characters. Women in literature were traditionally beautiful but helpless, ignorant of life's realities. The popular books of the day were the Graustark stories of Charles McCutcheon and the tales of Richard Harding Davis, and they presented women in this light. Even Jack's idols, Rudyard Kipling and Robert Louis Stevenson, wrote about women as minor characters, with negligible roles in the unraveling of the plot.

Jack had a daringly different approach in mind now. He would set the story during the Yukon Gold Rush, the period that he knew so well. But instead of having a heroine subservient to a masculine hero, she would be the daughter of a pioneer, born and raised in the icy wilderness of northern Alaska. She would be clever and strong, firm-willed, full of courage and determination. She would be the central character—not the man. She would be nothing like Belle Conquest, even though Belle had provided the germ of the idea. A title began to form in Jack's mind already—*A Daughter of the Snows.*

Exhilarated at the prospect of another story—even though he had a half dozen plots in mind now—he turned his attention back to his assignment with the police. Rollo's murder was a reminder of the seriousness of the threat against Belle Conquest. Yet the threat was not against her personally, but against the Rajah's Ruby. The most precious stone in the world.

The organization of the mysterious Glass coveted it, if Morley's theory was correct. The safecracking expert, Lou

Kandel, breaking out of San Quentin seemed to confirm it. But why the attack on Jack by the two *boo how doy*? The Chinese tongs were generally believed to be financed by money from China. Did they need to steal the stone? Perhaps the Chinese here were not as rich as people thought—thousands of them lived in squalor. Then there was How Chew Fat—he had suggested that two of the assassins were renegades working for Glass. Was that the truth or subterfuge?

Without paying much attention to where he was going, Jack found himself on Vallejo Street. He was pausing to decide which way to turn when a man came running across the street, calling to two others just in front of Jack. He was instantly on the alert. Two attacks on his life had sharpened his reactions, even when his thoughts were elsewhere.

The three near him looked like businessmen, but that could be a disguise. Listening to their raised voices, though, Jack knew that this was not an immediate threat. He caught the words "Union Trust" and "safe cracked." The men looked anxious, turned the corner and hurried along Sansome Street. Jack followed.

The Union Trust Bank was only a few blocks along Sansome Street, next to the London and San Francisco Bank, the German American Savings Bank and the California Bank. The three men ahead of him picked up another colleague on the way and excitedly told him the news. All four quickened their pace and Jack stayed close behind them.

The bank looked like it was under siege. Police wagons were drawn up on the street, keeping traffic away. Wooden barriers were still being unloaded and set up in position. Uniformed police swarmed everywhere. "Didn't know there were that many in the whole state!" Jack heard one wag say. The crowd was swelling; everyone was eager to know what was going on. Vehicles were stopping and the police were striving to move them along.

A few men, evidently reporters, were at the front of the crowd. Jack pushed his way toward them, using elbows and shoulders. "What's happening?" he demanded, and looked around for an answer. A couple of faces turned and looked blank. One man shrugged, but another said, "They found one of the vaults cracked during the night. Serves 'em right!" he added viciously. "And us on strike!"

A man in ordinary clothes came out and the uniformed police made way for him. Another followed—Captain Morley. They turned and went along the sidewalk, heading toward a police wagon about twenty yards away. Jack pushed his way out through the crowd and hurried down the street. He walked back onto the sidewalk so as to intercept Morley.

He knew it was not a good idea to be seen in public talking to the police captain. Morley had the same idea. He saw Jack at once but made no sign. When the two men drew level, Morley jerked his head toward the other side of the street and went on into the wagon.

Jack crossed the street and stood in the entrance of the Western Insurance Company. It was better than standing in the entrance of one of the banks, where the guards would be itchy and nervous. After a few moments, Morley came out of the wagon and, as he crossed the street, spotted Jack at once.

"This is as good a place as any," Morley said. He looked tired. "What brings you here?"

"Heard on the street that a vault had been cracked in the Union Trust. Anything about cracking vaults and safes gets my attention."

"If you'd heard any more, you'd have been here sooner," Morley said crisply. "This vault was rented a few days ago by Belle Conquest."

"Was the ruby in it?" asked Jack, shocked.

"A lot of her other jewelry was, but not the ruby. They got a fair haul but I'm guessing it was the ruby they were after."

"Does it look like the work of Lou Kandel?"

"Has his hallmark all over it. Only a handful of safe-

crackers in the country could break into that vault, and he's
the best of them all. Still, the city is teeming with malcontents, including all the strikers." Morley gave Jack a searching look. "Have you found out where she keeps that ruby?"

Jack shook his head.

"Can't you get close enough to her to find out?" Morley
sounded a little testy.

Jack decided it was not the time to mention how close he
had been just a short time before. "Not yet, but I think I
can," he said.

"Since the murder of that bodyguard, she must be nervous. Play on that. Make her more nervous, get her to trust
you."

There were some aspects of police work that Jack did not
like. He enjoyed the excitement and the danger, but using
other people's discomfort and fear to learn what he wanted
to know went against his natural principles of fair play.
Still, he told himself, it was for Belle's own good. He detected the hypocrisy in his own thoughts and added another
platitude: the end justifies the means.

Morley was looking at him intently. "You can do that,
can't you?"

"Yes," said Jack, mustering all his firmness.

"Another point. You have a lot of unsavory acquaintances—any of them belong to the Riders of the Rim?"

"Not as far as I know," Jack said. "I don't know much
about them. Gang of bandits, aren't they?"

"They robbed the Carson City Stage recently, a very professional job. They also held up the Bank of Sacramento,
just as efficiently."

"Think they are after the ruby too?"

"It doesn't seem to be their kind of job—" Morley broke
off as an insurance customer came out. He passed them
without a glance and they both watched him until he was
out of sight. Morley went on. "But the most valuable stone
in the world has got to be a magnet for any villain. Keep

your ears open and let me know if you hear anything of this crew."

"I will. There's something else I should tell you—somebody tried to kill me." He recounted the incident at the Tower Music Hall and his experience in the boiler.

Morley frowned. "Houdini brought his own people with him. We can't check them out as easily as we can our local criminals. Is someone on to you?"

"I don't know."

"Well, we can look on the good side of it. You've made someone nervous enough that he wants to kill you."

Morley returned to the police wagon across the street, and after a few minutes watching, Jack turned onto Pine and took the short walk to the Ferry Building.

He had declined to ask Morley what the bad side was.

Chapter 13

Luna's was a sharp contrast to the bars and music halls of the Barbary Coast. It catered to journalists, editors, magazine writers and visiting celebrities, such as novelists, poets and playwrights. It had the ambience of a men's club, and its polished dark wood floors, paneled walls, potted plants, and brass wall lamps would not have been out of place in New York or Philadelphia.

It had the reputation of having no address due to its corner location and absence of a street number. Jack always felt mildly uncomfortable there; he was certainly much more at home in the raucous, rowdy atmosphere found in most of the places he frequented. His usual reason for visiting Luna's was to talk to the redoubtable editor of the *San Francisco Examiner,* Ambrose Bierce.

The paper, already powerful, had climbed to dizzying heights under Bierce's thunderous pen. Bierce attacked religion, horse racing, lawyers, dogs, the police, the National Guard, bankers, shippers—and especially the Republican Party. It was said that every politician in California read Bierce's editorial column in the *Examiner* before eating breakfast.

As Jack had expected, Ambrose Bierce was at the bar, a Sazerac in front of him, one foot on the brass rail and a fist hammering home a point of rhetoric. The mahogany bar was resisting stoutly, but the red-faced man with Bierce wasn't. He said a few angry words and stomped off without as much as a handshake. Bierce turned to watch him leave with an expression of amusement on his face. As he did so, his eye fell on Jack.

"Ah, my young protégé. Still applying all the lessons I've taught you?"

Once again, Bierce took credit for encouraging Jack's writing career. Jack valued the older man's knowledge and experience and did not bring the point to argument. The two were an unlikely pair, and yet there existed an indefinable bond between them. Jack sometimes wondered how far that bond would stretch if tested, but such an occasion had never arisen.

"Hello, Ambrose. Yes, I must be."

"What are you drinking?"

Jack ordered a schooner of beer. On the bar stood bowls of frogs' legs, pickled squid and fried shrimp, and Jack helped himself. They were the only two at the bar, but the dining area looked busy, and subdued chatter and laughter came from the opulent lounges.

"You have a busy few days coming up, don't you?" Bierce asked. "All these openings at those disgraceful places of entertainment you patronize?"

"It is going to be busy," Jack agreed, "with Houdini, Eulalia Paradino and then Belle Conquest all having openings."

"You always have your ear to the ground," said Bierce. "You've heard about the vault being cracked at the Union Trust, I'm sure. With La Belle's jewels in it."

Jack smiled. Ambrose was ever the newspaperman. He might know more about what was happening in San Francisco than any other human being, and he never missed a chance to dig out any little detail that someone else might have learned or a competitor overlooked.

"As you well know, Ambrose, the Rajah's Ruby wasn't in that vault."

"That's the way I heard it," Bierce agreed smoothly. "I wonder where she keeps it. Of course, we haven't seen it yet. She may have pawned it already."

"She insists on wearing it every performance," Jack said, "so I'm sure she'll have it on Saturday evening."

"Speaking of a busy few days," Bierce went on, "this is extraordinary, isn't it? Three openings so close together? Is it good business?"

Jack took a long pull of beer, drinking it slowly. Bierce's mercurial mind usually raced from one topic to another. Why had he gone back to this?

"It is unusual," Jack said. He eyed Bierce. "Are you suggesting it has some significance?"

Bierce was more than twice Jack's age but he was spry and active, and his mind was one of the sharpest in America. "Any matter that the Big Three have their guilt-stained fingers in has significance."

"You're sure you're not getting paranoid about the Big Three?" asked Jack.

Bierce snorted. "Impossible! If I had a hundred suspicions—no matter how wild—about their dirty work, at least ninety of them would have some substance."

The Big Three were Collis P. Huntington, Fred Crocker and Leland Stanford. They owned the entire waterfront around San Francisco and controlled all the water traffic in the Bay Area, all the shipping going in and out of it and all the river traffic throughout California and adjoining states. They had built and owned all the railroads, including the transcontinental railroad that joined the east and west coasts of America.

Jack knew they were his friend's bête noire. Bierce never missed a chance to castigate them in his column, never failed to suggest that they were behind every crime and crooked deal, never overlooked an opportunity to blame them for lining their own pockets at the expense of the community.

All were multimillionaires who had vast resources at their disposal, but Bierce was one mouth they had not been able to close. Pressure on Hearst to restrain Bierce had been ineffective—he was one of the few men in the country to have as much money as they did.

"I would have thought they had more important things to think about than which opening nights are being chosen by which music hall stars," Jack said. He could not see the direction of Bierce's attack, but from long acquaintance with the irascible editor he knew how to chip away at his fund of knowledge.

"So would I," Bierce said disappointingly.

Jack reached for a couple of frogs' legs, then drank more beer. Bierce was not a blabbermouth by any means, but Jack knew that he would drop a few crumbs of information his way. The editor would consider it part of "training" his young protégé. Jack took a handful of pickled squid.

"The Virginia National Bank put up the money to reserve Houdini's booking at the Tower," said Bierce, sipping his Sazerac.

"Who owns that?"

"I don't know yet—I'm trying to find out."

"Banks don't usually finance theatrical shows," Jack said.

"Hasn't been known till now."

"Is this going to be in your column, Ambrose?"

"Not yet," Bierce said. "I'm going to give them a little more rope. But that's not all. Fritz Danner at the Midway Plaisance is feeling a financial pinch. He's taken a big loan—also from the Virginia National."

"That may not mean anything. With this strike on, it means there's a lot less money to spend right now," Jack said. "But the talk is that Fritz doesn't own the Midway—people say that two well-known San Francisco politicians really own it but don't want the voters to hear about it."

"Probably true," Bierce agreed.

His neutral tone prompted Jack to say, "And I'll bet you know just who those two are."

Bierce took another sip of Sazerac. He looked, Jack thought, like a cat appreciatively sipping cream. Carefully putting down his glass, Bierce said, "Right now, I'm hearing rumors about the Eureka."

"What sort of rumors? More about their financial difficulties?"

"Maybe, maybe something else."

"Eulalia Paradino is opening there. It's the first time a performance like hers has been put on in the Devil's Acre," said Jack, trying to nudge Bierce toward more revelations.

"So I understand," murmured the editor. "They say she has supernatural powers. I wonder if there are any more like her around? I might be able to use them—they should be invaluable in the newspaper world."

Jack grinned. "You don't believe in the supernatural, Ambrose. You've said so many times. Anyway, what do you want to do? Print tomorrow's headlines today?"

Ambrose smiled enigmatically. Jack tried another tack.

"What do you know about the Riders of the Rim?"

Bierce shrugged. It was a dismissive gesture. "A gang of part-revolutionaries, part-bandits, part-opportunists—"

"And discontented strikers?" Jack interjected.

"Yes. They've collected a few of those too. They even have a few misguided California patriots, fighting for independence from the Union, and some religious zealots who are still determined to avenge John Brown."

Jack knew that Bierce was strongly antireligion too, though he managed to control himself in print rather than offend readers. "What's their aim?" Jack asked.

"All of the above. They don't seem to have a firm leader, which is why they haven't made much impact. They've robbed a bank or two, and they held up a stage on the Nevada state line a month ago. Supposedly raising money, but they don't seem able to decide on which cause to donate it to—just themselves so far."

"Are they a threat?" Jack was trying to figure out what was behind Captain Morley's words.

"To whom or what?"

"The community."

"As I say, not so far."

"Could they be?"

"If they could be organized, perhaps," Bierce admitted. He shot a keen glance at Jack. "Do you know something about them?"

"No," Jack said. "I just heard about them recently."

"You'll tell me if you do," Bierce pressed. "About the Riders of the Rim or the music halls that are having financial difficulties."

"Sure," said Jack. "I'll even throw in how Houdini does his tricks and how the Paradino woman communicates with the dead."

Bierce threw back his head and laughed uproariously. "We'll make it a special edition that day!"

Jack grinned and ate some more fried shrimp. Bierce finished his Sazerac and called for another. "And a beer for my young friend here," he added.

"No, I have to go," Jack said.

"Gathering information?" said Bierce. He waited for Jack, who didn't react. "So you are on another investigation, aren't you?" Bierce went on. "You made a name for yourself as a law enforcement officer on the Fish Patrol; then you helped the police solve the murders of those dance hall girls. Now you're at it again. I suppose you're going to say it's confidential and that you can't tell me anything about it."

"You're too shrewd for me, Ambrose." Jack grinned. "No wonder they call you the best newspaper editor in the USA."

"What really flatters a man is that you think him worth flattering," Bierce said. "Now listen, young fellow, here's an offer that you might want to take up in the hope of gathering some useful information—whatever it is you're looking for. The new governor of California is giving a reception at the Presidio in a couple of days. I'll see that you get an invitation. Everybody will be there—well, everybody who is anybody."

"Houdini and the Riders of the Rim?" asked Jack with a smile.

"I'm expected to bring a few luminaries from the world of letters," Bierce continued. "You almost qualify for that, don't you? Now that you've made a sale to *Overland Monthly*?"

"It's a well-known magazine," said Jack stiffly.

"It is, it is," said Bierce. "I'm trying to get Stephen Crane. Oscar Wilde has just gone back to London unfortunately, and Kipling's still in South Africa. I asked W. S. Gilbert but he sent some sneering reply about nothing but Indians west of New York. Mark Twain's not well, so—"

"So you have to ask me."

"You will be an adornment to the occasion," Bierce said with a straight face.

Jack laughed. "You have a silver tongue, Ambrose. How could I refuse?"

Chapter 14

On his way to the Tower Music Hall, Jack went into the Midway Plaisance to make sure that no crises had occurred or seemed likely. There was no sign of Belle Conquest but one of her bodyguards was talking to Flo.

"All normal here," she told Jack with her engaging smile. The bodyguard gave Jack a slight nod and Jack supposed that he knew nothing of his status. Flo's friendly greeting apparently obviated any suspicion on his part, although Jack thought that perhaps La Belle had told the other bodyguards about Jack. Backstage, nothing was out of the ordinary and Jack was able to leave satisfied.

The Tower was already full when Jack arrived for the opening of Harry Houdini that evening. The posters outside showed him hanging upside down in a straitjacket with the new Brooklyn Bridge prominent behind him. "The World Famous Death-Defying Escapologist" proclaimed the huge letters.

Jack made his way to the bar. The crowd there was three deep but he was able to push his way through and get a beer. It was a mixed crowd, for although Houdini was not yet established as a major artist, he had attracted interest with his sensational escape at the pier. That had received lots of coverage in all of the San Francisco newspapers.

The orchestra was already in the mood, playing one of the popular songs of the day. Then Houdini came out to modest applause. He wore a black suit with a waistcoat and a white shirt with sleeves so long they protruded several inches over the wrists and flapped unfastened. His black bow tie and black shoes completed the outfit, but its modesty was more than balanced by the four nubile young girls in shimmering silvery blouses and bloomer-type shorts showing expanses of bare arms and legs.

As the girls moved around him in a languorous dance, Houdini plucked silver dollars from their hair, their clothing, their mouths and ears. The girls showed suitable surprise and tried to evade his grasp. More and more silver dollars appeared from under their arms and out of their clothing. The flow continued and the excitement of the audience grew. Many leaned forward, trying to see where the coins came from, for Houdini's hands flickered constantly and it looked for all the world as if he was actually pulling the coins from thin air.

The girls left the stage to enthusiastic clapping. Another girl in a smart blue uniform jacket with white piping joined Houdini now. The jacket was just long enough that she did not need a skirt and her legs brought whistles of approval from the male-dominated audience. Around her neck were draped several silk scarves in various dazzling colors. She pulled off a red one and handed it to Houdini. He twisted and twirled it, first to one side, then to the other, then high above his head.

Abruptly, he squashed the scarf into a ball, holding it out to the audience in his clenched hands. There was utter silence; then slowly he began to open up the scarf. It moved. He opened it more—and from inside the silken folds fluttered a live white dove.

As the applause swelled, the girl handed Houdini another scarf, yellow this time, and he repeated the trick. Even as the clapping continued, a blue scarf turned into a third dove.

The orchestra burst into H. W. Petrie's popular hit "Asleep in the Deep" as a further tribute to Houdini's underwater escape ability. The magician was now joined onstage by his brother, Theo, who was introduced by his nickname, "Dash. " Theo wore a light blue suit that distinguished him from Harry.

A steamer trunk was carried onto the stage. It was opened and shown to the audience, who could clearly see that it was empty. Harry then tied up his brother at the wrists and the ankles using bright red rope and put him in the trunk. He locked it and handed the key to a man in the front row of the audience.

He waved for a screen to be brought onstage and placed it in front of the trunk. He faced the audience and said, "When I clap my hands three times—behold a miracle!" He stepped behind the screen on one side, clapped, and almost instantaneously his brother emerged from the other side.

The gasps of amazement rippled around. Theo removed the screen and asked the man in the front row for the key. He unlocked the trunk, lifted the lid and aided the unmistakable figure of Harry Houdini out. The magician had his hands behind his back. He brought them out now. One of them held the bright red ropes.

The crowd went wild. It was not an entirely original illusion, but no one in the crowd had seen it performed so smoothly. How could the two have changed places so quickly? It did not seem possible. Jack applauded as loudly and enthusiastically as everyone else.

The first of several intervals followed. It enabled the waiter girls to replenish the drinks of the customers. The show would not be resumed until every glass had been refilled.

The next portion of the show was entirely an "escape" segment. Handcuffs, chains, manacles, leg irons, shackles and fetters were brought on and Houdini escaped from them all. Sometimes he did so behind a screen, sometimes facing the audience with his hands behind his back, sometimes in full view so that everyone could watch him escape. Men came up from the audience carrying unusual and fearsome-looking steel devices, which they fitted around the magician. Houdini slipped out of them all with baffling ease.

It was during the next interval that Jack noticed Jim Laidlaw working his way through the audience, greeting several patrons by name. Laidlaw completed his tour of the auditorium and headed for the bar, shaking a hand here and there. He finally came to Jack.

"Ah, my writer friend!" he said in his customary Western drawl.

"Wonderful show," said Jack. "This Houdini fellow is really magic!"

"I was lucky to get him," said Laidlaw. "He has been disappointed at not becoming better known in this country, especially on the East Coast, and was thinking about making a European tour. I am glad I could get him to come here first."

"He must cost plenty," Jack said.

Laidlaw waved a hand expansively. "I try to put on the best shows—you know that."

"Isn't the strike affecting your business here?" Jack asked.

Laidlaw looked around the crowded auditorium. "Does it look like it?" he asked with a happy smile.

Jack had to admit that it didn't. He tried another approach. "Still, you'll have some strong competition when the Paradino woman opens."

Laidlaw gave a shrug of disdain. "Who cares about dead people? The Barbary Coast is for the living! Look around you."

"Everybody is certainly having a good time tonight," Jack agreed. "You know, Jim, a lot of people are talking about the way Houdini feels about spiritualism. He can't be very happy about appearing across the street from Paradino, who claims to be the world's greatest spiritual medium."

Laidlaw smiled. "Makes very good publicity, doesn't it?"

"Is that all it is?" Jack asked innocently. "Just good publicity?"

"Oh, I know Harry gets excited when he talks about mediums and spiritualism and voices from the dead," Laidlaw said, "but I think he's sincere. He hates the tricksters who prey on widows, for instance. His attitude doesn't come from a desire for publicity, but if it gets him in the newspaper headlines, that's great!"

They talked for a few minutes longer; then Laidlaw continued his parade along the bar, shaking hands. The orchestra struck up with the title song from *The Wizard of the Nile,* last year's big hit from Broadway written by Victor Herbert.

The next segment began with a trestle table being brought onto the stage. One of the young women stretched out prone on it and Houdini stood behind it, facing the audience over the girl's body. Houdini's face took on a mystical look and he waved his hands, muttering unintelligible words. The orchestra's violins played soft music that climbed the scales, touching spine-tingling high notes. Houdini took two steps back and his arms moved higher.

Gasps came from the audience as the girl rose slowly into the air. Houdini stopped his movements and stood stock-still. The girl continued to rise. Another girl came out with a wooden hoop, which she handed to Houdini.

He passed it over the feet of the levitating girl and moved it slowly up her body, demonstrating clearly that there were no invisible supports. He took a bow as the applause swelled, then, using hand motions, brought the girl back down onto the table.

Houdini addressed the audience. "Ladies and gentlemen, I will now present the most amazing disappearing act on the stage today! In order to do this, I need four volunteers from the audience."

After some cajoling and sweet-talking, Houdini selected four men and positioned them a few paces apart in a line behind the table. He clapped his hands and two girls came onstage carrying a green folding screen, which they placed around the girl on the table. It lacked lower panels so that the audience could see under it and also under the trestle table.

Houdini repeated his show of waving his hands and murmuring strange words. The audience was rapt in silence; then cries rang out as the girl's hands could be seen waving over the top of the screen. Next her face appeared. She turned it, smiling, toward the audience first, then to the four men standing behind.

Using his hands, Houdini lowered her until she was just out of sight. The orchestra launched into "Say Au Revoir But Not Good-bye," the popular song by Harry Kennedy. No sooner had the melody become recognizable to the audience than Houdini clapped his hands and the girls whisked away the screen to reveal an empty table.

The applause was strong but tinged with an air of astonished disbelief. Houdini bowed politely, then thanked the four volunteers with a handshake each. He waited until they were off the stage; then he called them back before they could return to their seats. To one, he returned the man's pocket watch, to another his belt buckle, to the third an ornate studded tie clasp, and to the fourth a wad of bills.

"Count them, just to be sure," Houdini told him. It was just the right humorous touch to end the dramatic disappearance and the clapping increased.

As it finally died away, a voice called out, "Where's the girl?" Houdini pretended not to hear. He waved to the orchestra leader to strike up once more, but as he did so the cry was taken up by other voices in the crowd. "Where's the girl? Where's the girl?" surged around the crowd.

Houdini motioned to the orchestra leader and the music subsided. Houdini looked slowly from wall to wall, then to the back of the auditorium. Suddenly, he shot out a hand and pointed.

All eyes followed to a table near the back and a girl stood, then stepped onto her chair and onto the tabletop.

She turned on the same ravishing smile that had appeared over the top of the screen. Now the crowd really yelled and shouted and clapped until the ceiling rang with the noise.

It had been a short segment but it had the crowd arguing and guessing loudly in the ensuing interval. Jack was as vociferous as anyone else, full of admiration for the supreme showman. Again, the waiter girls came out to bring fresh drinks. Jack was about to order another beer from one of the overworked and perspiring bartenders when a face at a table not far away caught his eye.

Did he know the man? He looked familiar. Jack had a good memory for faces and names but he could not place this man. Perhaps he had never known his name, he thought, and turned to get a bartender's attention. Then it struck him.

He had seen the man after the stakeout at the docks and again after the near-wrecking of the Orpheum by Carrie Nation and her ladies.

This was not the corpulent man standing in a doorway watching him, but the one who had appeared out of the fog and asked Jack for a light, the man who had distracted him while the man in the doorway had disappeared. Jack recognized the clean-shaven face and the trim, tiny mustache—this was the man.

The other turned to look around the auditorium and Jack quickly averted his face, moving to bring another figure between them. When Jack saw him again, the man was speaking to someone at the table. Then he rose, threw some coins on the table and made for the door.

Jack did not know why he felt this to be important, but there had been something menacing in the way the toadlike man had been watching Jack, and the other had clearly been a decoy, so these two had something to hide. Jack drained his beer and headed for the door at a discreet distance from his quarry.

Chapter 15

Jack's experience as a law enforcement officer in the Fish Patrol had not been all in San Francisco Bay. At times, he had had to follow suspects on land in the expectation that they would lead to confederates. He had learned from the old hands most of the tricks of following without being spotted.

He called upon these skills now. The man he was following, lean and spare, had a rapid stride. Jack stayed on the other side of the street, about a dozen paces behind, so that he could keep the other in sight without turning his head.

The streets were busy. Men with poster boards advertising shows, bars and restaurants were on most street corners. There were drunks and those who intended soon to be drunk, a few toffs in fancy clothes that made them easy marks, the usual number of Westerners in high boots, fringed jackets and Stetsons, and the inevitable prospectors determined to spend the gold they had scrabbled for so desperately in the wilderness of the Yukon.

The man Jack was following took a left at Union Street, then went across Kearny and Grant. Jack hoped he wasn't heading for the cable car stop on Grant Street—that would increase Jack's exposure. Instead, the man went straight on, still at a fast pace. They crossed Stockton Street, where the man turned right. Enough people still thronged the streets to make Jack's task easier. He stayed with small knots of people, avoided standing out, moving from one group to another to keep up with the man's steady stride.

Halfway along Stockton Street, the man turned into the
Panama Hotel. It looked like a modest, middle-class place,
not a dump but not showy either. Jack crossed the street and
went into the lobby. It was small but not shabby. A potted
plant stood by the window near three chairs around a small
table. There was a painting of the California desert on one
wall, garish in browns and golds but imaginative. A fairly
clean, large window looked out onto the street.

Jack could hear voices but the clerk was not at the desk.
He saw the legs of the man he was following disappearing
onto the landing of the first floor, and Jack ran up the stairs
quickly. Peering between the rails, he saw the man go into
the first room on the left. Jack was moving toward the room
to see the number on the door when he heard a movement
behind him.

The man wore a dark suit and had a hard face. The hand
inside his jacket was in position to pull out a gun. "I'm
looking for Tommy Whelan," Jack said, using the name of
the owner of the grocery shop near his house. It was the
first name that came into his head. "I think he's on this
floor."

The man pointed a finger at the first door on the left. "Go
in."

His hand remained inside his jacket, and Jack had no intention of finding out whether it held a gun or not. His bluff
called, Jack opened the door and went in.

It was a typical hotel room, though larger than most, but
Jack had no time to study the furniture. Facing him was the
figure he had seen twice before, the figure that had been
watching him, the figure that he found threatening without
knowing why.

Seeing him this close, he found him slightly familiar,
though not just from those two encounters. That thought
was cut short by the slamming of the door behind him, and
without looking, Jack knew that the man who had been
guarding the door was now behind him.

The man facing him was dressed just as before—the

tweed suit, the waistcoat with the gold watch chain draped across it, the droopy gray mustache and the gold-rimmed spectacles. He looked fatter and older than Jack had thought, but this was the first time he had seen him up close. Again, that nagging thread of memory tantalized him—why did the man look familiar?

"Our paths keep crossing," the other observed. His voice was hoarse; possibly the man had consumption. He eased his bulky frame into a chair, wincing a little as he did so. Probably a rheumatic too, Jack thought.

Now that his head was not covered by the floppy black hat, Jack could see that his hair was thinning and only a few silvery strands covered his large head. He could also see that the gold-rimmed spectacles had extra-thick lenses. Behind them a pair of gray-blue eyes appraised him shrewdly.

Jack nodded. He was determined to say as little as possible until he learned who this man was and what his purpose might be.

"I understand that your name is Jack London. You write stories about your adventures at sea and in the Yukon where you searched—unsuccessfully, I believe—for gold. You worked for the California Fish Patrol as a law enforcement officer after a brief career as an oyster pirate. You have been called on by the police to assist them on occasion, due to the fact that you know nearly everyone on the Barbary Coast, especially in the bars and the brothels, the dives and the deadfalls."

It was a harsh assessment of Jack's range of friends and acquaintances and the places in which they could be found. Jack guessed at a religious or puritanical background that the other tried to sublimate without being fully successful.

Jack gave him a small nod. "You know who I am. Who are you?"

There was another man in the room, whose presence Jack had registered only peripherally. He was sitting in a far corner. It was the man Jack had followed here. He rose, put a hand into an inside pocket, and brought out a wallet that he opened and held for Jack's inspection. It read: PINKERTON DETECTIVE AGENCY.

The famous detective agency had been founded by Allan Pinkerton in 1850. In 1861, Pinkerton had used it to guard President Abraham Lincoln and the power and reputation of the agency had spread.

Jack's fervent support for American socialism made him aware that the Pinkerton Agency had been called in to smash labor union demonstrations on many occasions, sometimes when the local National Guard had tried and failed.

Connections clicked in Jack's brain. He recalled the copies of *Everybody's, Leslie's, Colliers,* the *American Magazine.* All had carried photographs of the man before him. He was James McParland, who had taken control of the agency when Pinkerton had died in 1884. The most famous case involving the Pinkertons had been that of the Molly Maguires. It had made headline news throughout the nation and was a tale familiar to every habitué of barbershops and hotel lobbies, where the *Police Gazette* and its competitors were consumed so avidly.

The Molly Maguires were a secret society of immigrant Irish coal miners in Pennsylvania. They led violent labor conflicts between mine workers and owners and were accused of murder in one of the most sensational trials of the century. Their name was based on an Irish heroine of the seventeenth century who led a revolt of peasant farmers against rent collectors. The members of the secret society frequently dressed as women to evade the authorities.

James McParland had become one of the best-known men in America, despite his efforts to keep his picture out of the papers. It had been his evidence that had led to the hanging of twenty members of the Molly Maguires.

Jack was silent at this realization and tried not to show his amazement. "So why are you following me?" he asked in as truculent a tone as he could muster.

"I thought you followed Henry here," said McParland in a slightly amused tone.

"I wanted to know what was behind your interest in me," said Jack.

"I can tell you that," was the mild reply. "We are trying to understand your concern for Belle Conquest."

So the Pinkertons were here to guard the Rajah's Ruby. Or was that it?

Jack decided to attempt some subterfuge first. "I spend a lot of time at the Midway Plaisance because of Flo," he said.

"Flo?" McParland repeated the name, looked at his lieutenants. Jack answered first.

"She used to be known as Little Egypt. She trains the dancers at the Midway now."

McParland looked from one to the other of his men.

Henry, the man Jack had followed, shrugged. The other man, still by the door, just looked blank.

"I have been going to the Midway to see Flo for some time," Jack added, "since long before it was known Belle Conquest was coming. Flo works a lot of hours, so when I want to see her, I have to go to the Midway. Ask anybody there."

"We will," McParland said.

Jack wondered who might have hired the Pinkerton Agency and why the detectives had been watching him even before he hired on to help guard the fabulous jewel. It seemed as if Captain Morley and his department in the police force did not know. Or maybe they did know—Morley's words came back to him now: "Other people are concerned about this situation and may be hiring people of their own." It would not be unknown for two organizations to be kept in ignorance of each other's activities, and it was not uncommon for several rival branches of law enforcement to be working on the same case. All agreed that much needed to be done to coordinate things, but nothing was being done. Jack could recall more than one incident in his days on the Fish Patrol when they had collided head-on with the San Francisco Police. Trust was a rare commodity on the Barbary Coast.

"Do you have a girlfriend at the Tower too?" McParland asked.

"No," Jack replied. "I went there only because I was fascinated by Houdini and his magic. I saw him at the docks and he invited me to visit him at the theater." He gave McParland an angry look. "Did you have me followed there? Perhaps it was one of your men who locked me in that boiler!"

McParland, amused again, looked at his two men. One shrugged and the other shook his head. "We were not responsible for that," McParland said. He adjusted his gold-rimmed spectacles and fixed Jack with a more intent look. "If some other person or persons did that, it must mean you are very unpopular. I wonder why."

He had made a bad mistake there, Jack realized. He should not have allowed his anger to get the better of him. If McParland thought Jack was entangled in something serious enough to get him killed, then he would be even more skeptical of his story so far. Jack knew he had to be more careful in his answers. This man was obviously an expert in interrogation and extremely clever.

"Perhaps you can save us the trouble of wasting a man on you," McParland said. "Tell me where you are going to be tomorrow night."

Jack saw quickly that his best plan was to tell the truth— at least initially. "At the Eureka Music Hall," he said with what he hoped sounded like instant candor. "Watching Eulalia Paradino."

McParland said nothing but his expression seemed to tighten. Jack wondered if he found the answer significant. He recalled Ambrose Bierce's words: "Extraordinary, isn't it? Three openings so close together?"

After a moment or two, McParland shifted his weight in the chair and said, "You attend a lot of shows."

"I spend a lot of my time on the Barbary Coast," Jack said. "I do see a lot of shows, but I find the one tomorrow night particularly interesting because when I was a child my mother made me take part in spiritualistic séances."

"Did she." McParland's tone conveyed nothing.

"I didn't enjoy them," Jack went on, "but Paradino sounds like an extraordinary woman. I can remember a few of the tricks my mother used. I'm curious to see if I can spot Paradino using any of them." That's close enough to the truth, Jack thought, that he can't pick any holes in it.

"Your mother hoaxed the public." There was scorn behind the words but Jack refused to be provoked, which he knew was the intention.

"She really did have powers that could not be explained," he said. "But at times, like all mediums, when she couldn't get any response from the spirits, she resorted to tricks."

McParland seemed to accept that explanation, though his demeanor did not change. "I'm glad we had this chat," he said with a slight wheeze. He moved a hand in what his men evidently knew to be dismissal. The one nearest the door went to open it. "You'll probably be seeing us as we go about our job," McParland said. "Although if we do our job properly, maybe you won't."

So they'd continue to watch him closely. Well, they had the manpower for it. Pinkertons were renowned for putting a lot of men on a job. When they had crushed the labor unions of the iron and steel workers at the Homestead plant of the Carnegie company a few years ago, it was said that they employed several hundred agents.

Jack nodded, went out and down the stairs. There was no sign of anyone at the desk or in the lobby as he went out. Presumably, the Pinkertons had commandeered the entire hotel.

Chapter 16

Jack was already into his daily writing the next morning when the mailman arrived. Jack was one of his steadiest customers, for manuscripts came back with soul-numbing frequency. Two rejections were on top of the short stack that Wally handed him with his usual apologetic grin. Jack had told Wally of his writing and Wally could now recognize reject envelopes as readily as Jack.

Next, however, was a letter envelope with the imprint of *Overland Monthly* on it. Jack opened it, wondering. He had no manuscripts out to them currently, and anyway, this envelope was not large enough to hold a manuscript. He read the contents with growing excitement. He put it down, then quickly read it again.

It was the offer of a contract! A contract for six stories! At last, he was on his way!

He read the letter yet again. The editor, Ninetta Eames, regretted that she could not pay more than seven dollars and fifty cents each for the stories. She promised, however, that the stories would be given prominence in the magazine and would be bound to attract the attention not only of reviewers but also publications on the East Coast that, the editor freely admitted, paid much more than *Overland Monthly*.

Jack felt a sag in enthusiasm at the sight of that fee, but his ebullience surged back at the thought of what a great showcase for his work the magazine would be. It could easily be a springboard to the future he envisioned but at times despaired he could ever reach. Among *Overland Monthly*'s regular writers were Charles Warren Stoddard and Bret Harte, both of whom were being vigorously promoted as outstanding talents. The magazine could do the same for him.

It was with a renewed vitality that he completed his writing for the day, and his step was light as he headed for the Midway Plaisance later in the afternoon. On the way, his head was buzzing with ideas. Six stories—he would need a lot of ideas for six stories, but he did not lack confidence that he could conjure them up very easily. Wolves were fascinating to a public not threatened by them—a story about a wolf must be one of the six. And there would be no difficulty in pulling out plots from his adventures in the Fish Patrol. . . .

At the Midway Plaisance, Flo was rehearsing her girls in a dance number that required gyrations not normally demanded of the human body. It was not Flo's specialty, the hoochy coochy, for that was very arduous and required much longer practice. Still, this number was strenuous and the girls were having difficulties meeting Flo's high standards.

As Jack approached, Milly, a tall girl with long blond hair, gasped, "Oh, Jack, thank God you've come!"

Flo looked about to make a sharp response, but she had a sunny disposition that rarely allowed her to dwell on any negative reaction. She joined the girls in the laughter and smiled at the calls that included words such as "dance slaves" and "need a union." She gave them fifteen minutes to rest, and as the girls walked away, Milly said, "Only fifteen minutes, Jack. You'll have to work fast!"

Jack gave her a playful slap and embraced Flo. "You're hot and you're sweaty," he told her.

"You've seen me both ways many times before," Flo said, her dark eyes sparkling. "This is the first time you've complained."

"It's not a complaint," Jack said. They walked to the

edge of the stage and Flo sank thankfully into a chair at the front row of tables. A banjo was being strummed somewhere backstage and the clatter of bottles came from the bar, where two bartenders were restocking shelves. The smell of beer and cigarette smoke that hung heavy in the air would never go away.

"What's new?" Flo asked. "I'd say you look like you have something to tell me."

"You know me too well. I don't want you going to the Paradino show and learning any mind reading—you're too good at that already."

Flo smiled her warm, sincere smile. "So tell me."

Jack told her of his contract with *Overland Monthly* and she clasped his hands in delight. "Jack, that's wonderful! You're going to be a famous writer! This is the breakthrough you've been wanting."

They talked about the contract and the writing future that it promised. Then Flo said, "I've been talking to Belle's bodyguards like you asked me. La Belle gets jealous every time she sees anybody near them, particularly another woman."

"And particularly you," added Jack.

"But she can't keep an eye on three of them all at the same time. Laurence, Teddy and Francis their names are. I played the wide-eyed girl fascinated by the big Broadway star."

"Flo, you're an actress as well as a dancer."

"I can sing too," Flo said indignantly. Then she smiled as she went on. "So naturally I wanted to know where the famous ruby is kept."

"Go on," Jack urged. "Maybe you can add detection to all your other talents."

"I talked to Laurence first. He just laughed and said, 'That's what everybody wants to know.' I asked Francis and got exactly the same reply. I guess Belle has them well trained."

"Apparently." Jack frowned. "Anything else?"

"This engagement was made at very short notice, Laurence told me. When I was talking to Teddy, he said that Belle really didn't want to come here—she thinks San Francisco is a hick town. But they offered her so much money that she couldn't say no."

"Hick town!" Jack said. "Who does she think she is?"

"She thinks she's the Queen of Broadway," Flo reminded him. "Trouble is, she's right. That's just who she is." She chuckled at Jack's expression. "Still, nobody can get away with insulting San Francisco as far as you're concerned, can they?"

"Right." Jack nodded. "But you know, that's strange. Fritz Danner is short of cash. Surely he can't afford to be paying an astronomic amount for Belle, even if she is big on Broadway."

"She's big here too. Always complaining about having to lose weight and always eating more than she should."

"Well," Jack said, "it's not much, but it's a start. We'll make an assistant detective out of you yet."

"So it's the other world tonight, is it?" Flo asked.

"Yes. I can't resist seeing this Paradino woman. Should be interesting. Tell me, is Fritz around?"

"Haven't seen him for days, but then he never is around much."

"I'll go talk to Andy."

"If you're thinking of looking for Belle after that, she's not here yet," Flo said with an innocent expression.

"Who? Oh, Belle . . . she isn't? That doesn't matter," Jack said and Flo smiled.

"I hope you're a better detective than you are an actor, Jack London!"

Jack chuckled and pushed his chair back. Flo stood and embraced him hard. "Be careful," she murmured in his ear. "Whoever you're with."

Andy was finishing supervising the hauling into the cellar of what looked like an endless stream of cases of beer.

He wiped his hands on a cloth and grinned at Jack. "Fancy a drink?"

Jack did fancy one but he was maintaining a firm control over his drinking habits. It was a subject that might be worth a story someday. He had been heavily under the influence of the demon drink but had been able to pull himself out of it. And he found now that, with his writing and these sporadic jobs of working for the police, he had enough to concentrate on that he no longer had as many temptations toward the bottle.

"Not right now, Andy, thanks. So Fritz is leaving you to it, is he?"

"That's nothing new. Seems to think the place runs itself." Andy's recent promotion to head bartender meant that he was mainly responsible for the day-to-day operations. Jack wondered just how much he knew.

"Business seems to be good," Jack said casually. "Must be making a lot of money."

Andy made a wry expression that was hard to interpret.

Jack pursued the thought. "After all, Fritz has been able to bring Belle Conquest here. Folks say she's the highest paid star on Broadway. Must have cost a big packet of money to get her."

Andy put a shot glass on the bar and poured himself a Jack Daniel's. He tossed it down and poured another. "Bowled me over, Fritz did, when he told me she was coming. Don't know where he got the money."

"You said you were doing well," Jack retorted. "Lots of business, making a lot of cash."

"I didn't say that, you did. Oh, we're doing well enough, but that dame is more expensive than the Brooklyn Bridge."

"Still," Jack said, "Fritz got her, so he must have the money."

Andy leaned over the bar, the second Jack Daniel's in his hand. "Or maybe he just knows where to get it."

"Everybody knows that—from a bank. Either hold it up or borrow it."

Andy chortled. "You've got that right, and Fritz is sure no bank robber. Doesn't need to be when he knows the right people."

Jack pressed Andy further. He was not likely to be in Fritz's confidence, but he was in a position to hear a lot of scuttlebutt. "The banks don't put money into Barbary Coast dives," Jack said. "They get a better profit elsewhere—railroads and shipping, for instance."

Andy downed the second whisky. "They put it into the Midway," he said assertively. "Fritz had talks with some moneyman. Talked every day, they did, for three or four days, till Fritz got hold of Belle Conquest and got her to come here."

"Hope the banks know what they're doing," Jack said. "Otherwise I may have to take all my money out of there and put it back under my pillow. Might be safer."

Andy laughed. "Banks don't ever put money in the wrong place," he said with a wink.

Jack declined Andy's second offer of a drink, then noted that Flo's rehearsal had resumed. He strolled casually backstage. Maybe Belle had arrived by now.

She emerged from a dressing room just as he was passing. Behind her he got a glimpse of a young man pulling a shirt over his head. Belle closed the door, giving Jack a provocative look.

"Rehearsing a scene," she said in that low, sultry voice. "Took several tries to get it right."

"Hope you finally succeeded," Jack said.

"Could have been better," she drawled. "Maybe it needs a new man. What about you?"

Jack felt his blood quickening but he answered calmly, "The first thing I wanted to ask you was about the ruby. Is it safe?"

"It sure is."

"When did you see it last?"

"It was there when I looked this morning," she replied, looking him in the eye. "Is that all you're concerned about?"

"First the ruby, then you," Jack said. "You say it's safe and I can see you look all right."

"Never better." She accompanied the words with a movement of one shoulder that was not quite a shrug but somehow an invitation.

"Are you still planning to wear the ruby onstage?"

"Sure. It's my good luck charm."

"I thought its reputation was for bringing bad luck?"

"Not to me," Belle said confidently. The statement was hardly out of her mouth when a scream echoed along the corridor.

Their eyes met. "Somebody's goosing one of the girls," Belle said, but there was the faintest quaver in her voice.

"I don't think so," Jack said over his shoulder as he ran toward the scream.

Chapter 17

The girl who stood screaming was one of the showgirls, Rachel. She wore only a skimpy skintight costume in green and white with bright green dance slippers. Her hands cradled her face in terror as her screams came in panting gasps.

Jack gripped her arms and shook her gently. "What is it? What's wrong?"

Her eyes were tearing and she was quivering with fright. She mumbled something Jack could not catch and he asked her the same questions again. This time, she managed to take her hands from her face and point to an open door. It was another of the numerous dressing rooms. Jack pushed the door wider and went in—to stop suddenly as he saw the body on the floor.

Rachel stood behind him, in the grip of a horrible fascination. "It's Francis." She said the name in a frozen voice and Jack recognized it as belonging to one of Belle's bodyguards.

He was a young man, in his early twenties. Tall and well built, he was wearing a light gray waistcoat with a pattern of thin blue diagonal lines, and gray twill pants. His normally handsome face was contorted as if in pain but no signs of violence were visible. Jack examined him and quickly realized that he was dead.

He was sprawled near a large padded chair, one arm draped on its seat as if he had been trying to get to his feet. Jack looked at the chair and the floor around the body. He could see nothing unusual. There was another chair, a large clothes rack, a chest and a dressing table with an oil lamp on either side of it.

"Call the police," said Jack sharply.

Rachel stood for a moment, still petrified, and Jack told her again, louder this time. She hurried away. Jack closed the door and walked through the room, looking everywhere. A knock came and Jack answered it. Another showgirl was there in street clothes. Jack had seen her but did not know her name. "Is Rachel here?" she asked, trying to see past him into the room.

Jack did not move, merely shook his head. "No, she just left."

"Is something wrong?" the girl asked.

"There's been an—an accident," Jack said. "You don't have to worry—join the other girls and don't leave."

He closed the door before the girl could ask more.

The police arrived remarkably quickly. First was the same lieutenant who had come when Rollo Masters had been killed. Jack recalled his name as O'Bannion. He was accompanied by a different uniformed officer. O'Bannion gave Jack a sour glare.

"You again? Why are you always here when a body is found?" His aggressive, accusatory tone told Jack he was in for a rough time.

"I'm here a lot, every day pretty near. I come to see one of the girls here, Flo. Ask Fritz or any of the bartenders. They all know me. They'll tell you."

He was saved from further harassment by the arrival of Captain Morley, who darted Jack a quick look, then took O'Bannion aside. They talked in low tones. The uniformed man kept a close eye on Jack, who gave him a reassuring smile.

The discussion went on. O'Bannion seemed to resent the presence of Morley, but he was not able to protest too much because the other man outranked him. From what Jack could gather, O'Bannion was puzzled as to how Morley knew about the crime so quickly. Morley was not being accommodating with his answers, but he remained coolly correct. Jack was not aware that Morley mentioned his name to the lieutenant but he evidently did so. Morley beckoned to Jack and they went outside.

Another uniformed officer was there and Morley told him to keep everyone away from the dressing room where the body lay. Morley took Jack to another dressing room and closed the door.

"You know the dead man?" he asked peremptorily.

"I don't know him, but Rachel, the girl who found him, says his name was Francis. He's one of Belle Conquest's bodyguards."

"Another one?" Morley showed what was for him unusual surprise.

"Yes."

"You think this is another warning?" He managed to avoid outright skepticism but an element of it was in his voice.

"I know I thought that about the murder of Rollo," said Jack. "Now I'm not so sure."

"I'll get the report from O'Bannion, but how did he die?"

"I couldn't see any signs on the body, but his face shows pain from some cause."

Morley stroked his chin. He seemed to be trying to make some kind of decision. He leaned back against the bare wall. "What do you mean?"

"The same as Rollo Masters," he commented.

"Rollo Masters was tortured to death. He was already dead when he was shot—that's why there was so little blood."

"What?" Jack was aghast. "How do you know that?"

"Belle Conquest put up the money for his body to be shipped back to St. Louis for burial—that's where he's from and his parents still live there. It was decided to embalm it for the journey. When the undertakers started the embalming, they called us at once." Morley paused. His face was taut. Jack wondered what was coming.

"The testicles are a particularly tender part of the body," Morley said, keeping emotion out of his voice with an obvious effort. "These so-called bodyguards seem to be sensitive young men. The torture of Rollo Masters was not over quickly, the police doctor says. I won't give you any details, but it must have lasted some time, and he died of heart failure from shock."

Jack gasped.

"Not pleasant, is it?" Morley said. "If the body hadn't gone for embalming, he would have been buried in the clothes he died in. We would not have known."

"Sounds like I was wrong," Jack said. "He must have been tortured to tell where the ruby was hidden."

"And presumably he didn't tell and this second young man—"

"Pain shows in his face," Jack cut in.

"Yes, and we'll soon know if he was tortured too. I'll have O'Bannion examine him now before the body is removed."

He pushed his lean frame from the wall and strode back to the other dressing room, then returned to Jack. "He'll let us know. So you haven't talked to this man?"

"No, but I have been told a few things said by the girls who work here." He related what he had heard from Flo and from Andy.

Morley listened with his customary attention. "I don't see how this ties in with the theft of the ruby," he said. "All these openings, one after the other, it's not normal on the Coast, is it?"

"It's rare," Jack said.

"Rare in the entertainment business maybe, but what does that have to do with crime?"

"I don't know," Jack admitted.

Their conversation was interrupted by O'Bannion, who knocked and came in, standing just inside the door. Morley went over to him and they talked briefly, quietly. Morley nodded. O'Bannion left, saying, "We're talking now to the girl who found him."

When he had gone, Morley came over to Jack, who knew what he was going to say from his bleak expression.

"This one was tortured to death too."

Jack repressed a shudder. Morley said, "The only reason for torturing the second bodyguard would be because the first one hadn't told them where the ruby was."

"I wonder if the second one would know when the first one didn't?"

"It would appear to be unlikely—in which case we may expect a third one to undergo the same thing."

"They—whoever they are—couldn't expect to get away with this three times in a row," Jack said. "Torturing and killing them in the theater where Belle Conquest is appearing is too blatant, surely."

Morley thought for a moment. "Your theory of intimidation may come into play here."

"And a disregard for anything the police might be doing," Jack added.

Morley shrugged. "We have a man watching this place from across the street day and night and another in the alley at the back. I'll see if they noticed anything. I may have to double that watch. I should have another man inside this place but he might be obvious."

"Can't you go out now and ask those two?"

"Not without giving them away," Morley said dryly. "But I'll find out soon enough. You'd better stay around here for a while. I'll talk to you again."

As Morley rejoined O'Bannion, Jack went into the theater, where girls in small groups stood talking in low anguished tones. Flo left one of the groups and came quickly to him.

Jack told her what had happened. Flo shuddered. "Poor Francis, he was such a dear boy. They all are." A flash of anger showed in her eyes. "All she thinks about is herself and her pleasures. These poor boys are being murdered for protecting her."

Similar words to those Belle had used herself, Jack thought, so perhaps she was not as selfish as Flo was suggesting. He said nothing on that point, though, and instead asked her, "The other two—Teddy and—"

"Laurence. An officer in uniform is talking to both of them now."

"So both of them have been here in the Midway?"

"Yes." Flo was quick to see the reason for Jack's question. "Surely you don't think one of them killed the others?"

"I don't think it's very likely, no."

"Do you have any idea who did?"

"Not at the moment."

"Or why?"

"The best guess at the moment is that the two of them were tortured to make them tell where the Rajah's Ruby is."

"That piece of rock! If that's true, it's living up to all the stories about it being cursed."

"You don't have any idea at all where she keeps it, do you?" Jack asked. "Does Belle send her bodyguards out on any errands, maybe putting it in or taking it out of wherever she keeps it?"

Flo shook her head slowly. "Not that I've noticed. There's a small safe in her dressing room, but it doesn't look very burglar-proof so I doubt if it's in there."

"And I don't suppose you've seen any strangers around? You've been rehearsing the girls all this time—has anybody come in or out that you don't know?" Jack smiled at the expression on her face. "Yes, I know the police will be asking you the same questions, but—"

"I'm sure they will, but no, I haven't. It's true we were all in the theater and would have seen anyone coming in that way." She hesitated. "Just that delivery . . ."

"What delivery?" Jack snapped.

"Man with a case of whisky."

"At this time of day?"

"I don't know what time whisky is delivered."

"Come on, let's find Andy, assuming he isn't already being interrogated."

Andy was standing near the bar, talking to two of the other bartenders. He turned to Jack. "Is it true, Jack? About another one of those boyos being killed?"

"I'm afraid so, Andy. Listen, have you had any deliveries today?"

"No, not today." There was concern on his face.

"I saw a man come in with a case of whisky on his shoulder," Flo told him.

"We've had no whisky delivered today," Andy said. "What did the man look like?"

"Well, I didn't notice particularly," said Flo. "He was dark, could have been Mexican."

"Did he see you?" Jack asked.

Flo understood the reason for his question. She shook her head firmly. "No, I'm sure he didn't."

Andy snapped his fingers. "Let's find the case."

They soon found it near the end of the long bar, half pushed out of sight. It was yellow and brown and Flo let out an exclamation as she saw it. "That's it—I remember the colors now."

Andy called to one of the bartenders. "Did you see who put this here, Ned?"

The man scratched a scrubby beard. "Sure, looked like a Mex. Said it was a special order, that we was short."

Andy shook his head. "We're not short of Jim Beam. Nobody ordered it." He looked at Jack. "Hey, you think it was him killed the boy?"

"Maybe. We'd better tell the police about this." In his mind, though, he was certain. At the same time, he was relieved that the man had not seen Flo and made her a target for murder too.

They found Lieutenant O'Bannion and told him. Andy

brought Ned the bartender over and had him repeat his story.

"Did you see him close?" O'Bannion asked.

"He sort of turned away, put the case down and left," Ned said uneasily. Jack wondered if he had reason for being nervous in front of the police.

"Did you notice anything unusual about him?" said O'Bannion.

"Nah, just a Mex—" He hesitated.

"What?" O'Bannion pressed.

"He had a scar here," he said, touching a finger to the edge of his mouth.

"What kind of a scar?"

"Maybe an old knife wound."

Further questioning produced nothing else and O'Bannion was about to move away when loud cries rang out. Belle Conquest, in a scarlet dressing gown and her blond hair perfectly coiffed, burst across the stage and hurled herself at O'Bannion.

"Tell me it's not true! Tell me that they haven't murdered my lovely Francis!" Her fists beat on the lieutenant's chest. His big hands closed over them. She tried to kick his shin in her fury.

"I'm sorry, ma'am, but it's true. We'll get the man who did it though."

Tears ran down her face, making it a grotesque mask as her makeup smeared and spread. Her body throbbed with grief and anger. She stood back and stared accusingly at O'Bannion and then at Jack.

"I want you to get the man who did it and kill him! Forget about protecting the ruby! Just find the bastard and kill him!"

"We'll find him, ma'am. We will," said O'Bannion gruffly.

Chapter 18

The Eureka Music Hall was a little smaller than the Midway Plaisance but the design was similar. The walls had been redecorated with murals showing ghosts floating in the air, mysterious shadowy faces looking down from clouds and coffins with their occupants climbing out.

Flo had insisted on coming with Jack and a small bribe had gotten them a table. They were listening to the orchestra playing "Will the Angels Play Their Harps for Me?" The place was full and more were still entering. It would be standing room only from now on and the bar was getting more and more crowded.

Jack had time to think about the murder of the second of Belle's bodyguards. The sight of the young man sprawled so ignominiously on the floor of the dressing room had affected him, but then the revelation had come from Captain Morley that Francis, and Rollo before him, had been tortured to death. Jack felt that his own vigilance was at fault, but he was not sure what he could, or should, have done. He was supposed to be protecting the Rajah's Ruby, not the bodyguards.

Flo broke in on his thoughts. "You're thinking about those two boys, aren't you?"

"Yes. Is that bauble really worth all this?"

Flo grimaced. "There's a story going around that Belle Conquest has offered a huge reward for the killers, dead or alive—is it true?"

"I haven't heard that but it could be."

"Yes, she's tough, but underneath it she's very sentimental," said Flo. "I think it's the kind of thing she would do."

Life was cheap on the Barbary Coast and a day seldom went by without at least one murder. The death of two boys who did not even live there was of little interest. They might rate a brief column in the *Examiner,* while the *Sentinel,* the official mouthpiece of the Christian Science movement, might use it as an example of divine retribution for a dissolute life.

Jack had had the opportunity to talk to Morley again before he left the scene of the murder. He had been told of the suspect using a case of whisky as cover and had spoken to his detective out front, who had seen the man come in carrying a case but thought nothing of it.

"Dark-faced, possibly Mexican and a knife slash at the edge of his mouth," Morley had said. "There's a chance we can pick him up."

Jack had said nothing. The chance was slight.

"I talked to the other two, Teddy and Laurence," Morley went on. "They're blue with fear. I've got men watching them."

"Did they tell you anything?" Jack asked.

"I got the impression that they don't know where the ruby is kept. The Conquest woman still won't tell."

"I can believe that those other two really didn't know," Jack agreed. "They would surely have told under torture."

"You can also believe that Belle Conquest is an obstinate and uncaring female," Morley said. "To her, the ruby is more important than human lives." His tone was sharper than usual, and they had parted with Jack realizing that Morley was getting angry with this case.

While Jack and Flo waited for Eulalia Paradino to begin her act, the orchestra struck up with James M. Black's popular hit of recent years, "When the Roll Is Called Up Yonder, I'll Be There." It was a song that had been taken up with enthusiasm by the revivalists, and its strains rang out every Sunday at their assemblies. But it remained a music hall favorite still. With the world's greatest spiritualistic medium about to appear, it was the perfect opportunity to play the tune.

The Eureka was jammed by now. Outside, Jack and Flo had stopped to read the colorful posters. "Tonight! The Sensation of the East Coast! Attend a Séance with Eulalia Paradino!" one proclaimed, while another stated, "See Her Converse with the Dead!" and a third asked, "What Do You Want to Ask the Dear Departed?"

Jack recognized a number of faces in the audience belonging to some well-known locals, and there was no doubt that the show was a big crowd puller.

As the orchestra finished its number, there was a lull. Jack took the opportunity to ask Flo about Eulalia Paradino. "So tell me about the star tonight. I'm sure you've got the full story on her."

"She was born in Naples, Italy. Her parents were peasants. She was considered simple as a child, but she performed some extraordinary feats: making glasses, bottles and tables rise into the air and apparently conjuring up faces and shadowy figures that terrified the villagers. A famous professor at Pavia University heard about her. He studied strange happenings like that. He tested her and said she was genuine. He brought in other experts and they all said the same."

"And she's been famous ever since."

"Traveled all over Europe and this country," Flo confirmed. "It was her own idea to put the séances on the stage, as she felt private séances did not help enough people."

The lights in the auditorium dimmed and an uneasy silence fell, a rare occurrence in the Eureka.

Performances in the music halls usually opened without any curtains, with a chorus number. The girls would come straight out dancing. On this occasion, though, an opaque white sheet was hung so as to block the audience's view. It now began to rise slowly and an audible murmur of apprehension replaced the usual cheers and shouts. The stage lights came on to reveal a sole occupant.

Eulalia Paradino sat in the center of the large stage. She wore a shiny black silk gown spangled with golden signs of the zodiac. Her face was white, in contrast to the black hair that hung down to her shoulders. Her age was hard to guess but Jack thought she must be about fifty, though her face was unlined. Her eyes were large and dark and she looked squat, sitting in a large wooden chair with her small hands, heavily jeweled, resting placidly on the heavy chair arms.

A slight mist hovered above the stage floor and added to the spooky ambience. In front of her and the only other object on the stage was a wooden table, like a kitchen table. On it were an oil lamp and two candles, a large handbell and a banjo. A young, fair-haired girl in a long white robe padded onstage barefoot. She raised each of the items in turn so that everyone could see them. She left and Eulalia Paradino spoke for the first time.

In a thick Italian accent she said slowly, "Welcome to all of you. It is so nice to see so many true believers. Tonight, I propose to contact the dead and I want you all to try to make the journey with me."

She paused and the audience was silent, hanging on her next words.

"First I must advise our friends on the other side of our intentions." She moved her head slightly to take in all the rapt spectators. "The lights will dim and I will ask if there is someone there to receive our messages. May I please have your full attention."

She hardly needed to ask that, Jack thought. A bowie knife falling to the floor would have alarmed the entire audience. The lights dimmed and the only sound was the wheezing of heavy smokers. Someone injudicious enough to clink a glass was told to shush by several neighbors.

Madam Paradino folded her hands on her lap and closed her eyes. Her breathing became deeper and deeper.

The unreal tranquillity that followed lasted less than a

minute. A gasp from a table near the stage alerted those farther back that something was happening, and Jack craned his neck to see.

The handbell was tilting. It did not fall, but suddenly rose and pealed out so sharply that several women yelped. It subsided to the table and was quiet; then notes began to strum out from the banjo. They were not recognizable as any tune, but their sequence was not unappealing. A few near the front stood in amazement, staring as the strings of the banjo quivered. Some audience members shouted at the people standing to sit down and others called for everybody to shut up.

Another apprehensive silence settled. Madam Paradino was breathing heavily. Her eyes remained closed and her breast heaved as in sleep.

"We are here. We are ready to communicate. What do you wish to ask?"

The outcry from the audience was like water rushing through an inadequate dam. Some cries were anguished, some wondering, some clamoring. An argument was breaking out on one side of the auditorium and the handbell rose into the air and rang loudly.

Jack thought it was like a school bell calling an unruly class to attention. The bell pealed out imperiously. Order was immediately restored and quiet prevailed once more. Eulalia Paradino's voice cut through the air but her accent seemed less obvious.

"Please do not be alarmed. Our friends on the other side want to help us. Does anyone wish to contact a loved one?"

There was no lack of responses. Most of the people knew someone who had passed on, and they were anxious to ask questions. A man in a smart city suit was first and loudest. He said he wished to talk to his brother, who had died recently. Before he could say more, Eulalia Paradino stirred in her chair and a voice that was completely unlike her own and unmistakably that of a man came from her.

He identified himself as Henry William, the brother of

the questioner, and the audience listened to a flow of questions and answers. Henry William liked it over there; it was different but pleasant, he said. He knew that his wife missed him but he was aware that she was not present because she was on her way to Chicago by train.

"That's right!" the man cried in amazement. "She is!"

Questions about husbands and wives, daughters, sons and parents followed in rapid succession and the accurate knowledge of the departed was unequivocally established in the minds of most. Remarkably, the voice of Eulalia Paradino changed with each character.

An unexpected laugh arose when a question about a departed friend was asked by a man in Western garb. "You shot me!" said a deep voice from the body of the spiritualist. "They should have hanged you, you son of a bitch!"

From the end of the bar, a man pushed his way through to stand where he could call out his question. He was clearly bursting to ask it and others deferred to his insistence. He had white hair and a stocky build and wore rough, ordinary clothes.

"My wife disappeared five years ago," he called out in an unsteady voice. "Is she still alive? Her name is Cecily. I miss her terribly. We were very close."

Eulalia Paradino raised her head slightly, her eyes unseeing. Then her lips moved. "I miss you too, my dear husband. I have been gone from your world for some time now but you should not worry. I did not suffer and am happy and content here." Pure and sweet, the voice was about to continue when, to the astonishment of the crowd, the man pulled off the wig of white hair. He straightened his posture and seemed to lose twenty years.

"You are a liar and a cheat," the man called out in a strident voice. "My wife is not called Cecily. She is not dead. She is here with me now. You are a fraud! You take people's money under false pretenses. You play on their fears and take advantage of their personal tragedies and bereavements."

He pushed out his chest and looked proudly around the auditorium. "My name is Harry Houdini. I am a professional stage magician. You are not a psychic at all. You have no special powers! I can reproduce any trick that you do—and not by psychic means but by physical means! I can—"

Shouts came and fists waved. Men stood and bawled threats at Houdini. The noise was deafening after the calm. Jack pushed his way to the bar and put a hand on Houdini's shoulder. The magician turned, about to defend himself, then stopped as he recognized Jack.

"Better get out of here, Harry," Jack said crisply. "This crowd might get ugly."

"I don't care!" Houdini was still tense with anger. "That woman is a menace. She—"

Jack was several inches taller and fifteen pounds heavier than Houdini. He was aware of the magician's great strength but he hoped Houdini would not use it to oppose him. Jack hustled the shorter man to the door before he could make up his mind to resist.

Outside on the busy sidewalk, Jack eased Houdini away, keeping an eye on the door to make sure no one followed them out. "What are you doing here, Harry?" he asked, a wry amusement in his voice. "You can get yourself injured doing that kind of thing."

Houdini was still fuming. "My show just finished. I put on the wig and rushed over here in time to hear that charlatan telling those poor people all those lies!" He was about to go on but Jack steered him in the direction of the Tower Music Hall.

He stayed with the magician all the way to his dressing room. "Good night, Harry. Be careful, will you? This town is rough. A lot of its citizens are not as civilized as the people you're used to back east. In many ways, this is still the wild, wild West."

Houdini gave him a half grin. "Thanks, Jack. I know you mean well. But that woman, and all like her"—he began to get furious again —"terrorizing mothers with stories about their sons, frightening poor widows, I just can't—"

"I can see you giving up magic and escapes one day," Jack told him, "and devoting yourself to exposing phony mediums."

Houdini nodded thoughtfully. "I may do just that."

As Jack left to return to Flo and the show, he found himself worrying about something that seemed to lie just beyond his grasp. What was it? A happening, a word, an action?

It was not just the special significance that the séance had for him, the memories of being forced to take part in similar ones by his mother and the man she'd married.

William H. Chaney had calculated horoscopes, lectured on chemistry, blasphemed the Christian religion and computed people's "nativities" based on the transit of the planets. He called himself the Professor and charged money whenever he could, making the most from séances. Jack felt that Harry Houdini had been right when he had criticized Eulalia Paradino, saying that she played on people's fears and took advantage of their tragedies.

So what was it? There was something in the scene he had just witnessed: a meaning, a connection that narrowly eluded him. What could it be?

Chapter 19

The knock at Jack's door the next morning while he was writing took him by surprise. Not another manuscript being returned surely? It was too early for that. When he opened the door, he was even more surprised. A Chinese stood there. He was a young man with bright eyes and a slight smile. The Chinese in San Francisco had a hard life and few of them showed smiles. Wearing a blue shift and blue cotton pants, he had a short pigtail under a coolie hat.

"Mr. Jack London?"

"Yes."

"I bring message from the revered How Chew Fat. He asks if you be so kind as to visit him."

Jack could not imagine what was behind the request but he quickly decided that there was no reason to refuse. "I would be pleased to do so. When and where?"

"At one o'clock this afternoon, if this is convenient. He asks that if you are so good as to agree, you be at the provision store on Dupont Street. From there, you will be conducted into his honored presence."

"Very well," Jack said. "I'll be there."

Leaving the Ferry building, Jack was delayed by a straggling column of hundreds of dockworkers pressing the cause of their strike, grim-faced but fortunately not yet suffering the pangs of extreme hunger. He felt sympathy for them because he himself had marched in several such throngs.

He wondered what chance the strikers stood against the Big Three, who could manipulate the economy with such selfish ease. Jack remembered the words of his hero, Eugene Debs: "We have been cursed with the reign of gold long enough. The time has come to regenerate society—we are on the eve of universal change." Jack went on his way when the strikers had gone by. This group seemed peaceful enough, but how much longer could the men last? Some strikes lasted for months.

He hurried on to Chinatown, where the giant red, yellow and green lanterns swayed in the breezes off the bay and white banners fluttered gaily, with black Chinese characters waving in and out of sight. Dupont Street was crowded with wagons, rickshaws and bicycles while smells of tobacco, incense, ripe fruit, meat and burning cooking oil filled the air. High-pitched Chinese voices clinked and clattered amid cries from the vehicle drivers to clear the way.

Jack passed the shop selling fruit and flowers with tall, slender pillars in front and went on to the provision store. The same elderly Chinese with a long pigtail addressed him, this time with increased politeness.

"Welcome to my humble shop. You are expected. My niece will conduct you to the honorable How Chew Fat."

The same young girl with the pale oval face came out as if she had been waiting for Jack. She bowed gravely to him, then turned and pattered on tiny feet through a curtain in the back of the store.

Jack expected to find himself going through the Chinese laundry as before, but instead they went into a deserted courtyard with lines of drying clothes rippling in the strengthening breeze. A door in a decrepit-looking building opened under the girl's hand and they went inside an empty warehouse. A wooden staircase led upward to another story, but the girl led the way in the opposite direction. Jack realized that once again they were descending into the underground world where forty thousand Chinese men, women and children worked and struggled, lived and died.

He felt a sense of foreboding. Was it a trap? No one knew where he had gone. He could easily be killed and his body disposed of—but why? He decided that was not the purpose of his invitation. But what then was it?

They went on through the subterranean labyrinth and Jack was soon lost completely. He had navigated boats, both small and large, over several oceans of the world, but within five minutes here he had not the slightest idea where he was in relation to the ground above. Already they had descended three stories—were there to be more? But no, the girl passed another stairway and went into a corridor with no side doors. At the end, she rapped on a dark wooden door. A peephole opened and quickly snapped closed, and the door swung on silent hinges. The girl motioned Jack inside, then turned and hurried back along the corridor.

Jack half expected to find himself in the same large room as before with its silken drapes, red-and-gold rugs and the silver and jade objects. He thought that they had probably approached the same destination by another route, but this was a different room altogether.

More modest and almost homey, its walls were painted in blues and browns and oranges, faded with age, depicting pastoral scenes. Heavy beams supported the ceiling and Oriental rugs covered the floor. The furniture was of the same heavy dark wood seen frequently in Chinatown. A large desk with stacks of papers and an ornate bronze lamp dominated one portion of the room. Jack was astonished to see that near the lamp stood a telephone.

He hardly had time to observe these features because at a large table in the middle of the room sat How Chew Fat. The table was bare. How Chew Fat motioned for Jack to sit in an empty chair opposite him.

He wore the same Mandarin-style clothing as before, but this time the long coat was saffron yellow, the cuffs on the long sleeves and the wide trousers the same color. His protruding eyes still oozed the occasional tear, and he wiped each one away with a delicate lace handkerchief.

"You are still writing stories?" His voice was high and each word came out distinctly separate from the others. His thick blubbery lips moved very little as he spoke. The vacant eyes showed no emotion.

You didn't bring me here to ask that, was Jack's immediate reaction, but he said, "Yes. I just got a contract for six more."

"Offer is from *Godey's Magazine* or *Overland Monthly*?"

Jack was startled, but determined not to show his surprise, he said in a neutral tone, "*Overland Monthly*."

"Does not pay well but has excellent reputation," the Chinese commented, and Jack reflected ruefully that he could not have summed up the magazine better himself.

"Our Chinese community here has many investments in American business world. Newspapers, magazines are some of these. Is necessary therefore to know such things."

Jack nodded. That plus the telephone on the desk was a partial explanation. He waited for the other to continue.

"No more attempts on your life since we talk last." It was a statement as much as a question. It was time for Jack to take the initiative in the conversation.

"As a matter of fact, there has been an attempt, yes." He went on to describe being locked in Houdini's boiler backstage at the Tower Music Hall. How Chew Fat listened with neither interruption nor any sign of paying attention. Then his blubbery lips moved as he said, "Not action of Chinese. Perhaps by helping police, you become a nuisance someone wish to remove."

So much for initiative, Jack thought. This cunning Oriental was one step ahead of him all the time. Unable to think of anything to say, he remained silent.

"It is our custom to eat at this time," said How Chew Fat. He waved an arm as if to make a meal appear. "You will join me, please?" He dabbed his lips with the handkerchief.

Jack was getting used to being surprised. "Thank you, yes. That is very kind of you."

"But first," How Chew Fat said, "there is one thing."

Jack waited. The Chinaman shuffled in his chair. He seemed to grow several inches in height, as if his body were stretching. The blubbery lips contracted into a straight, tight line. The vacant look in the pale eyes turned into a keen, appraising gaze. His entire demeanor had changed, and when he spoke again, his voice was deep and full.

"It often suits my purpose to have people regard me as a simpleton, a buffoon. It puts me in a more advantageous position."

Jack stared, amazed at this transformation, hardly able to believe that it had happened before his eyes. It could have been a totally different man facing him.

"However, I use that guise only with those I do not know or trust." His English was now impeccable, Jack noticed, and only the slightest sibilance betrayed his Oriental heritage. "Once I have established in my mind the true nature of the person I am talking to, I consider that it would be dishonest to continue the pretense. So I will now order the meal and we will talk man to man."

He rapped lightly on the table. Two very elderly women in long Chinese robes came in. One spread an immaculate white damask tablecloth and the other put down a tray bearing a silver teapot and two exquisite china cups in saucers. She poured and steam rose as she placed a cup in front of each of them.

She left and the man opposite Jack continued. "How Chew Fat is not, of course, my name. I use it to conceal a stupid character. My real name does not matter. I have a position on what you would call the board of directors of the Six Companies. This position involves most of our connections with the Occidental world."

They drank tea. Jack had tasted Chinese tea before but this was infinitely more subtle, yet richer at the same time.

The women returned and trays were unloaded. Plates of sparkling white porcelain with gold edges were placed in front of them and How Chew Fat waved a hand. "Please help yourself. Would you like to start with the shark's fin soup?"

Jack was still trying to recover from his astonishment at the radical change in the character of the Chinaman. He nodded. More dishes came. One bowl contained steamed eels and another lacquered duck with water chestnuts, bamboo shoots, soya beans and almonds. Bowls of white and yellow rice, dark brown crinkled mushrooms and tiny rice pancakes were placed on the table as the women came and went. Beef cubes in a thick sauce had a gingery taste and chicken slices had been cooked in jasmine oil. How Chew Fat described each dish to Jack, who had eaten Chinese food before but never a banquet like this.

"I come from the Canton region of China," How Chew Fat explained. "It is considered to be the gastronomic capital of my country."

The meal was punctuated only by comments on the food, and Jack knew that this such conversation was the Chinese custom. But he didn't mind. He just reveled in the exotic feast, which was quite a change from the bar food he usually ate.

It was not until the table had been cleared that How Chew Fat sat back. "When you were here on the previous occasion, you told me of two Chinese who had attacked you. I told you that they were *boo how doy* who had broken an important rule in our society and been banished from it. I also told you that they are placing their skills at the disposal of white men in San Francisco."

Jack did not need to ask what the other man meant by "skills." He meant their ability to kill swiftly and efficiently. Jack was lucky not to have been among their victims.

"One of these men is now using a disguise to make it easier for him to operate in the white man's area. He has used walnut juice on his face and hands to make him look like a Mexican. His eyes are Oriental but not unlike those of the people belonging to some Mexican Indian tribes. He has one distinguishing mark also—a knife cut at the edge of his mouth."

Jack nodded. "He has just committed a murder," he said.

The Chinaman's eyes clouded. "I was afraid that might be the case. I fear that he may kill again soon."

"Why did you bring me here?" Jack asked abruptly. He knew that the Oriental way was to be more subtle and indirect, but he was forthright in nature and suddenly felt impatient at this polite talk about murder.

How Chew Fat nodded in understanding. "You are a young man and impatient to see retribution. Your Occidental way is more impetuous than ours. I know that. Very well, I will tell you. We are forty thousand Chinese trapped—most of us belowground—in your city of San Francisco. We do not interfere in your affairs unless they endanger our future. Unfortunately, such a situation now threatens."

"What situation?" Jack demanded.

"Its constitution is not yet clear. The components are being manifested but the connections are uncertain. More than that, I cannot tell you, but I can assure you that San Francisco faces a greater hazard than it has ever faced before."

Jack was stunned by the pronouncement. "You say these two *boo how doy* may kill again? Is this one of the components of the dangerous situation that you're talking about?"

"It is. I can tell you one thing that may be helpful—the other *boo how doy* is said to be changing his appearance too so that he can pass as white."

"Is the man with the scar on his mouth with him?"

"Probably. In their activities as *boo how doy,* they operate as a team. I must tell you though that the Suey Chun tong is very unhappy about these two men. They consider them renegades and traitors. They may be trying to bring them to justice."

"You mean hang them?" Jack asked, but he thought he knew the answer.

"A similar fate but much less formal," said How Chew Fat, confirming Jack's suspicion. "Now I have more interesting gossip for you."

Jack smiled at the word "gossip." "What would be really interesting would be the identity of Glass, or whoever is giving orders to these two renegades," he said.

"That is precisely what I am about to tell you," the imperturbable Chinaman said. "I am sure you are familiar with the term 'the Big Three?' "

"I was afraid of that," Jack said grimly. "They're behind this?"

"So it is believed. Their orders appear to be transmitted through a city councilman called Stanley Hogben. His role is unclear but the finger points at him unerringly."

"I know who he is. I don't like him." Hogben had once sent toughs to drag Jack off the stage when he was addressing a socialist rally in Oakland.

"You may use this information as you wish," said How Chew Fat. "My main concern is for my own people. I do not wish to see them hurt in an affair that is not of their making."

"Nor do I," Jack said, "but if the Big Three are transmitting through Hogben, then what about Glass?"

Jack hardly expected any reaction from the Chinaman, nor was there one. The man answered cryptically, "I believe the name Glass hides the identity of a real person who is behind many crimes in San Francisco."

"I appreciate your trusting me with this information," said Jack. "I hope it will be a help in preventing the dangerous situation you refer to."

"I hope prevention is possible," said How Chew Fat gravely.

How Chew Fat moved gently in the direction of the door and Jack accepted the hint. As they walked together, the

Chinaman said, "One final question—what do you know of a plot to burn Chinatown?"

Jack looked at him amazed. "Burn Chinatown? What do you mean? Why would anyone do that?"

How Chew Fat fluttered a hand, a gesture more in keeping with his disguised mannerisms than with his real ones. "You have heard nothing of it. That is plain. Maybe it is a rumor, possibly baseless."

They exchanged farewells. Up close, the Chinaman looked older than Jack had previously thought—ten years older at least, but perhaps that came from the authoritative manner and expansive knowledge of this new persona, such a contrast to the fat, blubbery-faced individual he had met at first.

Jack was still pondering the seriousness and the nature of the looming threat that How Chew Fat had spoken of when the slim girl appeared and conducted him through a series of completely different passages, stairways and corridors. They finally emerged in a shop that buzzed and shrieked with the cries and calls of dozens of Oriental birds in cages. Jack stood there and looked for the girl but she had already disappeared from sight.

Chapter 20

Fraser Street was only a short walk away from the edge of Chinatown and Jack went directly to the Plucked Chicken, the bar where Morley had told him he could leave a message. That early in the day, only a handful of deeply dedicated drinkers was there. Two slouched over the bar and three men who looked like dockworkers were at a table covered with glasses and bottles. Cigarette ash was strewn on the floor around them and their card game was noisy and argumentative.

The place was sparse and none too clean. Two dim lamps shed a miserable glow, which partially revealed the dirt and dust. An unshaven bartender emerged and glared at Jack as if irritated at being disturbed. Jack ordered a beer, and when it came he asked casually, "Niccolo in today?"

"Haven't seen him in days," was the grunted reply. Jack drank his beer. The card game continued and the two at the bar continued their silent drinking. Jack waited hopefully, but when nothing had changed after about fifteen minutes, he finished his beer and left. He walked to the cable car stop on Powell Street and joined the half dozen people standing there waiting for the next car. A man came up to stand near him.

"You looking for Niccolo?"

His voice was thin and reedy and his appearance was similar. His face was sallow but his eyes were lively.

"Yes, I am," Jack said.

"What's your name?"

"Jack London."

The other nodded and jerked his head. The two of them moved away from the cable car passengers. This man, Niccolo, looked vaguely familiar, Jack thought. He had seen him recently. Then it struck him. He was one of the two drunks at the bar.

"You got something for the captain?"

Jack told him of How Chew Fat's warning but without identifying his source. He told him of the two *boo how doy*.

"One of the *boo how doy* has already been made to look like a Mex," Jack said. "The second is trying to look white."

"Grant Street near Union Square," Niccolo said thoughtfully. "There's a character there calls himself a doctor, specializes in making Orientals look like whites, bleaches their faces and straightens their eyes."

Jack then passed along the information on Councilman Stanley Hogben. Niccolo nodded and frowned. "He's mixed up in this, is he?" he mused. His gaze focused on something over Jack's shoulder.

"Something wrong?" Jack asked, turning, but there was no one near.

Niccolo shook his head. "No. It's okay."

"You know something else about Stanley Hogben?" asked Jack.

"His name keeps coming up. Captain's got a man on him. But what's this dangerous situation in the city that you're talking about?"

"I wish I knew," Jack said. "I'll pass on everything I hear," he added, hoping that would prevent the other from probing too deeply into Jack's source.

The worn, tired face put on a slight grin. "I can understand you don't want to tell me where you got this information," Niccolo said. "I don't like to reveal my sources either." He glanced both ways along Grant Street; then as he turned back to Jack, he said sharply, "Damn, there they go."

Jack looked over his shoulder to see what had been attracting Niccolo's attention. Three men were crossing the street.

"They're the three you saw in the Plucked Chicken," Niccolo said. "I was trying to catch what I could of their conversation—we think they belong to that gang, Riders of the Rim. I ought to follow them but I've got another fellow coming in with an urgent message in a few minutes. Got to wait for him."

"Let me follow them," said Jack on impulse.

Niccolo hesitated, then nodded. "Okay, but be careful. We don't know enough about these ruffians yet."

"All right."

"And I'll see the captain gets your stuff right away."

The three pursued a none-too-steady course as far as the corner, then turned on Clay Street, which was busy with carts and wagons being loaded with fruit, vegetables and fish for delivery. Pigtailed Chinese in blue denim and conical straw hats padded along, shoulders bowed under loads dangling from bamboo poles. Harsh cries and barked orders rang out and horses whinnied and pawed the ground, impatient to go. It was easy for Jack to keep the men in sight.

As they passed Front Street, it was clear that their destination was the Embarcadero, with its long row of empty wharves and unnaturally quiet warehouses stretching in both directions from the Ferry Building.

There was less cover for Jack, so he stayed close to buildings to be less conspicuous, but the three did not look back. Jack had a fleeting thought that it was a trap and that Niccolo was not a policeman—perhaps he was not even Niccolo at all! But Jack's obstinate streak and the lure of excitement had the upper hand.

A warehouse looked empty but one of the three opened a large door and they all went in. Jack waited, observing the quiet scene. From along Drumm Street came a solitary man who seemed to know where he was going. He went in the same door as the three; Jack took a deep breath and followed suit.

It was a huge building, and at one end a sizable crowd had accumulated. A man was speaking from a makeshift platform but was not getting the crowd's full attention. Feet shuffled and conversations came from muttered groups. Jack found it easy to wend his way among them and get close enough to hear, but not too close should he want to make an early escape. He picked up the thread of the speech.

"We are living in the most prosperous and enlightened country in the world," he was saying in a loud voice. "Yet we have today ten million people living in poverty. These ten million people are, in fact, dying, body and soul, slowly but surely, because they have nothing to eat.

"We know this, but what are we doing about it? We are letting our less fortunate comrades die a hideous death from starvation. . . ."

He went on in the same vein, protesting, cajoling, condemning, until a big man in a striped suit came out and interrupted him.

"Thank you, comrade, for your heartfelt words. We indeed sympathize with our unhappy comrades. Here is another voice to tell us what we can do to help them." He waved to a prosperous-looking, well-fed man with a plump, florid face. "We all know him and we welcome him today—Stanley Hogben."

Hogben bounded up onto the stage and Jack leaned forward eagerly. The man in the striped suit gave Hogben a big buildup. He referred to his experience as an assessor, a tax collector and a land committeeman—all positions, thought Jack, where opportunities for bribes were plentiful.

He was an officer of the Law and Order Party too, added the striped-suit man. This was a new political party, replacing the Vigilance Committee, whose members' activities as vigilantes had been responsible for a partial cleanup of the crime and corruption in San Francisco. As the powers of the vigilantes stretched farther and farther outside the law, however, the group became more and more high-handed and ruled by personal gain. Street hangings with only a farce of a trial and without any defense became common.

The army had been called in to disband them. It was at this point that the Law and Order Party was formed and relative calm prevailed under a false assumption that these were men with higher motives. It took the penetrating voice of Ambrose Bierce and the *Examiner* editorial columns to point out that most of the Vigilance Committee officers had become the officials of the Law and Order Party.

Hogben began his talk with a condemnation of the companies that owned the docks and the ships that lay idle. "They are bleeding us!" he thundered. "They are taking the bread out of our mouths!" He went on like this for some time and the anger and indignation of his listeners grew until the tin roof of the warehouse flung back the echoing cries.

Jack had the opportunity to look at the members of the crowd. Many were unemployed dockworkers, some were disgruntled miners who had spent all their hard-earned gold and others were sailors, shore-bound by the strike. He even saw two Chinese in laborers' clothes. He also noticed that there were others in the same mold as the three he had followed there. They were strong in number and loud of voice. When Hogben made a crucial point, they were the first to shout. These men were a rallying team, whipping up support and inflaming the rest.

"Most of you are sympathizers, friends of our cause," he bellowed. Then he paused in his peroration, flung out an arm and pointed at Jack, who was not far from the front of the crowd.

"But a few spies invade our meetings, and there is one of them! He calls himself a writer but I say he is a spy for the bloated bosses, those who grind us down, keep us from working, cause our starvation—and if we die, don't give a damn!"

The fiery words brought forth angry murmurs. As heads turned in his direction, Jack felt a wave of animosity and those surrounding him began to shrink away. For a second, he stood paralyzed by the suddenness of the accusation. The cries grew louder, fists shook.

Jack waved his hands above his head, appealing for quiet. At first, there was no change in the dangerous mood of the crowd, but as he kept waving, the noise level subsided just enough for him to be heard.

"Some of you know me," Jack shouted. "I am a socialist! I have been a member of the Socialist Party in Oakland for ten years. I have been arrested and put in Oakland jail for being a socialist. I say any man is a socialist who wants his government replaced by a better one! But I am not an anarchist and—"

That enraged Hogben. His face red, he yelled, "Don't you accuse us of being anarchists! Don't try to cover up your spying tactics that way!" He raved on and Jack was astonished at his extreme reaction.

A man near Jack seized his arm and started to hustle him away. Another grabbed Jack's other arm. Both men were strong and well trained. Struggle as he would, Jack could not free himself from their grip. "We'll take care of him!" one of his captors shouted as they dragged him away.

They pulled him through the crowd, where fists still waved and epithets were yelled. They dragged him through a door—then to Jack's amazement, they released him. One of the men dropped a bar across the door to secure it. The other grinned at Jack.

"McParland told us to keep an eye on you. Said you were a bit of a hothead. Better get out fast. Go that way."

The rehearsal under way at the Midway Plaisance was at the frenetic stage. Belle Conquest, in her full finery, was shouting orders and hurling criticisms in all directions. She wore her full stage makeup, including eyelashes long enough to be seen from the back rows. Her attire was an

evening dress, presumably for the role, tight-fitting, cut low
on the breasts and cinched snugly at the waist. The dress
was an eye-catching yellow and green and it was strained to
its limits by Belle's suggestive wiggles and writhing con-
tortions.

Jack had to admit that she kept these to a minimum of
movement while still achieving the maximum of effect. Sitting at a stage-side table and nursing a refreshing beer, he
was finding the performance a fine cure for his exciting
visit to the meeting of the Riders of the Rim. Was that who
they were? If he had stayed longer, he might have found
out. On the other hand, he might be nursing broken bones
or worse. How had Hogben known him and why was he so
vehement against him?

"No! No! No!" Belle screamed and the orchestra died
down obediently. She pointed an imperious forefinger at
each end of the chorus line. "You girls are supposed to
swing out into a half circle there! Haven't you rehearsed
this at all?"

She threw a glare at Flo, who wore the shimmering gray
one-piece outfit that she often donned for rehearsing.

"No, we haven't." Flo's light, clear voice contrasted
sharply with Belle's loud, brassy tones. "This is one of the
changes you made." Jack noted the restraint in Flo's answer.

"That's what rehearsals are for!" Belle snapped. "Try it
again!" She turned angrily to the orchestra. "Well, what are
you waiting for?"

Flo's well-trained girls quickly went into Belle's next
number, which she immediately claimed was being played
too slow. "If Only I Was a Lady" had been one of her big
hits on Broadway. Belle blamed Flo for the tempo, shouting
that the orchestra was slowing in order to keep pace with
the chorus. After further altercation and a couple of run-
throughs, they had it right. Belle squirmed her way into the
"I'm Just a Prisoner of Passion" number and Flo slipped
from the stage to join Jack.

"She's taking the deaths of those two boys very hard," Flo said in her gentle voice. "It's making her bitchy."

Two deliverymen came in and stared goggle-eyed at the stage. "Sorry, fellows. No free shows—and this lady's very expensive," said Flo.

They gazed fixedly at the stage. "She looks worth it," said one of the men.

"Do you have those new costumes?" Flo asked.

"Yes. Where do you want them?"

Flo took them backstage and returned to Jack. "New costumes?" he asked.

"New and unusual." Flo smiled. "You'll love them."

The dance became more sexually suggestive as another of Belle's bodyguards joined her. "That's Teddy," whispered Flo. "He's been knocking back the whisky. He's nervous as a cat. He'll catch hell if Belle hears about it. She doesn't drink herself and she doesn't permit anyone around her to drink."

The orchestra played louder as the dance flirted with obscenity. "They'll love this at the opening," Jack said.

Belle twisted her body in an explicitly sensual movement and Flo murmured, "One role she'll never be able to play is sweet Rosie O'Grady."

"She knows show business," Jack said admiringly.

"You can call it bad taste," Flo said with a nod, "but it's made her the biggest star on Broadway, and it will make her the biggest star ever to appear on the Barbary Coast. She'll sell more seats than Lillian Russell or Lillie Langtry. She has tremendous gusto and vitality and it comes through on the stage. Audiences love her because she doesn't shilly-shally. She doesn't try to suggest sex—she shows it in every word and every move."

"Don't talk anymore," Jack murmured, his eyes on the stage. "You're distracting me." Flo gave him a jab in the ribs with her elbow.

Belle found fault with the closing of the number and yelled for Flo, who went over at once. Jack chose the moment to make his way unobtrusively past the stage and into the area behind it. Coming toward him was Louis Lahearne. Jack deliberately blocked the narrow corridor.

"Just having a look around," Jack told Belle's manager breezily. "Making sure that everything's all right." He still did not know if Belle had told Lahearne that he had been hired to guard the Rajah's Ruby. The other man did not question Jack's authority to be back there, so he presumed the manager knew.

"Is Belle's other bodyguard around?" Jack asked.

"Getting ready," Lahearne answered. "Belle wants to run through one of his numbers."

When Lahearne made as if to push past Jack, the writer remained immobile and asked, "Anybody else here?"

"I haven't seen anybody," said Lahearne, and then Jack let him pass.

It was quiet with almost all the performers on the stage, and as Jack went by a dressing room door he heard the clink of a glass and the gurgle of liquid. He grasped the doorknob firmly, turned it and opened the door a few inches.

Laurence, Belle's bodyguard, was slumped on a sofa, and with him was a woman Jack recognized as one of Flo's chorus girls. Rita was a handsome but hard-faced girl, and Flo had told Jack that she was a minor problem due to her preference for women rather than men. Some of the other chorus girls had complained about her to Flo. Yet here she was with Laurence. They were drinking whisky—Jack could smell it from the door—and both were barely half dressed. They were too occupied with each other to hear the door and Jack closed it carefully.

He completed his tour of the backstage area and found nothing else unusual. He went back to the auditorium, where Belle's voice was like a trumpet, complaining about the timing on another number. Jack tried to exit unobtrusively but Belle spied him.

"Jack, come on up here! We need another man for this scene!"

Jack stopped. He had faced raging typhoons on the Pacific and Chinese assassins with knives and garrotes, but being on the stage with Belle Conquest was a concept that terrified him more. Yet he could not just walk away. He glanced at Flo, who stood there with an amused smile, waiting to see his reaction.

He was still hesitating when Laurence came up the side approach to the stage. His stride was unsteady, and when he came near Belle an aroma of alcohol must have reached her. She snarled something at him, not loud enough for anyone else to hear. He smiled foolishly and struck a dance pose. He reached one arm around Belle and pulled her into the next number before she could react. The orchestra, wanting to get the rehearsal over, obligingly struck up with "What Is It, If It's Not Love?"

Jack saw his chance and hurried out the door.

Chapter 21

It was the first time Jack had been inside San Francisco's Presidio. As he entered now, he was elated that Bierce had invited him to attend this notable occasion, but he was also aware that "the Presidio" had become such a part of the language of the city that its true significance was becoming lost. It was a landmark building, but so old that it was taken for granted by most San Franciscans.

Jack had done his research as meticulously as he did for his stories. He knew that in 1774 the Spanish viceroy in Mexico had begun the construction of a new presidio in San Francisco, modeling it after the presidio built three years earlier at Monterey. Here, as in Monterey, a mission had been erected at the same time, but it was the presidio that was such an important part of the city.

The Spanish meaning of the word was "garrison," and that was its primary function. Just down the coast from Seal Rocks, it consisted of several rows of long, low buildings with a large flag flying from a very tall flagpole.

At the guard gate, Jack had his name checked on the guest list. He wore his best suit—his only suit—which he had checked out that morning from Lou Treager's pawnshop. He felt it was safer there.

Small flags lined the wide path that led to the nearest of the buildings, where two soldiers stood on duty. A steady stream of formally dressed men and women were ahead of Jack as they alighted from coaches and carriages, a large

number of which had already accumulated. He went up the
three steps and inside.

The army had done its best but it was still a barracks building. Nevertheless, the flags that covered all the walls gave it a
somewhat festive air and subdued the military image. Jack
noted that in addition to the Stars and Stripes, the Bear Flag
of the state of California was prominent. The others were presumably company and divisional flags and award pennants.

Oil lamps had been installed in place of chandeliers, and
an orchestra of about ten was playing a lilting minuet, successful in adapting their brass dominance to this more sedate occasion. Long tables were spaced throughout the
room, laden with enticing-looking food, while around the
walls were tables serving as bars, a colored man behind
each one. Men and women in their finery were clustered in
groups, chattering and gossiping.

One man detached himself from a group and, as he was
walking across the room, caught sight of Jack. He was
dressed in a black cutaway suit with a wingtail tie and a
shiny white shirt with pearl buttons. Hap Harrison was the
owner of the Cobweb Palace, one of the premier music hall
saloons on the Barbary Coast. Hap was proud of the fact
that he was a veteran of the War Between the States, although he omitted to add that he had fought on both sides.

Hap Harrison was a tall, gangly man whose limbs seemed
awkward in movement. He was not cross-eyed, but he had an
unfocused gaze in which his two eyes seemed to operate separately. They swiveled in different directions, making it impossible to tell if one was false. Hap was genial and friendly
but a tough man to cross, and Jack wondered if the ten-inch
bowie knife he wore in the Cobweb Palace to deal with recal-
citrant customers was concealed under his elegant clothing.

"Jack, my young friend!" he beamed. Hap had been
shown one of Jack's short stories and believed that he recognized himself as one of the characters, an irascible but
kindhearted saloon owner. Jack had always preferred not to
tell him that the original was a different saloon owner al-

together, because Hap's version resulted in an unusual bond between them.

"You look real swell, Hap," Jack told him.

"Got to, with a crowd like this!" Hap said. "Haven't seen such a turnout since Teddy Roosevelt was here."

"Oh, you get crowds nearly this big at the Palace," Jack told him.

"Yeah, not as rich though." Hap grinned. "Lot of money in this room."

"A lot of power too."

"Certainly is." Hap's double-barreled gaze swept the room. "Don't see too many music hall owners here."

"Aren't many respectable ones," Jack pointed out.

"And there might be less in the future," Hap said darkly.

"What do you mean?"

Hap refocused on Jack. "Somebody's trying to buy up music halls on the Coast," he said in a confidential tone. "Don't know who, it's being kept quiet but I hear Jim Laidlaw at the Tower has had an offer."

One eye swung across the room while the other turned to Jack. "There's Martin Beck over there. Got to talk to him."

As Hap left, Jack caught sight of another familiar face, which belonged to a good-looking man with an athletic bearing in a very expensive suit with shiny lapels. It was Richard Harding Davis, probably the best-known war correspondent in America. The two of them had met briefly several times. Jack detested Davis's novels as being too effete and polite but he respected his courage and professionalism as a journalist.

Davis was described as "the most admired and envied man in America today." His dashing exploits, his news-gathering expeditions to all parts of the world, where he hobnobbed with world leaders, and his well-written dispatches, usually from the front lines and almost always, according to Davis, under fire, probably justified the description. Jack admitted his own envy and had a secret determination to be a war correspondent himself one day—provided it did not interfere with his intention to be a great novelist.

They greeted each other warmly and Davis, as usual, opened the conversation on his favorite subject—himself.

"As you know, Jack, I have been in South Africa, covering England's war with the Boers for the *New York Herald*. Let me tell you, it's neither an interesting country nor an interesting war. Do you know, I went a week without food at one time? But I had the chance to spend a few days with Mr. Winston Churchill, and that made it worthwhile. I believe he will be a great man one day, mark my words."

"You took your wife with you, I understand," Jack said.

"Only as far as Cape Town. Then I went on to Ladysmith. The siege was still on when I arrived, and I had the good fortune to be able to watch first the British Army under Lord Roberts and then the Boers."

"The Boers are an anachronism," Jack said, knowing that Davis would disagree with him. "It's the Anglo-Saxon people against the world and the English people are in the vanguard. Economics are at the foundation of all their actions and foreign holdings are vital to their existence."

Their discussion went on until Ambrose Bierce strolled across and took Davis by the arm. "Back from the wars, Richard, I see. Come and tell me all about it. Perhaps I can persuade you to be our guest columnist. . . ."

Jack helped himself to the heaps of shrimp and oysters on one of the tables, then went to the nearest drinks table. The attendant offered him a glass of wine but Jack refused—he hated wine, having gotten drunk on it at the age of seven. A bottle of beer was poured into a fancy glass stein, and he was turning to see who else he knew when a large figure loomed before him.

The thinning hair and the few silvery strands covering the large head were the same. The thick-lensed, gold-rimmed spectacles, the droopy mustache and the shrewd blue eyes were undoubtedly those of James McParland, head of the Pinkerton Detective Agency. In place of the tweed outfit he had worn before was his tails suit, shiny black.

"I have to thank you for those two men of yours at that

meeting," Jack said after McParland greeted him politely.
"They will have told you about it. There might have been a
nasty turn of events if your men hadn't intervened."

McParland nodded. "They told me. You evidently have
interests ranging beyond the spiritualist woman and the
connection with your mother's séances."

McParland had a knack for making statements that sounded
harmless yet hinted at other, deeper layers of knowledge.
Jack had no intention of getting into a sparring contest with
him. He said only, "Thanks for the help anyway."

"In the future," McParland said, "you will have to be
more careful."

"I will," Jack said.

"The reason I say that," McParland went on, "is that we
are pulling out tomorrow."

"Pulling out?" Jack could not keep the surprise out of his
voice.

"Yes. Our activities here are terminated."

Jack eyed him for a moment. It was impossible to read
the man. "Terminated? You mean finished?"

"Terminated," McParland repeated.

"Have you accomplished what you came to do?" Jack
asked.

"There are other assignments for my men. I have to get
them reestablished."

Jack was trying to fit the significance behind McParland's words into the pattern of events. So the Pinkertons
were not there to guard the Rajah's Ruby. Had the ruby
been stolen already? No, that could hardly have been
hushed up.

"Be careful, young man. Be very careful," McParland
said, then limped away.

Jack looked around to see if Bierce was in sight. He
probably knew about this astonishing development already,
and if he did, he would have had time to make some judgment on it. But Jack could not find him. He did see one
very recognizable figure—the high domed forehead with a

noble cast and the heavy beard and mustache made him unmistakable. It was Collis P. Huntington, one of the Big Three. He was in an earnest discussion with a man Jack knew to be Rudolph of the wealthy Spreckels family.

On the other side of the room, Terence Caraher was not talking—he was preaching. He was preaching now to a small gathering that listened with only partial attention. His technique was understandable, for preaching was his business. The Reverend Caraher was pastor of the Roman Catholic Church of St. Francis and, more important from the point of view of the Barbary Coast, chairman of the Committee on Morals.

An Irishman who had come to the United States twenty years earlier and started his work at the Mission of San Jose, he was now the voice of morality in San Francisco and the leader of the crusade to clean up the city. He waged incessant warfare against the red-light district of the Barbary Coast. He blockaded the brothels, wrote inflammatory articles in the newspapers naming the wealthy and often seemingly respectable owners of those establishments and hauled offenders into court.

Jack found it hard to assess those listening to him now. The odds were that some proportion of them might eventually be among his victims. He kept doing more and more to justify his nickname of "Terrible Terry." A few of those listening might be sympathetic, but right at that moment the reverend was condemning public dancing as both vicious and immoral. He called San Francisco's cable cars "dance halls on wheels" and described roller-skating rinks, which were just becoming popular, as "dangerous to both body and soul, frequented by the worst elements of society."

If the Reverend Caraher had been invited to this occasion, then perhaps Carrie Nation was here too. But she was not in sight, and Jack supposed that even if she were invited she would refuse to attend, especially if she knew of the steady business at the drinks tables around the room.

Jack ate a few more shrimp and a couple of salmon sandwiches, then some of the mussels in an Italian sauce. He re-filled his beer glass and was surveying the room when he saw Bierce waving to him. He was with a man in full tails.

"This is Wilford Barcroft, our new governor." To the governor, Bierce said, "This is Jack London, a young man who is starting to make a name for himself in the world of letters. He is destined to be a great writer one day. I am helping him as much as I can," he added.

The governor acknowledged Jack cordially enough. He was a short, stout man with a carefully trimmed beard and mustache of the type popularized by Ulysses S. Grant. His voice was gruff, no doubt from the barking of orders. Clearly, though, he was anxious to get away and spend his time talking to citizens more influential than a writer in his twenties, however promising.

He excused himself and Bierce watched the governor strut away to talk to the mayor, Hiram T. Nelson. Bierce's shrewd eyes under the fair, bushy brows flickered across the assembly.

"Looking for a good target for tomorrow's editorial, Ambrose?" Jack asked.

"I was just thinking," said Bierce, "that this is a perfect opportunity for a group of villains to get together. And there are plenty of them here." His eye alighted on a circle of guests and he nodded in that direction. "There's an arch-villain there, for example."

In the center of the circle was a heavy, red-faced man with a bearing that indicated he was used to dominating any assembly of which he was a part.

"Fred Crocker," said Jack. Crocker's picture appeared in newspapers and magazines frequently, and there was no mistaking the harsh features. Bierce criticized and casti-gated Crocker at every available opportunity—Crocker and his fellow members of the Big Three. "I saw Huntington," Jack said, "talking to Rudolph Spreckels, but I haven't seen Stanford. I hear he's ill."

Bierce grunted unsympathetically. "Haven't seen him. Ill or not, he's probably up to some rascally activities elsewhere."

Jack grinned. Bierce would ascribe any crooked activity in that part of California to the wicked machinations of the Big Three. Leland Stanford had recently donated a hundred thousand acres of prime California land on which to build a university and endowed it with a grant of thirty million dollars—on condition it was named after him. Ambrose Bierce was still using that in his columns, hammering at what he called "spurious generosity."

Crocker was waving his arms, accentuating some point in his discourse. He was not quite as hard-drinking, profane and bull-voiced as his father—whom he had replaced in the Big Three—but he was a hardheaded and ruthless businessman who had been the first to see the immense value of a railroad through the Sierras. The building of the Central Pacific Railroad had been the major factor in linking the east and west coasts and creating the incalculable business increase that had provided. Bierce never failed to accompany any mention of the railroad with the fact that it had been built at the cost of ten thousand lives.

"I wonder what he's saying?"

"I'll tell you in my column tomorrow."

"But you don't know, Ambrose."

"Let him sue me," Bierce said indifferently. He paused as he spotted another face. "So Jim McParland is here. He doesn't attend many social functions."

"A farewell appearance, I suppose," Jack murmured.

Bierce glanced at him sharply. "You didn't read that in my column in the *Examiner.*"

"I probably will," Jack said. "But no, I didn't. McParland just told me."

"Did he? You detective types have to stick together, I suppose."

Jack grinned. "I hardly qualify for that description. I did run into him a while ago though."

"He's not usually that communicative," Bierce said. "Does he confide in you a lot?"

Jack shook his head. "No confidences. Since he told me he was leaving, though, I've been trying to figure out what the Pinks did while they were here and if they finished whatever it was."

Bierce grunted. It was one of the noncommittal grunts he was so practiced at and could be read a number of ways. "So the new governor arrives and the Pinkerton boss leaves," he said. "What do you think of coincidences, Jack? Do you believe in them?"

"They do happen—but are you saying these two events are connected? I don't see how they possibly can be."

Bierce brushed a finger across his luxuriant mustache. "The next few days may tell us," he said slowly, and was about to go on when his gaze fell on someone and his eyes brightened. "I need more material for my column tomorrow. Here's a likely victim."

The subject of his gaze was a tall, upstanding man of spare figure and piercing eyes. His face was gray and lined and his mouth tight. His thin hair was carefully spread but still did not cover his large head. His formal suit was tailor-made and looked very expensive.

"Mr. Robert Windham," murmured Bierce. "You'll have to excuse me, Jack. Time to earn my salary."

He walked off to greet the other, whose name was familiar to Jack as one of San Francisco's most prominent businessmen. He had made money in railroads and banking and was involved in numerous enterprises.

Before Jack could look for another familiar face, he was approached by a man in a formal suit that made its wearer look uncomfortable. It was Harry Houdini.

After handshakes, Jack said to Houdini, "I think you'd rather be somewhere else than here, Harry. Surely you know how to escape."

Houdini smiled weakly. "I don't enjoy social functions, especially when they are as formal as this."

"I think you only feel really at home on the stage," Jack said, and Houdini nodded prompt affirmation.

"Still, I suppose it helps at the box office," Jack could not help adding. At that moment Bierce returned and he and Houdini exchanged greetings.

Houdini was looking keenly at the other guests. "Is she here?" he asked. "That terrible woman?"

"Harry means Eulalia Paradino," Jack explained, but Bierce was already nodding.

"The contest still rages, eh, Harry? Determined to expose the fakes and the frauds?"

"With every fiber of my being," Houdini said fiercely. "The woman is a menace." Bierce and Jack were given another vigorous denouncement of the spiritualist, which was halted only by the arrival of Martin Beck.

The impressario seized on Houdini. "I'm glad you finally got here, Harry. Listen—there's a man over by that table— tell me, have you ever been to Australia? No? Good. Now the deal is this. He wants . . ." He led the magician away by the arm and Jack turned to speak to Bierce, only to find him staring fixedly across the room.

More guests had come in and the room was almost as full as it could be and still permit movement. The orchestra had increased its volume just enough to be heard but not enough to drown the myriad conversations.

"See something worth printing, Ambrose?" Jack asked.

"That door over there." Bierce directed his intense gaze and Jack followed it. "Just going through it now," Bierce said.

Jack caught only a glimpse of the man but recognized him instantly. "Hogben."

"Yes, Stanley Hogben."

"Everyone seems interested in him these days," said Jack.

"Everyone?"

Resisting giving a direct answer to that, Jack said, "I blundered into a meeting, several Riders of the Rim, among others, and Hogben was running it. He denounced me and I was nearly lynched."

Bierce chuckled unsympathetically and his attention remained on the far side of the room. "I know this building. That door goes to a corridor with only classrooms for cadets. They can hardly be in use tonight, but do you see those two other fellows going there too?"

Jack strained to see. "I can see one of them—why, it's Lem Tullamore!"

"The owner of the Eureka?" asked Bierce in surprise. "That's an unlikely pair."

"It is," Jack agreed, "but I can't make out who the other man is, too many people. He may make it even more unlikely."

"I can't see him clearly either. Now tell me, Jack, am I getting paranoid or do you agree that some kind of clandestine meeting is about to be held in one of those classrooms?"

"I don't think you're paranoid, but I may be prejudiced. I'd suspect Hogben of any kind of skullduggery."

Bierce fluffed his luxuriant mustache again. "Pity I'm getting too old for investigative work. If I were a few years younger, I'd want to go find out what those gentlemen are up to."

Jack grinned. "You're sending me off into dangerous territory, Ambrose! I'm not even armed."

"You're a brave young fellow. I only wish I—"

"I know you do, Ambrose, spoken like a true commander. If I'm not back in a half hour, tell McParland not to pull his agents out just yet," Jack said and set off across the room.

Chapter 22

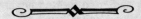

Jack strolled casually out the door and closed it behind him. A corridor stretched from the banquet hall the length of the building and was lined with closed doors. These must be the classrooms, as Bierce had said. Jack listened but could hear nothing. He walked cautiously down the corridor and put an ear to each door in turn. About halfway down he was rewarded by the sound of voices, but try as he might, he could not distinguish what was being said.

He tried the door of the room next to it. It opened and he went into near darkness, and as his eyes adjusted he saw light coming in from a window, just enough to make out black shapes. Desks and chairs were all he could initially see, but on one wall, as he approached it quietly, he found a large sink and stacks of cups, saucers and glasses.

A sudden idea struck him. He picked up a glass and carried it over to the wall. It was a trick he had learned in jail. He pressed it tightly against the wall and put his ear to it. He could hear Stanley Hogben's voice, but not enough words came through clearly. He repositioned the glass and kept moving it around until he found a good spot.

"Everything's ready." The phrase chilled Jack when he heard it. He held his breath as he listened for more. One of the others was speaking now, but his voice was suppressed and Jack could not make out any words. Then Hogben was replying, but he must have been moving as he spoke, for his voice came and went.

"Opening night" was another phrase Jack made out. Did

Hogben refer to Belle Conquest's opening night? He tried to hear more but the third man was speaking now, still indistinctly, perhaps from the other side of the room.

When Hogben replied, his voice was loud enough to make Jack start and almost drop the glass. He had to be just on the other side of the wall. His words were clear in Jack's ear: "the Midway and then the Eureka. . . ." The voice was lost as Hogben presumably turned away.

Another man asked an inaudible question, and Hogben must have turned again, for Jack could hear him ask, "Where can I get in touch with you during the day?" Jack held his breath again, desperately anxious to hear the answer. He heard the other speak but could make out nothing. He tensed again as Hogben repeated the other's words.

"The branch on Leavenworth—right."

Jack could hear little after that. The door of the other room opened and Jack listened as footsteps sounded on the hardwood floor. Two of the three were walking back into the banquet room.

Jack could not follow immediately, even though he was anxious to see who the third man was. Which had left first? He had no way of knowing, but it did not matter. He could not risk being seen. He heard the door close a second time and listened to further footsteps. He waited a safe few minutes, then went back into the banquet room.

A few more people had arrived. The orchestra was still playing enthusiastically, though its brassy outbursts betrayed its military band origins. Jack saw Hap Harrison weaving his way through the knots of people. Some might have thought him inebriated, but Jack knew better than to jump to that conclusion.

"Having a good time, Hap?" he asked.

"Lot of nice people, really nice people."

"Seen the Belle of Broadway?"

Hap looked at him in surprise. "No, is she coming?"

"I thought she might," Jack said. "She seldom misses a chance like this."

"Opens tomorrow, doesn't she?" Hap's eyes roamed in different directions.

"She does. Should be a great occasion."

Hap spotted an acquaintance with one of his eyes and headed off in that direction. Jack decided on another beer and was on his way to the nearest bar when Captain Morley came toward him. There was no hint of any official capacity. He wore smart formal attire as if he were accustomed to it. With him was an elderly lady wearing a towering silvery hairpiece and a flowing gown.

Jack started toward him, his hand reaching. For a long second, their eyes met. But Morley's stride did not slacken, and he turned his head to say something to his companion as they walked past. Jack felt rebuffed at first. Surely this was a social occasion—a few friendly words would not be compromising. Jack decided to give Morley the benefit of the doubt. Several villains were already in the room; maybe there were more.

Martin Beck came by and waved amicably. He had a wealthy-looking man by the arm, no doubt a potential backer of a show, and was talking volubly. "If I can get Lillian Russell, I'd be prepared to bring Dubarry from New York," Jack heard Beck saying. "It's a huge hit there and I'm sure the San Francisco audiences would love it. I was thinking I could also get . . ." They walked on, Beck talking, the other nodding.

Jack looked for Morley. Perhaps he had left the woman he was with and Jack would have the chance to talk with him. He needed to pass on the information he had just gathered. Maybe Morley would have some ideas on the identity of the man with Hogben and Lem Tullamore. He looked through the room, hoping that the woman's tall hairpiece would make her easy to find. It was in vain—neither Morley nor the woman could be found.

Harry Houdini was in the middle of a large group. He looked marginally more at ease and his expansive arm movements suggested that he was explaining some of his escapes. Then Jack thought no, he wouldn't be explaining them—he'd be clarifying how difficult they were.

Stephen Crane was the first writer Jack encountered. "Are we upholding the literary profession between us, Jack?" Crane smiled. He looked terrible, wan-faced and pitifully thin.

Jack knew that he was in an advanced stage of tuberculosis, but he seemed cheerful. He admired Crane not only for his prose and his poetry but now for his courage. "I really thought *War Is Kind* was a great collection," he said. "I am not a writer of poetry myself—I've tried to write it but I just can't do it. I'm amazed at how you can write both."

"Thanks, Jack," Crane said. "Not too cynical for you?"

"Not for me. Have you had that criticism?"

"Oh, yes. The editor and I had a few arguments over it."

"You evidently won," Jack said. "Well done. In fact, ever since *The Red Badge of Courage,* you've gotten better and better. I still think 'The Open Boat' one of the greatest of all short stories."

Crane smiled wryly. "I had to get shipwrecked and almost drowned to get the material for that, although I didn't intend it that way."

Jack grinned appreciatively. He knew that Crane had, in fact, been shipwrecked off the coast of Florida and given up for lost. "Well, as you say, Stephen, we seem to be the only upholders of the writers' banner. I haven't seen any others, have you?"

"No. Kipling is still in South Africa, and I doubt if Oscar Wilde will be here in the near future, much as they like him. Seen Frank Norris lately?"

"No," Jack said. "As far as I know, he's still writing his novel about the wheat business and how it's controlled by the railroads."

"The first in a three-novel series, I believe."

"Yes. He has a title now—it gave him a lot of trouble but he finally selected *The Octopus*."

"Very descriptive. Frank has a great flair for the melodramatic. Oh, Bierce is here," Crane went on, "and in good form as usual."

Crane began to cough and Jack waited sympathetically, knowing that Crane hated any show of solicitude. Finally he recovered, his face ashen. He gave Jack a pallid smile and said, "Think I'll go in search of more writers," but Jack was sure that he was going outside or perhaps leaving.

He looked for Morley again but could not see him. He strolled through the crowd, seeking the tall hairpiece. At last he spotted it and squeezed past tightly packed guests. The lady was talking to several men and women but Morley was not among them.

Jack saw Bierce waving to him and went to join him. With him was a man Jack recognized immediately, although he had never met him. Bierce introduced them. "Jack, this is Bret Harte. Bret, I don't think you know Jack London."

They shook hands. Harte was in his sixties, tall, well built, with masses of white hair and a thick mustache. A monocle screwed into his right eye gave him an appearance of eccentricity. His cutaway coat, striped pants, embroidered vest and spats added to it. He had a haughty manner but Bierce's presence seemed to moderate it.

"I've read some of your short stories," Harte told Jack. "You have a great future."

"Thanks. That means a lot, coming from you. You used to be editor of *Overland Monthly,* didn't you?"

"Yes, and I've read some of your stories in it."

"Bret's living in London now," Bierce said. "Been there— how long, Bret? Nearly twenty years, isn't it?"

"Yes, but I still keep up with you young, up-and-coming writers."

"And still enjoying living there?"

Jack knew that Bierce had loved his life in London and might never have left but for the climate, which had severely affected his health.

"It was like a sluggish nightmare at first," said Harte.

Then with a flash of the egotist that his appearance suggested, he added, "But it finally got used to me."

"Jack has many of your writing preferences," Bierce told Harte. "He likes to write about miners and gamblers, and his descriptions of the Yukon are nearly as powerful as some of your work describing the Gold Rush in California."

Harte nodded approvingly and Jack said, "I remember that piece you wrote criticizing white Californians for their part in a massacre of Indians. It was masterly."

Harte smiled ruefully. "Yes, that was for the *Northern Californian,* a fine paper. Unfortunately, the townfolk weren't concerned with the literary quality of the piece— they forced me to resign from the paper for the sentiments in it. They don't like to be criticized for their treatment of the Indians."

" 'The Luck of Roaring Camp' was great too," Jack said.

"That was in *Overland Monthly,*" Harte told him. "Californians didn't like it either when it was first published." The sad smile appeared again. "I seem to have a knack for upsetting magazines."

"But it later became a classic," Bierce assured him. "Made your reputation nationwide."

"Mainly on the East Coast," said Harte.

"You were the first to establish what they now call 'local color writing,' " said Bierce. "Before you, writers wrote mainly plot and character—you added a style that captured the feeling of a place and the people who live in it. A very difficult thing to do."

The three discussed writing and its trends further, oblivious to the more frothy and social conversations around them. Harte was clearly—and understandably to Jack—disgruntled at the failure of the Western states to acknowledge his work. He spoke disparagingly of their scanty interest in literature and praised Easterners for their advanced culture.

Bierce eventually left to pursue yet another newsworthy source while Jack and Bret Harte continued their discussion. When Harte was pulled away to give an account of life in literary circles in London, Jack made a final circuit of the room, exchanged a few words here and there with acquaintances, then slipped out into the night to ponder the evening's events as he headed back home.

Chapter 23

It was a cool, breezy day with a high haze obscuring the sun and Jack found the walk from the Ferry Building invigorating. From the outside the Plucked Chicken looked even more dismal in the absence of sunshine, and Jack entered to find the interior not only just as dismal but empty. Not merely of customers but completely empty—there was no one behind the bar.

The door had been open, though, so someone must be around. Perhaps the bartender had gone to get something from the cellar or the storeroom. Jack put a foot on the bar rail and banged his fist. "Anybody here?" he called loudly. He thought he heard the faint clink of glass but no reply came.

He walked along the bar to the end, where a door at the back was closed. Jack went around the end of the bar and tried the door. It opened into a storeroom, and as his eyes became accustomed to the gloom he could see the place was empty.

He went to the beer pump. Some none-too-clean glasses were near it, and Jack selected the cleanest and put it under the pump. He pulled. It was turned on, so someone must be here. Foam and beer gushed into the glass. Jack made sure it was full, pushed it along the bar and returned to the customer side. With a foot back on the bar rail, he raised the glass and drank.

In the mirror above the bar he caught a glimpse of movement behind him. He froze in the act of swallowing and nearly choked. When he had cleared his throat, he examined the mirror without being too apparent. Nothing moved. He half turned, with the glass in his hand, and drank again, his eyes alert. No one else was in the room.

Chairs were in position at the tables, so someone had made an effort at tidying up after the previous night. Most of the ashtrays had been emptied and the tables cleared. He turned back and looked at the mirror. Then he saw movement again.

It came from a large closet, the door of which was opening very slowly. Jack put down his glass. The clink was the only sound to break the silence. Jack contemplated leaping over the bar, where he'd have a little protection, but the door was still moving open and nothing had appeared. Then suddenly a face showed.

It was deathly white and the eyes glared horribly. The door opened farther and the face came into full view, followed by a body. It crumpled to the floor, and Jack stood transfixed for a split second. The closet was fully open now and held no further terrors. Jack ran to the body.

It was Niccolo, the police agent. He was dead, shot in the chest. Blood covered the front of his shirt. His flesh was warm—he had not been dead very long. Jack had seen many dead men in his time but he never got used to them. He felt an overwhelming sadness, even though he had barely met the man. Behind him there was the slam of doors and two men walked in.

They were roughly dressed and moved with purposeful intent. "You the man Niccolo was waiting for?" one of them asked in a grating voice. Both looked tough and hard. They were experienced too. They spread out as they approached him.

"Came in for a drink," Jack said. He stumbled over the words, hoping he sounded drunk.

Both men looked at the body of Niccolo at his feet. One of them motioned to the other to look behind the bar. Jack's glass of beer stood there, half empty.

"He drew you a glass of beer and you killed him," the second one said, his voice equally uncompromising.

"No, no, I didn't," Jack protested. He was not sure who these men were. They might be police, but if so, they ran no risk of it being suspected from their appearance.

"You'd better come with us," one said. Jack tensed, ready to make a dash for the door, assessing his best route. The two men had separated enough to leave a gap between them, but they looked as if they might be as fast as they were tough.

They moved in on him, a concerted course that indicated practice. Jack started forward but the two edged closer, both taking out coshes. Jack feigned hesitation, then charged, trying to burst between them.

One swung his cosh at Jack's chest. It stung and delayed him a vital second, and that was all the other man needed to crack him on the back of the head. Jack saw the room dissolving into a shapeless mass of images as a second blow brought a numbing pain and complete darkness.

Was he emerging from the darkness or was he part of it? He recovered consciousness with a full memory of the scene in the Plucked Chicken and the two blows on the head, but were his eyes open? If they were, why couldn't he see? He felt a surge of sudden terror—was he blind? The pain in his head pulsed and he groaned aloud. He sat still.

The pain subsided to an agonizing ache but he could see no glint of light. He held a hand before him but could see absolutely nothing. He touched his face. He moved his hands around. He was lying on a rough floor. He crawled along and winced as he bumped into a wall.

At least he wasn't blind. He was in an underground chamber—San Francisco was honeycombed with them. There must be an entrance somewhere though. He waited as the pain at the back of his head settled to a dull gnawing; then he explored the space he was in.

It was not large and his spirits rose when his fumbling

hands found a heavy door in one corner, but it fitted tightly. A large lockplate secured it and there was nothing to get hold of, no protrusion, just a keyhole. He sat, dejected. His headache increased and he slid into a twilight phase of disjointed dreams and uneasy sleep.

He awoke to find a dim light shining on him. His befuddled brain, still hurting, was slow in realization. At last, he finally comprehended that two men were standing in front of him, shadowy figures, nothing more than outlines. A third man came and stood in the doorway, holding a lantern.

"What were you doing in the Plucked Chicken?" came a harsh voice.

Jack swallowed with difficulty. He managed to say, "Went in for a drink."

"The man you killed was a police agent. Did you know that?"

The less said the better seemed like a good policy to Jack. "No."

"Why did you kill him?"

It was time to retaliate. "Who are you?" he asked in a croaky voice.

"Never mind. We're asking the questions. Have you been in the Plucked Chicken before?"

He might have been seen, so it was safer not to lie. "A couple of times."

"Why?"

"Went in for a drink. Sure could use one now."

"How well did you know Niccolo?"

The questions were coming fast. Fumbling for an answer was not difficult. All he had to do was concentrate on the pain in the back of his head.

"Who?"

"The man you killed. Was he the bartender?"

Did they genuinely not know? Or were they testing him? He decided to stay close to the truth.

"Last time I went in there, different man tending bar."

"What did you talk to them about? The bartender and Niccolo?"

"Didn't talk, just drank."

The two withdrew a few paces and whispered. The third man, the one with the lantern came and joined them. The pain from his head seemed to spread through his body. He could not make any move at escape right now; he was much too weak.

Perhaps they believed him, or perhaps they had to confer with a boss. Were they police or villains? Surely the police would have put him in a police station. Still, Jack had no illusions about the force. They were known to use brutal and thoroughly illegal methods when slower ones failed. Could they be some self-appointed vigilante group? He hadn't heard of one operating recently, but such organizations surfaced frequently.

They all left. The door clanged shut and all light went with them. A key crunched in the lock and the tongue slammed home. Jack was left once again in pitch-darkness, and he wondered if he would ever see the yellow gleam of the sun again.

Jack had no idea how much time had elapsed, but when he awoke his head still ached, his stomach growled with hunger and he was so parched with thirst that he had difficulty summing up enough saliva to swallow.

He became slowly aware that the door had opened. A shaft of light illuminated a figure, which was pushed in and fell beside him. The door slammed, the lock ground with metallic screeches and the dreaded darkness descended again.

Jack could hear heavy breathing, then a rustling as his new cellmate moved around. "I'm in here too," Jack said, and the movement stopped, as if the newcomer had not known the cell was occupied.

Jack sat up, forcing his aching limbs to move. "I don't know how long I've been here but I've been interrogated once. This place seems impossible to get out of—there isn't a hint of light anywhere." His dry throat made talking difficult, but he felt a little better now that he had been able to move and talk.

"Why are you here?" The voice had just a trace of a foreign accent.

Jack didn't know who this man was. He might be a plant, a more subtle way of getting information out of him. He decided to give away as little as possible.

"A man was killed. They're accusing me of killing him. I didn't do it."

"Who was the man killed?"

"A man in a bar. You wouldn't know him."

There was a silence. Then the other man said, "I have some matches." Clothing rustled. There was a rattle, followed by a scratching sound and pale yellow light flared. A match was held close to Jack's face. In his turn, Jack saw only work clothes and an indistinct face under a large cap.

There was a loud intake of breath. "Jack! Is that you, Jack?"

The match moved, came closer, but Jack could not make out any features. The voice came again, "Jack? Jack London?"

The accent, the voice—both began to sound vaguely familiar. The match illuminated the other's face and one hand pulled back the cap. Jack could hardly believe his eyes. Was he still dreaming?

"Harry?" he asked incredulously, "Harry Houdini?"

Jack kept to his story. He amplified it a little but gave away nothing about his mission. He hated to deceive his acquaintance, but this was no time to betray confidences. The magician accepted Jack's account without question, anxious to tell why he was here.

"I brought several of my own team with me to San Francisco, but as I always do, I took on a few local men. One of them aroused some suspicion when one of my team noticed that he carried a gun. The same man was then reported to

me as being seen drinking with some men who were believed to belong to a gang called the Riders of the Rim."

The match went out. Jack spoke in the darkness, the fact
that he was no longer alone making him feel better. "I've
heard of them," Jack said. "They're malcontents, troublemakers, rebels—"

"Well, this man we suspected received a message. I saw
him read it and slip out in a suspicious manner. Rather than
risk one of my own team, I followed him myself. He joined
a half dozen men in the back room of this bar on Harding
Street. Before I could learn anything, a sentry I hadn't noticed hit me on the head. They asked me a lot of questions.
I didn't tell them who I was. I was afraid they'd ask for a
ransom. Then they threw me in here."

Jack's laughter brought an angry snort from Houdini. "It
is not funny! I do nothing to be treated like this! Who are
these men? Rebels, you say? Troublemakers? Why do they
want to make trouble for me?"

"They caught you spying on them, Harry. They suspect
you of being a police agent." Jack controlled his laughter.
"But that's not why I was laughing."

Houdini lit another match. "Then why laugh?" he asked,
still petulant.

"Of all the people to put in a locked cell with me, who
better than the world's greatest escape artist?"

Houdini grunted. He gave an involuntary chuckle; then
the chuckle gave way to laughter. Jack joined in and Houdini dropped the match. The two threw their arms around
each other, laughing uncontrollably. They stopped more
quickly than they had started, both aware that they did not
want to attract the attention of their jailers.

"I do my escapes on stage." Houdini was still grumbling.
"I am not prepared for this."

"When you're in a sack, in a box, inside a crate and ten
feet underwater, you're just as much in the dark as you are
here," Jack argued.

"I am not prepared," Houdini repeated obstinately, but

Jack heard him moving to the door and sliding his hands over the lock. There came other strange and unidentifiable noises. Minutes passed.

"What do you think, Harry?" Jack asked.

There was a silence and Jack was about to ask again when metal scraped on metal and the door swung open.

They crept outside and closed the door silently. They were in an empty chamber with crumbling dirt walls and a dirt floor. A wooden ladder led to an upper room, with daylight showing. They climbed the steps carefully. In the upper room were signs of habitation: a table with the remains of meals, chairs and packing crates. Houdini put a finger to his lips. His hearing was abnormally acute, Jack realized. He now could hear the murmur of voices from the next room.

They moved quietly through another empty room. Through a window, they could see and hear a street with people passing, the hum of wagons and the clip-clop of hooves. Jack was reaching for the handle of the door to go out onto the street when the door opened and a man came walking in.

He stared at Jack, then at Houdini, as surprised as they were. Jack recovered first. He hit the man hard in the throat, saw him reel back. It was not a blow he used often, for there was the danger of causing choking. He had seen men die that way. But he had needed to prevent the man from crying out. He followed out into the street, where the man was clutching his throat, trying to breathe. He hit him hard on the end of the jaw where the sensitive nerve is located. The man fell like a log.

No one was near. A head across on the other sidewalk turned in mild curiosity, but Jack and Houdini did not wait. They raced down the street, which Jack recognized instantly. "We're on Filbert Street," Jack gasped. "We'd better separate, Harry. You go that way. I'll go this way." Houdini gave him a startled look, nodded and hurried off.

Chapter 24

Jack's head ached but he was determined to make sure that his information reached Morley. He made his way to the Produce District, where Morley had given him an alternate contact. The fish market on Davis Street was open. Fish were being gutted and chopped, readied for the next morning's sales.

"I'm looking for Noah."

A youngish man with fair hair came forward, wiping his bloody hands on a cloth. "I'm Noah."

Jack paused, instantly wary. The other noticed his hesitation and laughed. "I'm Noah Junior. You want to talk to my father?"

After a couple of minutes, a large, barrel-chested man came out. His beard covered most of that ample chest. He examined Jack closely.

"Who are you?"

"My name is Jack London."

"So what do you want? Some fish?"

Jack hesitated. Surely Morley had told Noah about him. Jack ran a hand through his hair and said, "I used to be known as the Prince of the Oyster Pirates."

Noah Senior grinned. "Yeah, you fit the description. Let's go into the ice room."

It was a large chamber with padded walls where fish of all descriptions lay packed in ice. It was freezing cold, and Jack could hardly imagine a safer place for secrets. Before he could speak, though, Noah said, "The captain's in the neighborhood. I could have him over here in ten minutes. Better than you going to him. This is a real good place for reports."

"I can believe it," Jack said. "But I can't survive ten minutes in here."

Noah's beard opened and he grinned again. "You can wait downstairs. Like a bowl of shrimp while you're waiting?"

When he came in, Morley looked as dapper as if he had come from eight hours of sound sleep. Jack felt a little resentful, because his head still ached. He wasted no time in preliminaries. "You must know about Niccolo?"

Yes. I just heard about it." His face tightened. "He was a good man and a valuable agent."

Jack filled him in on the suspicious rendezvous at the Presidio, then went on to tell him of his incarceration and subsequent rescue by Houdini.

"By the way," Morley said, "I didn't acknowledge you at the banquet because that woman I was with may have important information."

Jack frowned. "Who is she?"

"She's the wife of Robert Windham, a power in the business world of San Francisco."

"Oh, yes," said Jack, "Ambrose Bierce mentioned him. Is he connected with all this?"

"I'm trying to find out," Morley said. "You think the three who interrogated you believed what you told them?"

"I think they were uncertain."

"Probably." Morley nodded. "If they had been sure, they probably would have killed you." He looked keenly at Jack. "Do you need any attention? Noah has a man here with some medical training."

"No, I'm all right. Got a headache and I need a little sleep, but then I'll be back to normal."

"What's your next move?" Morley asked.

"I'm going to keep a sharp eye on Hogben. It's got to lead somewhere."

Morley nodded. "We're running low on reliable trails to follow, and I have the feeling that we are getting close to the boiling point in this affair. All right, watch Hogben. Keep me informed."

By the time Jack arrived home, his head felt as if it were splitting apart. He doused it with cold water, but when that did not help, he lay on the bed, intending to rest a short while. When he awoke it was pitch-dark, and on looking at his alarm clock he saw to his amazement that it was almost four o'clock.

He climbed out of bed and soaked his head again. It felt better, and though he did not feel like writing, he forced himself to add a few more pages to the manuscript of *A Daughter of the Snows*. He did not reach his daily target of a thousand words. This was a difficult portion of the book and he had to push his memory back to the howling snows of the Yukon and recall the biting cold, the frequent hunger and the utter weariness of a day's digging for gold.

Then he read some Robert Louis Stevenson, this time *Kidnapped*. He admired Stevenson's clean descriptive prose and was sure that his own writing improved merely by reading the work of the great novelist.

A cup of strong tea and two slices of bread did duty as breakfast and took away the last lingering pains in his head. He dressed differently today. Instead of his usual seaman's sweater, he took out a light linen jacket. It had taken his fancy when he had seen it in a shop window. He had been flush with money at the time, an unusual situation, but no sooner had he bought it than he had doubts that it might be too "sissified." He had never worn it, but he was about to set out on the trail of Stanley Hogben, and anything that would change his appearance was needed. This was the perfect garment.

After slipping it on, he examined himself in the mirror.

His wavy brown hair was a distinguishing feature, he knew. He wetted it down and brushed it until it lay flat. Still it would dry out before long, he thought, and go back to its customary unruly look, so he put on a cap with a large peak.

Pleased with this rudimentary disguise, he cast his mind back to his short period in the university drama group at Berkeley. It had been a brief phase and had ended when he decided he was too much his own man to act like someone else. Nevertheless, he had played small parts in a few plays, and in one of them he had portrayed a dandy from the East Coast. He had put on a lisping accent, which he tried again now. It quickly came back to him and he felt it added to his new character.

Jack crossed on the ferry and took the cable car, alighting near Union Square. He walked up to O'Farrell Street, a large envelope under his arm. He paused to look at himself in a shop window. At first glance he felt he was not easily recognizable, and he went on, heartened.

Morley hadn't seemed too surprised that Stanley Hogben was a suspicious character. He kept turning up in the investigation, and Jack wondered again who the third man with Hogben and Tullamore at the Presidio had been—someone who was possibly higher in the criminal organization. Keeping a closer watch on Hogben's activities might reveal a new clue, so Jack's destination was the Law and Order Party headquarters.

It was possible that Hogben was there, although by no means certain. Still, it was a place to start, and Jack walked into a long, low-ceilinged room with posters covering the walls. It was crowded with desks, many with typewriters and others with piles of leaflets. People scurried to and fro, mostly men, but a few women too. Jack scanned the room quickly but did not see Hogben.

One young woman with an armful of posters stopped and asked Jack, "Were you looking for somebody?"

Jack smiled and held up the big envelope. "I have an important package here for Mr. Hogben."

"I'll take it and give it to him," she said. "Just drop it on the desk there."

"I can't do that," Jack said. "I have instructions to give it to him personally."

She frowned and shuffled the posters into a more comfortable position. "He won't be in today. Can you come back tomorrow?"

"It's fairly urgent," Jack said. "Do you know where I can find him?"

The posters were slipping and Jack helped her slide them onto a desk. "Just a minute," she said, and went across the room to confer with a bearded elderly man. She returned and said, "He's at the Geary Street office, just by Van Ness."

Jack thanked her and followed the directions. It was a similar establishment, formerly a shop but now a political substation. He entered cautiously, not wanting to walk right into Hogben, but it was immediately evident that the councilman was not there. Jack repeated his story to a harassed-looking fellow with pince-nez glasses.

"Mr. Hogben's not here. He—ah, let me see, where is he? Ah, he just went out. He's meeting Congressman Phelps."

Jack brought out his key words, "urgent," "important" and "have to give it to him personally." The man glanced at the large envelope over his glasses. "Important? Ah, well, yes, in that case you might catch him. He's going to the Richmond Café on Larkin Street."

Jack walked quickly along Van Ness Avenue, which was named after an early mayor of San Francisco. It carried a lot of traffic, mostly wagons of produce and goods, although with the docks idle, the traffic today was light. He reached Clay Street and was turning to go down to the well-known Richmond Café when he spotted Stanley Hogben ahead of him. Rotund and with a walk that was almost pompous, he was easy to follow.

Jack stayed at a distance and watched him enter the café. He waited a few minutes. There was no reason to believe that Hogben was using any subterfuge and was not inside the café. Jack was certain he had not been spotted.

He went to the window and held the envelope up to cover most of his face. His hair was drying out, he noticed, and beginning to spring up from under his cap. He pressed it down hard with his fingers and tucked it in as best he could. He could see Hogben and another man at a table. Jack withdrew across the street and kept watch. People went in and came out. In less than a half hour the two of them came out and stood before the door, talking. Then the other man walked away down Clay Street, and Hogben turned in the opposite direction. He crossed Van Ness.

Jack frowned. Where was he going?

Hogben did not look back, and Jack was still sure he had no idea he was being followed. The streets grew quieter, with little traffic and fewer and fewer pedestrians. Jack crossed Gough Street. A heavy cart, pushed by one man and pulled by a second, passed in front of him, blocking his way. When it had gone, Jack sought the now familiar figure of Hogben.

He had disappeared. Jack looked in all directions but there was no sign of the man. This was impossible! Jack took a few steps farther and spotted a black slit in the side of a building just down the street. It was a narrow alleyway. Hogben must have gone down there. He walked quickly to it.

It was gloomy down the alley and Jack walked carefully and quietly, stepping around piles of trash. At the end it opened onto another street. He was just in time to see Hogben enter a large, dilapidated building.

Jack waited in the end of the alley. After a few minutes, two men came along and went in by the same door. No sooner were they inside than another followed them. After a few seconds of consideration, Jack crossed the street in pursuit.

Chapter 25

The door opened readily and Jack found himself in what seemed like a small theater. Tall screens just inside the entrance darkened the area, and he could see sputtering oil lamps behind them. Without exposing himself, he peered around the screens.

A circular arena, like a miniature stockade, was surrounded by rows of wooden benches. Forty to fifty people were there, all men. An unusual sound arose and Jack saw that in the circle, which was covered with sawdust, two men were each holding a large rooster, which was crowing and cackling. The purpose of the place became instantly obvious—there was to be a cockfight.

Jack felt a relief. At least he could pass as just one of the crowd. He sought out Hogben, making sure to stay out of his vision. Hogben was talking to two other men, one on either side of him, both fairly well dressed. He studied them—wasn't one of them familiar? At first, he couldn't make the association; then—of course!—he was the man Jack had fought with during the stakeout with Sergeant Healey on the waterfront. He was the man who had been identified as Manny Thurston, the onetime gambler and known killer.

Jack felt his blood quicken. He was on a hot trail here. Hogben had led back to Thurston. Jack reexamined the man on the other side of Hogben. Did he look familiar too, or was that too much to expect? The man wore a hat, which was not large, but it shielded the top of his face and made recognition difficult. Jack could not be sure but he had a strong suspicion that this was Lou Kandel, the safecracker escapee from San Quentin. He had not seen that man as closely as the other because Healey had been struggling with him. Still, he had to keep this trio under observation.

He chose a seat on the top row. He sat among several well-dressed men so as to be less noticeable. Hogben and his companions would have to look back up and over their left shoulders to be able to see Jack. He was almost out of the circle of light cast by the nearest lamp. When one of the three heads did turn in his direction, Jack exchanged a few words with the man next to him so that, at a glance, he would look as if he were one of the party.

A loud squawking quenched all further conversation. The two handlers had "introduced" their birds to one another and a trained hatred of any other of their species took over. Both cockerels flapped furiously, kicked and snapped, trying to reach each other. Bookmakers were circulating through the crowd, taking bets, calling out the odds.

The contest began. Unlike human opponents who might size each other up first, these birds were trained for one thing only—fighting. They fought from first being released, pecking and biting and trying to rake the other with their steel-tipped claws. One was a magnificent golden-brown bird with a vicious eye, while the other was almost black in color with powerful legs. Sawdust sprayed up as the two battled for survival, each seeking the deadly blow that would fell its opponent.

The crowd was obviously composed of men who were regular followers of this sport. They cheered and yelled loudly, giving advice to the birds, which already had their own battle plans. The noise filled the arena.

No quarter was given—it was a fight to the death. Both contestants were trained to maim or blind and then kill. Blood soon spattered the sawdust, the smell of it sickly sweet. The crowd got more and more involved, whooping and shouting. The bookmakers circulated again, offering the chance of placing a new bet or increasing an existing one. Bets could be placed as to how long the contest would last, and already many had lost money, wagering on an early win by one bird or the other. Now those punters were placing new bets, trying to recoup their losses.

The crowd roared its approval as the birds reached a frenzy of biting and slashing. Their eyes glittered with malevolence and bloodstained spittle dripped from their beaks. The two handlers urged them on to even greater efforts. The small space reverberated with the noise of the crowd, while in the ring the two contestants battled their hearts out, as if fully aware that only one of them would emerge alive.

Jack was not a lover of blood sports. Too often, in the Yukon, he had been an observer of dogfights, for in that environment any kind of sport or contest was a welcome diversion from the harsh conditions. In the back of his mind he had an idea for a story about a dog, perhaps part-wolf, that was trained for fighting, but his usual problem with plot had stopped the idea from progressing any further.

It was not difficult for him to divide his attention between the combat in the arena and the trio he was keeping under observation. None of them had looked around again, and they did not appear to be conscious of being watched. Jack studied, one by one, the figures around the trio. First, he watched those on the row in front, then on the row behind, then at either end of the same row. His head no longer hurt, but he intended to take every precaution not to suffer any more blows.

He concluded that the trio had no bodyguards with them. They probably considered that Kandel's credentials as a killer and an escapee from San Quentin and Thurston's reputation as a killer made protection unnecessary.

By the time he had reached that decision, the duel was in its final stages. The once-golden bird, proud and fierce, was now a heaving bundle of ragged feathers, while the black cockerel, bleeding from almost as many wounds, still pecked and stabbed savagely.

The handler of the golden bird was waving in submission and trying to get his opposite number to restrain the black demon, which refused to stop his murderous attacks. He wanted to go into the ring and retrieve his bird but knew better than to risk the ferocity of the winner, still pecking and clawing the corpse.

Bookmakers were circling, paying out and collecting. It all seemed fairly orderly. Two men in overalls were waiting to sweep the blood-soaked sawdust out of the ring and replace it for the next fight.

Jack's trio sat talking for a few minutes. They had apparently had a few bets among themselves and were arguing over payment. The next contest was about to begin when the trio rose and headed for the door.

Jack waited, watching for others leaving. One harmless-looking young man seemed ideal and Jack joined him, asking if he had made any money. They were chatting like old friends when they went out into the rain.

It had turned into a damp, chilly night. The rain was fine but persistent and a gusty wind flung up sprays from the ground. It was perfect weather for shadowing, thought Jack. The trio would be less inclined to look behind them, and if they did so, less likely to see clearly in the wet gloom.

They would probably get a cab, and if so, Jack would follow in one. He was watching the trio carefully and at the same time keeping an eye open for cabs, but none appeared. The trio did not seem too concerned about the rain. They walked on to Stockton Street and turned. Jack was beginning to form an idea of where they might be going after a cockfight, and his guess was proved correct in a few minutes.

The location of every brothel on the Barbary Coast, whether it was a crib, a cow yard or a parlor house, was indicated by a red light that burned above the door from dusk till dawn. Stockton Street and the streets around it had countless red lights burning. Jack passed one with a copper plate attached to the door below it. It announced:

MADAM LUCILLE
YE OLDE WHORE SHOPPE

But the trio passed it and continued. French parlor houses were at the height of their popularity at this time. The Parisian Room, owned by Marcel and Jerome Bassity, was near the next corner. On the right were the Negro cribs, and after them many such dens filled with Mexican women. But the trio went on and Jack followed cautiously. The rain had stopped but the air was heavy with moisture, and another shower might come at any time.

They continued past more French establishments. Some had open windows with bare-bosomed women leaning out and loudly describing the delights to be found inside. It was a popular superstition in San Francisco that redheaded women were exceedingly amorous, and one such famous character on the street, Iodoform Kate, had made—and saved—enough money from her prostitution to open her own place. There, she installed only red-haired women.

They passed Kate's establishment; then a few doors beyond it, Jack slowed. The trio had stopped to knock at a door. A red light burned above it, but from this distance Jack could see no sign.

The door opened and the trio disappeared inside.

Jack stood there, undecided as to his next move.

Chapter 26

The rain began again. Jack moved against a wall to gain some temporary shelter while he pondered his next move. His natural inclination was to go straight into the brothel, remaining true to his preference for direct action. But he had grown up quickly, and even before he had reached the age of twenty he had learned the merits of prudence and caution. He told himself that he had a great advantage over others if he could achieve the perfect balance between impulse and discretion.

Inside, he might meet the three men he had followed, all of whom might recognize him. Hogben knew him the best. He had fought with Thurston, and they had come face-to-face, literally. The third man, Kandel, had seen him during the fight at the docks, but perhaps not clearly. Jack knew his disguise was good from a distance, but closer inspection might expose it.

If they were there for the obvious purpose, he might not encounter them at all. They might be too occupied already, though that depended on what kind of place this was. He studied the building. It was three stories and had once been a private residence. When such places were transformed into brothels, the interior design was altered to provide as many additional bedrooms as possible.

This was most probably a parlor house rather than a crib or a cow yard, more upper-class than the other two. It was, therefore, suited to the three men he was following, Jack thought, as they were more upper-class than the ordinary criminal.

His conclusion came from the consideration that, if he did not go in, he would learn nothing. If he went in, there was some chance of making progress in this case. He adjusted his cap to cover the top of his face better, pulled up the linen jacket around his chin and walked boldly up to the door.

The brass knocker, which showed tinges of green from the damp San Francisco air, made an imperious sound. There was no answer and Jack rapped again. Soft footsteps came and a small panel in the top of the door opened. After a pause, a chain rattled and a bolt scraped. The door opened.

A very tall Negro stood there. He wore smart black-and-red livery and would have done credit to many homes on Nob Hill. He blocked the doorway and did not attempt to move aside. "Name?" he demanded.

"Jack Prentiss." When his mother had almost died giving birth to him, she had been so weakened that the doctor recommended a wet nurse, a local black woman known to one and all as Mammie Jennie. She had lost her own baby in childbirth, and for the first eight months of Jack's life she had suckled and cared for him as if he were her own child. It was a tribute to her that her name was the first that came into his mind.

The Negro looked him over. "Who recommended you?"

This must be a higher-class place than Jack had supposed. "Councilman Winkler," he said after the briefest of pauses. Winkler was known as something of a hell-raiser in political circles and no one in San Francisco, especially his own supporters, would have been the least bit surprised to learn that he was a client there.

"I don't know him," the Negro said.

Jack managed a short laugh. "He probably doesn't use that name when he comes here."

After another brief pause the Negro opened the door. "Come in."

The parlor was a potpourri of garish rugs, erotic paintings, gaudy couches and divans. A heavily gilded table had on it one of the new electrical musical instruments with a curled black horn and a stack of black disks. Another table, carved from dark wood, held several bottles and glasses. The air was thick with perfume and gilded chairs stood around. None was occupied, Jack was glad to notice. Hogben, Kandel and Thurston must have been through there and gone to the rooms upstairs, past the heavy curtain that was the only other means of access.

"I'm Madam Lila."

The Negro had disappeared and in his place stood a handsome woman, tall and smiling. Dark hair was piled high on her head, held in place with silver combs that gave her the appearance of even greater height. Her eyes were large and luminous and her mouth large and generous. Her makeup was heavy but carefully applied. She wore a multi-layered garment of reds, yellows and browns in a silky material, a large string of pearls and silver shoes with turned-up toes.

"Jack Prentiss. Glad to meet you, ma'am," Jack said politely.

She gave him a swift appraising look but her words were warm and receiving. "You from out of town, Mr. Prentiss?"

"Been out of town quite a while, ma'am. But it's good to be back in San Francisco." Jack thought that was as ambiguous an answer as he could concoct on the spur of the moment. To be an out-of-towner was to risk exploitation, for San Franciscans saw the rest of the country's population, outside of that in New York and Chicago, as easy marks. On the other hand, admitting that he was a San Franciscan was too risky.

"And what can I do for you this evening, Mr. Prentiss?"

She might have been asking for his order in a tearoom. He tried to look embarrassed. In truth, he was a little. He was not an habitué of brothels. He had been in a few in the Orient while on the *Sophie Sutherland* seal hunting in

Japanese waters, but he had been thoroughly drunk on each of those occasions and he remembered little of them.

"I heard you had some nice girls here," he said, being hesitant.

Madam Lila took pity on this callow, inexperienced youth. "We have some very nice girls—some very friendly American girls, a few sweet little Oriental girls, some adorable girls from the West Indies. . . . In fact, we can satisfy your taste, whatever it is."

"Can I see some of them?" Jack asked, playing for time until he could decide what his next move was to be.

"Of course. First, let me get you a glass of wine." From the carved wood table she brought him a glass of white wine. Jack detested wine, especially red. He could barely tolerate white, and on this occasion, he only sipped it.

Madam Lila went out through the curtain and returned with six girls, who formed a selection from each of the groups she had mentioned. All wore scanty underwear, mostly in red or black, and high-heeled slippers. Two looked hard and tough, but the others seemed pleasant and smiled shyly.

"How many girls do you have?" Jack asked.

"Twelve," said Madam Lila, "and they are all very carefully chosen." She went on to describe their attributes and the rules of the establishment, which ensured the client that the girls were medically inspected regularly. Jack knew that, though most places said this, it was rarely true.

"Can I see some others?" asked Jack.

Madam Lila hesitated, about to make another pitch for the girls present, but then nodded. "Very well. It's still early and we are not busy yet. You are lucky—we can give you a big choice."

"Good," said Jack. He sipped from his glass and grimaced. There was a strange expression on Madam Lila's face, but she took the girls out and returned with six more, about the same proportion of experience and apparent virtue. He was thinking hard. He had seen all twelve now.

Where was the trio Jack had followed? They must be upstairs, and yet all the girls were supposedly there.

Madam Lila was regarding him oddly. Jack smiled and
sipped more wine. From a floor above, a male voice called
out, but Jack could not hear what was being demanded. He
recognized the voice though—it was Stanley Hogben's. It
came again, louder, though the words were still not distinct.

"You will have to excuse me for a moment," Madam Lila
said. "I'm wanted upstairs."

As she turned to go, Hogben's voice came once more. It
sounded closer.

Jack was in a quandary. If he went upstairs, he might
easily walk into Hogben, Kandel or Thurston. But he could
hardly stay here without making a choice of girls, and if he
tried to leave, it would seem very suspicious.

"I, er, see you have some nice girls, but I . . ." His voice
was like a mumble, even to himself. The girls looked at him
curiously, and at a wave from Madam Lila, they walked out.
The tableau seemed to tilt sideways like a disturbed photograph on a wall, and the girls looked as if they were being
poured out of the end of the picture.

The wine tasted unpleasant on his tongue. Jack wondered
if there was something in it as the scene dissolved into gray
and then black and then nothing.

It seemed like only minutes. He came to consciousness
with his mouth burning and his stomach churning. Instinctively, he felt his pockets. They were empty, all of them. He
had been rolled—a good old Barbary Coast custom. He
knew the technique. A brothel owner would size up the victim and decide whether to take his fee for a girl or drug him
and take all he had. Jack concluded Madam Lila had taken
him for an out-of-towner and more profitable if treated in
the second manner.

Jack got to his feet. God bless Madam Lila—she had
possibly saved his life. He could not have been spotted by
any of the trio he had followed or he would have been dead

by then. He staggered a little but his equilibrium returned almost at once and he went down the alley. Piles of rubbish were scattered everywhere and oil drums serving as trash containers overflowed. He walked cautiously, watching back doorways, but saw no one.

He had to tell Captain Morley of this as soon as possible so the police could mount a raid. He walked on toward the end of the alley. It opened onto another street, but when he was still about ten yards short of it, a figure stepped out in front of him. Jack slowed but the figure did not move. Jack stopped, uncertain.

The figure came down the alley, directly at him, walking purposefully. Jack could distinguish nothing about it. It was just a silhouette, seemingly clad in loose, shapeless garments.

It came closer and closer, moving slowly, ominously. A noise came from behind Jack, vague and indeterminate. He resisted the temptation to turn at once, his attention still on the form ahead.

He heard a thin, whirring sound. It seemed to come from above him, and he realized too late what it was—a thin wire dropped past his face and pulled tight around his throat.

Chapter 27

Jack's disguise saved him from instant death. The high collar of the linen jacket and the way he had pulled it up to hide the bottom part of his face obstructed the razor-sharp wire and prevented it from severing his windpipe. The tactic of the garroter was to kill his victim in the first few seconds. Many experts in the use of the weapon could decapitate a body with that first motion. Even if the prey survived that initial vicious onslaught, his natural instinct was to try to grab the wire and drag it loose. That usually gave the garroter time to pull and twist again, and very few survived the second assault.

Jack's brain registered the attack and realized why it had not been immediately successful, but he also knew that seconds were vital. Before the assailant could readjust the position of the steel wire so as to cut directly into the flesh of Jack's throat, Jack flung himself backward with all the strength and weight he could muster.

The garroter let out a gasp as the air flew out of him. He crashed to the ground with Jack on top of him. One end of the garrote wire loosened and Jack reached up and pulled it free. By then, the second man had raced at him.

Jack was aware of the technique of the two-man team from their previous encounter. They were the same two *boo how doy* who had tried to kill him after he had left the Midway Plaisance some days ago. He assumed they would use the same murderous tactics as before—with the knife man keeping in front of him so as to allow the garroter to approach him from behind.

Something was different about the knife man though. In the dim light of the alley, Jack could see the glint on the silvery blade of the long knife. That was not it. It was the way the man held his left arm that bothered him—then the same dim light showed a blade in the other hand too. It was a shorter stabbing knife.

Jack rolled off the body beneath him, keeping his arms close to his sides so that he could go farther. He leaped to his feet and faced the two assassins. He could just make out the Mexican-appearing features of the one and the unnaturally white face of the other.

The knife man feinted with the long knife. The garroter hung back. He had to wait to get behind Jack, who edged away to get his back to the wall. He tripped on a pile of garbage and the two moved quickly to take advantage but stopped as he recovered. They spread farther apart, menacing shapes in the dim alley.

Jack cursed himself for not bringing a gun. But then it had started out as only a stalking mission to follow Stanley Hogben. Still, it would have been taken when his pockets were emptied and its presence might have aroused suspicion. He tried to spot something he could use as a weapon but could see nothing other than the piles and sacks of garbage.

The *boo how doy* with the knife came at him in a single-minded rush, fast sure steps, the long knife held out at full arm's length. Jack twisted to protect his stomach; then the Chinaman's shoulder hit him in the chest. Jack half turned to jab a hard left, then a right, swinging quickly to keep the other from using that knife.

The Chinaman's left hand came up, the short stabbing knife aiming straight for his body, but he was still slightly off-balance and Jack squirmed clear as the short but deadly blade slashed by, only inches away.

Where was the other one, the garroter? He had merged into the gloom of the alley and Jack had lost sight of him in the intensity of the knife man's charge. Then he saw him creeping in from the right, but he had only a split second to register his position, for the knife man recovered and came at him again. He was waving the weapon from side to side now, long sweeping arcs that might tempt a novice to follow its path with his eyes.

Jack just kept his gaze firmly on the man. He watched him come closer and closer. Jack's foot kicked against another pile of rubbish but met with some resistance. It must have been a sack. Then the two rushed him, the knife man from the front and the garroter from the side.

The knife man was closer and therefore the more immediate danger. Jack bent down and picked up the sack. It was heavier than he expected and he frantically pushed it at the knife man as the blade flickered at him, and then he saw the blade going into it.

To Jack's horror, the sack moved in his hands just as the blade entered, and he realized it was a body. It must be a bum or a drunk, but it had been a man. The *boo how doy* was a trained and efficient professional, but he too was taken by surprise. As the knife dug deep, the full weight of his thrust behind it, he must have known that it was a human, and that fractional delay was vital.

Jack let go of the body and shot a driving straight left full into the Chinaman's face. His unnaturally white features were a pale blur and a groan came from them. Even as Jack's fist hit him, the assassin made a desperate effort and pulled out the knife, but a pitiful moan from the body distracted him. It was another fateful delay, and Jack followed up his advantage. He smashed another straight left, his full body weight behind it, into the Chinaman's face, then a powerful short right hook into the same target.

He would ordinarily have placed one of those blows to the body, but he could not see plainly where the *boo how doy* had his left hand, the one with the short stabbing knife in it, and he did not intend to risk slicing his hand on it. The unfortunate hobo let out a dying groan. The *boo how doy* was flung backward by the force of Jack's powerful blows.

His long knife clattered to the ground even as the garroter leaped at Jack.

That man could not have known that the sack was, in fact, a body. All he could have known for sure was that his partner had been knocked out and lay inert on the ground. He was certainly a professional too, thought Jack, and though his attack position was not ideal—a garroter always preferred to approach his victim from behind—he hoped to make up for it by speed.

The *boo how doy* had a reputation for being without fear, and their extensive training gave them an understandable confidence in their own abilities. When given an assignment to kill, they invariably carried it out with speed, precision and skill. That one almost succeeded.

He swung his garrote slowly, ready to lash out at the least opening. The razor-edged steel wire was still a very dangerous weapon. It could chop off a hand or dig deep into the flesh, and Jack hastily backed away to keep out of reach of that deadly loop. They faced each other silently. Jack edged around to keep the two bodies between them— the dead hobo and the still-inert knife man.

The Chinaman was determined to get it over fast. He rushed at Jack again and Jack retreated a few steps. He realized that the garroter had forced him away from the knife on the ground, which the Chinaman reached down and snatched. He charged at Jack, who feinted to one side, then grabbed the wrist that held the knife as it flashed past him only a handbreadth away.

They swayed and struggled. The Mexican-like features were clearly visible now, even the cut at the edge of the mouth. Hot, fetid, garlic-laden breath, washed over him, but Jack held on, keeping the knife away. The Chinaman tried to pull his arm loose but could not. He tried to swing the garrote wire at Jack's face with his other hand but Jack twisted at the wrist, eliciting a grunt of pain.

If the *boo how doy* wanted to end it quickly, so did Jack. The knife man, knocked out by the punches to the face, would not stay that way for more than a few minutes. He could recover at any moment, and one on one was infinitely preferable to facing two of these proficient killers. Jack relaxed his grip on the other's wrist and the man attempted to pull it loose.

Jack instantly renewed his grip, putting all the power of his two arms into it. He twisted the arm holding the knife. The Chinaman resisted, straining the opposite way, breathing heavily. Jack found the energy to twist a fraction harder. The Chinaman fought to counter him, and it was the opening that Jack was straining to achieve. He reversed his grip, using the strength of the Chinaman against him. The knife raked past Jack's chest and rammed into the Chinaman's own body.

A hideous gurgling signified the life force flowing out of him, but Jack was in no mood to take chances. Before the other could recover, he pulled on the hand and the knife and rammed it home again. The man slumped. Jack took his full weight, then let him slip to the ground. Jack straightened up, breath coming in great gasps, heart pumping. Then to his chilled horror, a hand grasped his ankle.

It must have been an instinctive action, the natural impulse of an assassin to fulfill his mission, for the knife man on the ground had not fully recovered. Moving while still only partly conscious was a mistake that cost him his life. Jack kept his balance on the leg that was being held and kicked out with the other. The Chinaman yelped in pain as Jack's boot struck his elbow. At the same moment, there was a metallic clunk and Jack saw that the short stabbing knife had fallen out of the man's other hand. Jack grabbed it and drove it into the middle of the man's chest.

He took a few minutes to recover. He had killed several men in his short, eventful life, but he had never gotten used to it. He resented the flow of exultation at having proved his superiority over those who wanted to kill him. But it was this primal urge that had allowed mankind to survive and to have reached this stage in its advance toward the superman—the *Ubermensch.*

He made sure first that both Chinese were dead. Then he examined the bundle of rags that had once been a person. He was pitifully small and thin, no wonder Jack had been able to pick him up. He too was quite dead.

Jack took both the knives, then hunted around for the garrote. When he found it, he went through the pockets of both *boo how doy.* The white-faced one had five silver dollars and several smaller coins—a lot of money for a Chinese. He also had two cable car ticket stubs and a short chain with three tiny carved ivory figurines on it. The other had three silver dollars, smaller coins, and a used train ticket.

He went through their pockets again, making sure they were now empty. He pulled one body against a wall and piled rubbish sacks over it. He dragged the other two farther away and did the same with them. About to leave, he dropped the long knife near them. The police were hardly likely to expend much effort over two Chinamen and a hobo found dead in an alley on the Barbary Coast.

He went down the still-silent alley and on into the gaudy brightness of Stockton Steet.

Jack felt sick to his stomach as he walked. It was due, he knew, to the death of the hobo in the alley. He felt little remorse for the deaths of the two *boo how doy.* They had been trying to kill him and he had defeated them in fair fight. Besides, they were professional assassins and killing was their trade—it had rebounded on them.

The hobo was a different matter and Jack nursed a profound sadness for the poor wretch. Jack had spent enough time as a hobo himself to know what it was like to be alone, penniless, and without the slightest inkling of when the next mouthful of food would come.

Jack had been a railroad hobo, riding the rods, and the memory came back to him, as it often did, of the time when a spark from the engine set his coat on fire as he clung to the platform boards beneath the train. Holding on desperately with one hand, he tore off his coat and saw it instantly whisked into the massive roaring wheels only feet away.

He recalled too begging for food at farmhouses and wrapping rags around his blistered feet when he was left behind by Coxey's Army on its way to Washington. On the lighter side was living in the track-side camps with their blazing bonfires and warm camaraderie. The adventure path, Jack had called it then. He tried to remind himself now that it had been the wanderlust in his blood that had impelled him—but then he wondered about the dead hobo. What had driven him to life in an alley? Had it been poverty, lack of employment, drink, disillusionment?

The nearest Jack had come to dredging the depths of despair had been in Yokohama, on shore leave from the *Sophie Sutherland*. He had spent two weeks there, drinking warm sake and existing in a hazy world without meaning and without purpose. His recollections of those two weeks always made him shudder, for his was usually a mind of relentless drive and determination. To think of drifting in an alcoholic fog of oblivion was repellent to him now that he was so engaged in a life of writing and action.

Had the hobo been driven to a hopeless life in the alley by such thoughts? Jack had learned much in his two dozen years—more than many learned in a long lifetime—and he had learned above all else how to put things out of his mind and concentrate on necessary realities.

The air was still heavy with rain but Jack found it invigorating and he walked at a steady pace. He went as far as California Street, then turned and went on toward the Produce District and the fish market on Davis Street. This time Noah was in the shop arguing over the price of a shipment with a young man who talked about his shop in Sausalito. Their business concluded, he took Jack into the ice room and closed the door.

"Captain's not around—won't be talking to him for a while unless it's something real desperate," he told Jack.

"It is desperate," said Jack. "This information must get to the captain right away. Just past Iodoform Kate's, there's a red-light place called Madam Lila's. The top floor is a hide-out and I'm pretty sure that Manny Thurston and Lou Kandel are there. If the captain can mount a raid right away, they should catch them, but he must be careful—the brothel may connect with other buildings."

Noah's eyes widened and he pursed his lips in a soft whistle. "Sounds like you've been busy."

"Also tell him there're three dead bodies in an alley behind Stockton Street. But tell him not to waste time looking for who killed them."

Noah was looking at him with new respect. "You have *really* been busy! We have an emergency route for very important messages—and this is one. I'll see he gets this right away."

Chapter 28

It was late afternoon as Jack made his way to the Midway Plaisance. It was to be Belle Conquest's opening night and Jack was all too well aware that the cryptic words he had heard at the Presidio—"the Midway and then the Eureka"—seemed likely to refer to coups that were being planned, and the attempted theft of the Rajah's Ruby seemed the most obvious first part of it. But how was it to be done? That was much less obvious. Then the other phrase he had heard came to mind—"the branch on Leavenworth." What did that mean?

The indefatigable Flo was rehearsing her girls in groups of three on the stage with the pianist keeping them in time. The staff was busily cleaning and polishing in preparation for the big night. Behind the bar, bottles rattled and glasses clinked as stocks were filled. The smell of beer and tobacco remained, though the aroma of crushed flower petals fought for assertion.

"Got to stretch a little further, Grace," Flo called out to one of the girls. "Reach out—way out—more—that's good." She gave Jack a cheery smile that raised his spirits. It was always uplifting to see her heart-shaped face and bright eyes, which were seldom glum or melancholy.

"Everything normal?" Jack asked.

"Yes. Just some last-minute rehearsals. We want to be as near perfect as we can." That sounded like Flo, ever striving for perfection.

"Nothing unusual? Nothing at all?" Jack asked.

"Take a break, girls. Five minutes." The three girls slumped into sitting positions, glad for a chance to relax. Flo came over to Jack. "No, nothing at all." She questioned him with her eyes. "Are you expecting trouble?"

Jack hesitated. It was no use trying to fool her. "Yes, it's possible."

"What kind of trouble?"

"I don't know. I've picked up bits of information here and there. They don't add up too well, but they do point to something happening tonight."

She sighed. "I'm running out of ways to tell you to be careful."

Jack moved closer and said in a low voice, "I need to tell you to be careful too. I have no idea what's being planned. Anyone here in the Midway may be at risk. These are dangerous men with no regard for life."

"I know." Flo shuddered. "Those two young men . . ."

Jack gave her a kiss and a pat on the shoulder. He went to the storage room behind the bar, then down into the cellar, where he examined all the exits. A uniformed policeman was making a patrol outside—one of the precautions remaining after the deaths of Rollo and Francis.

In the corridor, a door opened and Belle Conquest came out. She wore only a purple dressing gown with purple-dyed fur trim and purple slippers with long, turned-up toes. Her painted mouth curved into a smile as she saw Jack.

"Jack! You've come back to see me! It's about time, you naughty boy, you! Where have you been?"

"Looking out for you, Belle," Jack said. "Making sure that ruby is safe."

"And is it?" she asked coyly.

"I'm sure it is. Otherwise everybody would have heard."

"Ah, so you know where I keep it?"

"No," said Jack, "but I'd bet it's still there."

She nodded a head toward her dressing room. "Want to come in and see where I keep it?"

"Not in there, I hope," Jack said. Confound the woman—

he never knew when her innuendos contained any of the
truth and when they did not.

"I was going to ask Laurence what he's doing for the next
half hour, but I can ask you." Her eyes shone with invitation.

Jack tried to look official. "I have to be sure all the precautions have been taken for tonight," he told her sternly.

"Perhaps fifteen minutes would be enough." She moved
closer and took his hand. "Don't worry about precautions—
I'll take care of those."

Over Belle's shoulder, Jack caught sight of Laurence
coming along the corridor. "Here comes Laurence now," he
said loudly. "I think he's looking for you."

He left quickly, before she could protest. On the streets,
he passed an unruly gang of about twenty dockworkers carrying homemade banners protesting their treatment and demanding to return to work. At the Eureka, nothing looked
out of the ordinary. He tried the front door but it was
locked. He went around to a back entrance and a truculent
face demanded to know what he wanted. When he said he
wanted to know if everything was all right, the man snapped,
"Yes, it is," and slammed the door.

The Tower was slightly more friendly. Houdini was not
there, he was told; he had gone to the hardware store and
livery stable on Montgomery Street to collect some items
he needed for the act. He preferred to do this errand himself, apparently, because he liked to keep his secrets from
becoming public.

Jack's investigating activities were cutting into his writing time, so he made the most of the next few hours working on *A Daughter of the Snows*. He had a name for her,
Frona Welse, and she would be twenty years old. It was a
little young for such an intrepid and resourceful heroine,
but Jack liked setting himself challenges, and this forced
him to convincingly present the conflict between youth and
experience. Until now, his most effective feminine por-
trayal had been an Indian woman, Oportuk; so this was to

be a major leap in his development and he was excited at
the feeling of the progress he was making.

He had reached a point in the story where the spring
thaw had begun, and he was mentally picturing Frona
Welse in a canoe racing along amid massive, cascading
blocks of ice. In his mind too was the final, climactic scene,
which he wanted to set in a miners' court. He was intrigued
with the idea of an unofficial court, illegal but implacable
in its resolve to obtain primitive justice.

He returned to the Midway Plaisance dressed in his best
suit, the second time he had worn it in two days. It was the
custom of many music halls to open a new and important
show with a performance at eleven o'clock and a second
show afterward. On this glowing occasion, the place was
filled early and the orchestra was keeping the impatient audience partially entertained with a selection of tunes from
popular Gilbert and Sullivan musicals. A lively rendition of
"Three Little Maids from School" was causing a few toes to
tap as Jack walked in. He had already reconnoitered the rear
of the building. A uniformed police officer was patroling and
another man, leaning against a corner, looked like a "flycop,"
a detective in plain clothing.

He looked over the audience. He thought back to occasions in the Yukon, especially in Dawson, when the management insisted on the patrons checking their weapons at
the door. It might have been a good idea here, though it was
probably decided against as being below the dignity of such
an exalted establishment as the Midway.

It looked like an affluent crowd. Admission was by ticket
only, which had permitted a measure of control. Jack searched
the faces but could not find any that looked suspicious. He
had arranged for a tiny table by a side wall, but before he
went to it he went backstage once more. One of the more
muscular of the Midway's bouncers—which it did not admit
to possessing—knew him, gave him a nod and let him pass.

Flo was having a few final words with her girls. She

gave Jack a smile. "All clear back here," she said in a low voice. Jack returned her smile and walked down the corridor, hoping he would not meet Belle, who might decide she had ten minutes before the curtain rose. He could hear her voice from one of the dressing rooms. She sounded as if she were berating one of her bodyguards for some inadequacy. Jack returned to the front and had a few words with a couple of the bartenders before taking his seat at the table. He felt the tension inside him and took some deep breaths.

The orchestra enjoyed a breathing spell after its onslaught against Gilbert and Sullivan's music; then at about ten minutes past eleven, the lights dimmed. The strains of "Temptation Is a Woman" rose above the excited chatter of the audience, which slowly subsided as almost everyone recognized the title song by Will Rossiter from Belle's Broadway hit of the same name.

The stage was empty but there was a hearty round of applause for the set, which was an effective waterfront scene with flashing red lights outside a bordello described as Satan's Hideaway.

The chorus girls began to drift onstage, some with an arm around a man, others clearly dressed to attract one. They began to form a pattern that became a sensuous dance; then at its climax in both sound and passion, the lights flashed in a frenzy and Belle emerged.

Her crimson-and-black outfit clung tightly to her body but revealed her legs and most of her breasts, and she moved with the grace of a panther. A large hat and long gloves were in the same crimson and black, but even this dazzling and provocative outfit and its gorgeous, larger-than-life wearer took second place.

The Rajah's Ruby had been widely publicized in all the San Francisco newspapers and everyone knew what it looked like, but no one was prepared for the reality of the magnificent stone between her breasts. The gem was radiant with the redness of a setting sun. It was the size of a duck's egg but it appeared bigger in the glaring stage lights. Glistening shafts of ghostly red stabbed out toward the audience.

Belle stood and basked in the applause, letting the audience gasp and shout in a storm of acclamation. Her wide, red-lipped smile and the wicked glint in her large expressive eyes brought ovation after ovation. And she hadn't done a thing yet, thought Jack in admiration.

The program was not a taxing one for the star, nor did it need to be, for the applause was tremendous whether she sang or danced or merely swayed her hips and batted her eyelashes. Stanley Carter's hit song "You're Not the Only Pebble on the Beach" started the adulation; then a number made famous by Anna Held, "Won't You Come and Play with Me?" was given a decidedly sexual slant by Belle. She did not have to change any words—she knew exactly which ones to emphasize to give them a totally different meaning.

She followed that with Baldwin Sloan's song "When You Ain't Got No Money, You Needn't Come Around," but the words to this were Belle's own and owed little or nothing to the original lyrics by Clarence S. Brewster.

Flo's girls came in for their share of well-deserved clapping with a couple of expertly done chorus numbers; then the show ended as it had begun—with another dazzling display of the famous Rajah's Ruby. It was a toss-up whether Belle or the ruby received the loudest ovation.

Throughout the show, Jack had been on the alert. His eyes moved continuously over the crowd, sensitive to the smallest movement. Sometimes it was hard to see because fans stood to clap and cheer. At the end, as Belle took a third and then a fourth curtain call, Jack felt great relief and joined the standing crowd.

He pushed his way through the knots of satisfied customers and went past the stage to the dressing rooms. It was then that he heard shouted words and cries from female voices—cries of anguish.

Chapter 29

A dark-faced, long-jawed man with an Army Colt pistol in his hand stood at the door of the first dressing room. The door was open and he was herding Flo and the girls into the room. The gun swung menacingly at Jack as he went to Flo's side.

"It's all right, Jack," she said quickly. "Don't cause any trouble—not now."

Farther down the corridor, another man stood with a revolver. Jack could hear Belle's voice raised in anger but he could not see her. She sounded strident and forceful and did not seem to be in immediate danger.

Behind Jack came Louis Lahearne, Belle's manager. He looked at Jack; then his eyes widened as he saw the Colt revolver. "What's going on? Where is Belle?" he shouted.

"She's all right," Jack assured him. "There's not much we can do at the moment." Lahearne saw the other armed man and his face turned red with anger, but he only sputtered a meaningless protest.

Both gunmen looked trained and capable. They held their weapons with an easy familiarity. More Riders of the Rim, Jack supposed.

Belle's bodyguards stood there looking helpless, and the first gunman locked them along with Flo and the chorus girls into the dressing room. The noise from the auditorium could be heard clearly, still loud and clamorous. Adding to it was the triumphant beat of the orchestra reprising Belle's popular numbers. It was probable that the audience had no idea what was happening backstage.

The gang was well rehearsed. A third man came out of Belle's dressing room with a similar Colt pistol in one hand and something wrapped in a woman's garment in the other. He gave a nod to the other two.

Another dressing room door was opened and Jack and Lahearne were pushed into it. The key was turned in the lock.

Gurgles came from a large closet and Jack opened it to find the bound and gagged uniformed police officer and the flycop from outside. "Untie them," he snapped to Lahearne. "I'll try to get this door open."

It was too stoutly built for him and easily resisted his efforts. When the two policemen were released, they were full of curses and questions that Jack cut off. "Let's get this door open first."

From the inside, it was no easy task, even for the four of them. A panel finally splintered and they tore aside pieces to enlarge the hole, but by the time they were out a group had gathered. More people came from the auditorium as the news spread. Lahearne hurried to find Belle, then came back to say her door was locked.

Jack went to the dressing room in which Flo and the girls were trapped. "Flo, it's Jack! Can you hear me?"

Her voice expressed relief. "Jack! You're all right?"

"Yes. Hold on. We'll have you out in a minute."

The two police officers had left but several men from the audience eagerly volunteered to break down Belle's dressing room door. "Always wanted to do this," one of them panted.

Others threw their weight against the door of the room holding Flo and her girls. When they were all released, Flo, with her customary insight, asked, "How was it that we were all locked in? I've never seen keys for all these doors before."

One of the girls offered an answer in the form of another question. "Notice we're one girl short?" Another said, "It's that bitch, Rita." Other girls chipped in with similar comments and it was soon apparent that Rita, unpopular with the other girls and now absent, was a renegade who had been seen with questionable characters and had undoubtedly been in the pay of the Riders of the Rim.

Another policeman who had been on duty outside was found in the alley, unconscious. Louis Lahearne appeared. "Belle's fine. They didn't harm her."

Jack nodded. "All they wanted was the ruby."

At that moment, Belle's dressing room door opened and the star herself emerged. There were gasps. Belle wore a smug smile.

She also wore, on her sumptuous décolletage, the Rajah's Ruby.

Andy, the head bartender, came hurrying into the corridor at that moment and stopped at this spectacular sight. "Lawdy! Ain't I glad I lived to see this!"

"I thought I saw the gang going out with the ruby," Jack said in disbelief.

"You did, honey," drawled Belle. "This here's my spare."

Flo let out an unladylike whistle. "Spare! How many do you have, Belle?"

"The one those louts took from me was a phony," Belle said.

"And that one?" asked Jack. "Is it real?"

She swaggered a step closer and stopped with her breasts only inches away from his pointing finger. "Maybe it is, and then again, maybe it ain't."

"Several men have died defending the one they thought was real," Jack said harshly.

Belle's tough facade wilted and her face contorted. "I know and I feel terrible about it. Those poor boys." She turned away with a sob and ran back to her dressing room. Jack felt a pang of remorse but remembered Morley's opinion of her: "an obstinate and uncaring female." Was Morley right? Or was Belle that good an actress?

He said to Flo, "I have to get over to the Eureka right away. Something is going to happen there."

"That's what I came to tell you," said Andy, his eyes still wide. "There's a riot going on in the street there. A gang of Houdini supporters marched against the Eureka with banners and posters. The Paradino woman's supporters are trying to stop them."

A concept was forming in Jack's brain. Things were becoming clear. "I have to go—see what I can do," he said.

Andy shook his head. "It's too dangerous, Jack. It could spread, you know the hotheads in this town. Anyway, it would take an army to stop those people."

"An army . . ." Flo said.

"What is it, Flo?" Jack didn't like that tone of voice. He had heard her use it before. It meant she had something in mind.

"Give me five minutes," she said.

Less time than that had passed when the remnants of the door banged open and an astonishing parade emerged. At the head of the line came Flo, followed by her girls. It was their costumes that caught Jack's eye immediately. They were evidently the ones that had been delivered during Belle's rehearsal.

The costumes were prim and severe, a jarring contrast to the daring and scanty attire usually seen in the Midway Plaisance. From ankle to neck, the girls wore black alpaca with high white collars, white bibs, black bonnets with strings under the chin and high-buttoned black boots laced all the way. It was the uniform worn by Carrie Nation's wrecking crew.

On closer scrutiny, though, the severity of these costumes was different from those on the women who had wrecked the Orpheum. It was the severity of allure rather than the severity of constraint. These costumes were tight at the waist and padded at the bosom while the derrieres were tantalizingly rounded.

Jack gaped in amazement as the women marched past him. Most of the girls looked suitably grim and a couple had wicked smirks. It was the ax that each carried balanced on her shoulder that caused him to chuckle.

Flo broke ranks to come back to him. "What do you think, Jack?"

"Carrie Nation's army to a tee," Jack sputtered. He leaned forward to examine one of the axes as it went by. The blade gleamed purposefully but it was only painted wood. "Amazing," he admitted.

"We could probably get Carrie herself to do this if she were here," said Flo, "but unfortunately, she left town. Went to reform Carson City."

Jack shook his head. "I can't let you do it though. Not if you're thinking of going over to the Eureka."

"Why not?" Flo thrust out her chin. Jack knew that aggressive gesture. "You told me how Carrie Nation and her army wrecked the Orpheum," Flo went on. "There wasn't a finger raised to stop them. If an army of men went to Montgomery Street now, blood would be all over the place—but an army of women! They won't dare stop us. But we can stop them!"

"Flo, it's too risky," Jack said weakly. He knew when he had lost an argument with Flo, but he felt obliged to try.

"Girls!" Flo shouted, overriding his words. "Forward march!"

The situation on Montgomery Street looked ugly. Banners waved, proclaiming, "Stop These Fakes and Phonies!" and "No Swindlers and Tricksters Here." One read, "Protect Our Families from This Woman," but the man carrying it looked very unlike a family man. Angry shouts condemned Eulalia Paradino as cheating bereaved men and women while equally angry voices were raised defending her as genuine.

Posters demanded, "Call Out the Militia! San Francisco No Longer Safe," "Protect Our Citizens." The dusty street looked as if it were to be the scene of carnage. Fists were shaking and sticks waved threateningly. A skirmish broke out but the involvement was short. Two men ran away, jeered by the crowd. The mutinous rumble increased and a major confrontation looked inevitable.

The noise subsided miraculously as Flo's army marched right into them. A bewildered silence fell and the demonstrators dropped back in awe. Jack was aware that he could do nothing, but he followed the army. It split into columns, effectively breaking up the crowd. The girls marched right into them, cutting them into smaller groups. The hotheads were still shouting and Jack saw a number of them trying to bunch together. All looked like toughs, probably members of the Riders of the Rim. One of them seemed to be giving orders, rallying them for further mischief. The danger was still not over. Flo's army had achieved a vital delay, but what else could she do? If the Riders of the Rim wanted to use violence, Flo and her girls were in trouble.

Across Montgomery Street was the Tower Music Hall; a few figures had emerged from that building onto the sidewalk. Jack saw Houdini standing there. He hurried over. "Harry! Know any good tricks?"

Houdini frowned, his puzzled gaze still on the crowd milling around in the street before the theater. "Tricks?"

"No time to explain. Some ruffians have gathered a following. Damage may be done and people hurt. The crowd's too big and could be easily led. We've got to divert them."

"Who are those women?" Houdini, still bewildered, looked over the black-clad female force.

"Carrie Nation's Reserves," Jack cried. "Quick, there's no time to lose. Show 'em some tricks!"

The Riders of the Rim were dispersing through the throng, shouting exhortations, yelling threats and complaints, and the responsive, angry murmurs were swelling again. Banners were being put back up and a return to the belligerent mass of before looked inevitable.

Houdini turned to one of the men with him and snapped words. Two of them went inside and returned immediately with a table, which they set on the sidewalk. With a lithe bound, Houdini was on top of it. One of the men had gone back inside and came out with a baffled-looking fellow carrying a trumpet.

The anger in the air was almost palpable. The strident notes of the trumpet chopped through the tension like musical knives and startled faces turned. Voices—even the louder ones—were drowned in the trumpet blasts.

"Never mind music—just make it loud!" yelled the man who had dragged the musician out of the orchestra and was evidently quicker witted than the others.

By the time the trumpet player had emptied his lungs, there was a temporary hush on that block of Montgomery Street. By then, Houdini was ready. One of his aides handed him a glass of water. He raised it in the air, showing it to the crowd. His movements were rapid and deft, and the street was even quieter as all eyes were on the master magician.

With a flourish, he drank the water to the last drop. The aide took the glass as Houdini struck a pose, his head raised. He opened his mouth, then reached in theatrically with one hand and pulled out a large blue silk handkerchief.

The awed gasp that went up was hushed by others as Houdini pulled farther to show that the handkerchief was tied to another, this one bright crimson. More cries followed, for yet another handkerchief came out, saffron yellow—then deep purple, then pristine white. Out they came, every conceivable color, each tied to the next. The cries subsided as people tried to figure out how the trick was done. Some edged sideways to get another view but shook their heads because the handkerchiefs were indeed coming out of Houdini's mouth.

The seemingly infinite coil of dazzling silk colors formed a pile on the ground in front of the table. It grew larger and larger. When it was certain that the endless issue could not continue, it kept coming and coming.

Jack was as mystified as everyone else, but he tore his attention away from the illusionist and ran an eye over the assembly in the street. They were spellbound, but Jack also

noticed that most of the Riders of the Rim types were gone.
The immediate danger was averted.

At last, Houdini twitched a finger at the trumpet player,
who gave him a triumphantly patriotic burst of Francis
Scott Key's "Star-Spangled Banner" just as the last handkerchief came out—it was not a handkerchief, though, but
instead a large Stars and Stripes.

The applause was enormous. Their wrath forgotten, his
audience yelled for more and Houdini obliged with his nee-
dle trick, which he performed during his act at the Tower. It
was another crowd pleaser, in which Houdini apparently
swallowed a length of thread and a packet of sewing needles. After drinking water to wash them down, he showed
his mouth to be empty, then slowly drew out one hundred
needles, all neatly spaced and threaded onto the same
length of thread.

While the trick was still being watched with bated
breath, Jack slipped through to Flo, who was looking very
prim and sedate in her black uniform, which fitted her
curves in an enticingly unecclesiastical way. She and her
girls were just as transfixed by Houdini as everyone else.

Jack gave her a tight hug. "You don't listen when I tell
you to be careful, do you!"

Flo laughed merrily. "It's usually the other way around."

"Still," Jack went on, "you were marvelous. You saved
the day."

"Is it over?" Flo's dark eyes looked anxious.

"Most of the troublemakers have gone. It's over for
now."

"I'd better march the girls back," said Flo, disentangling
herself from Jack's arms. "We may as well get some more
publicity for the act!"

Chapter 30

When he returned to the Midway Plaisance, the first person Jack encountered was Captain Morley. He stood in the auditorium. Cleaners were at work and the place had a forlorn look, as if saddened by its demoted status. "I thought you had this place well guarded," Jack said angrily.

"I thought so too," Morley said, not sounding in the least apologetic. "Tell me about the robbery here," he urged. "I've had a few accounts. I'd like yours too."

Jack told him, including the events outside the Tower.

When he finished, Morley whistled softly. "She's one in a million, that girl."

Jack was thinking, Morley wasn't here and he wasn't at the Tower. Where was he? A suspicion that had been half formed for some time was hardening. He knew nothing about Morley, not even which branch of the police force he was in. Could he be involved in these crimes? It would be a perfect cover. He seemed honest and reliable enough, but Jack had met a number of cops who had been found to be taking bribes, men he had thought to be of the highest integrity. What about Morley?

"You got my information on the red-light place on Stockton Street?" Jack asked.

Morley's expression eased. "Yes. We got Kandel and Thurston. Well done. A good thing you told me about the building. We caught them getting onto the roof—they could have gotten into an adjoining building and escaped. We missed Soapy Groves, unfortunately. The explosives expert had been hiding there but he wasn't there when we raided. We have all his possessions though."

"What about Hogben? Did you get him?"

"Yes, and he's got some expensive lawyers trying to get him out."

"You still have him though?"

"We certainly do, and I intend to hold on to him until this is all over."

"Can you do that?" asked Jack.

"Even if I have to move him from jail to jail all through the city of San Francisco," Morley said grimly.

Jack felt a little more reassured about Morley. "That's good, because I think we're approaching a climax."

"In what way?"

"A lot of things have become clear in the last few hours," Jack said. "Until now, I had not connected the theft of the ruby, the Riders of the Rim, the stirring up of a battle between Paradino's followers and Houdini's supporters, the strike, McParland's presence and the calls for the militia to turn out. But now I see that they're all part of the same plot."

"Go on," Morley said.

"All right. Here's what I think. Glass wants the strike ended. He hired McParland and his Pinkertons to do it. They've done that kind of thing before, but those days are over. They can't get away with physical intimidation and having a lot of men killed any longer. McParland is smart enough to realize what he was involved in here and told whoever hired him that he was pulling out.

"Fritz at the Midway has not been flush with money lately, yet he was able to get hold of a large amount of money to bring Belle Conquest here. The Rajah's Ruby would not only be a big crowd pleaser, but it would be a lure for every crook in the state. Kandel was brought here to crack a safe or two and Soapy Groves to blow up any that Kandel couldn't pick. Glass, or the Big Three, if they are behind him, didn't want the ruby—Kandel or Groves could have it. Glass just wanted turmoil and lawlessness."

Morley looked interested. "Ingenious," he said. "You mean Belle Conquest and her ruby were just a lure, and a clever means of paying the bill."

"Next," Jack went on, "I think the same person advanced money to the Eureka to bring Eulalia Paradino and to the Tower to bring Harry Houdini."

"She is certainly a drawing card," admitted Morley, "but Houdini hasn't quite made it to the top yet. Still, I suppose his appearances in jails and police stations and shows like the one at the docks are spreading his name fast."

"I think there was another motive with Houdini," Jack said. "Glass knew how Houdini detests phony spiritualists and that having these two right across the street was like throwing kerosene on a fire."

"Glass's purpose being riots." Morley nodded. "Hmm, the idea has merit. But then we have the city in turmoil. What does that accomplish?"

"It allows the proclamation of civil disobedience and gives the governor reason to call out the militia."

Morley regarded Jack sharply at these words.

"I took classes at Berkeley," Jack explained, "local and state law."

"You intended to become a lawyer?"

"No. The Socialist Party has asked me a couple of times to think about running for mayor of Oakland."

A hint of a smile began to form around Morley's mouth but he suppressed it. "You're an ambitious young fellow."

"Only if I decide to run," said Jack.

"Hmm," Morley said again. "The militia, of course, would have the power to order all the strikers back to work. Normally, only the president can call out the militia. There is one exception—"

"Under California law, the governor can do so if it is an emergency. He could say that the strike made it an emergency. Then the shipowners and the dockyard owners would have won without having to pay higher wages or improve conditions."

"I suppose," Morley said thoughtfully, "that the shipping and dock owners would spend this much money bringing Belle Conquest, Houdini and Paradino. Pennies, that's all it is, pennies, compared to the cost of a hundred ships tied up."

"Exactly," said Jack.

"It's true that the governor is the only man with the power to call out the militia," Morley said. His voice was musing, as if he were thinking out loud. "But he's new in the job. He's only been here a few days. He might be very reluctant to use that power."

"That bothers me too," admitted Jack. He had gone this far with Morley. Perhaps his suspicions were unfounded after all. Until now he had been willing to trust the man.

"These Riders of the Rim," Morley continued. "We have never clearly established their position. Do you have any ideas on them?"

"A lot of them are professional outlaws, many are skilled gunmen. They are the backbone. They've recruited malcontents, out-of-works, hangers-on, men looking for easy pickings. These are not really a threat. They've been paid mainly to swell the numbers."

"They may be more of a threat than we think," Morley said. "In a city controlled by the militia, there would be lots of opportunities for a paramilitary organization like theirs to fill their own pockets."

"Do you have any idea who Glass is?" asked Jack. He had hoped to catch Morley off guard but there was no sign of success.

Morley shook his head. "I have ideas but they don't fit together yet. I have to make them fit together soon though. You and the girls and Houdini averted disaster tonight, but Glass—whoever he is—is a very dangerous man. We have to get him before he can come up with another scheme."

"Anything I can do to help?"

Morley rubbed his chin reflectively. "There is one route you might pursue."

"What's that?" Jack asked.

"That conversation between Hogben, Tullamore and another man during the reception for the new governor at the Presidio. Do you know who this other man was?" Morley asked.

"No, I couldn't see him."

Could the other man have been Morley? The thought flew across Jack's mind as he spoke. No, he concluded, I would have recognized his voice, wouldn't I? Did I hear him that clearly? Still uncertain, he hurried on. "Does 'the branch on Leavenworth' mean anything to you?"

Morley considered. "It's a long, busy street."

"It runs all the way from Fisherman's Wharf to Market Street," Jack agreed.

"Wells-Fargo has a branch office on it."

"Could that be where Belle Conquest really keeps the ruby?"

"I might be able to find out," Morley said. His voice changed. "And now I have some more questions to ask around here. Perhaps I can get a bit further with these Riders of the Rim. We're building quite a file on them."

Jack watched him go. Surely he must be a reliable police officer. . . .

Chapter 31

Jack's doubts about Morley were still not fully resolved the next morning. He pushed them aside for the moment. It was still dark at six o'clock when he resumed work on *A Daughter of the Snows*. To Jack, words were the greatest things in the world—descriptive words; graphic words; musical words; powerful, sharp and incisive words. He read books with a dictionary always at hand.

He would scribble down on sheets of paper words he had not encountered before and stick the sheets into the crack between the wood and the mirror above his bureau so that he could repeat and memorize them while he shaved and dressed. He strung clotheslines across his room, and with clothespins fastened small notes, each bearing a new word. Every time he walked past one, he would stop and repeat it several times. Nothing gave him a greater thrill than to search for—and find—the perfect word, the one that expressed his meaning precisely and completely.

Three hours later, he breathed a sigh of satisfaction. The story was moving along well. He needed a break. After a moment's thought, he took out the small box in which he had put the contents of the pockets of the two *boo how doy*.

The cable car tickets were for the run from Central to Powell. That told him little, because Powell was only minutes from Chinatown. The ivory figurines were evidently amulets of some kind, a sort of good luck charm. Well, any assassin would want to ensure a lot of that, thought Jack, though this one had chosen the wrong charm.

He was about to put the box away when he looked at one
of the coins. The silver dollar was shiny and new. He
picked up another, then lined up all eight of them—a sizable amount of money, but then he knew that *boo how doy*
were well paid. These coins were really new though. All
had that year's date and all gleamed with the sheen of the
mint. He put one in his pocket and went out, stopping at the
corner to get a newspaper.

The *Chronicle* had a big story on page one—how a riot
had developed, how threatening it had become until an
"army" of women, dressed like Carrie Nation's formidable
unit, had marched right into the rioters. The story went on
to tell of Houdini's magic acts, which had finally quelled
the unrest and brought peace to the city.

Talks between the ship and port owners and the unions
had been arranged, another article reported, and it was
hoped that a peaceful settlement was at last going to be
found.

Jack smiled to himself, put the paper in his pocket and
took the ferry across to San Francisco.

On the ferry ride, he looked down into the churning
white water and thought about which bank would be the
most helpful. His knowledge of banks was not extensive.
But he believed that the Canadian Bank of Commerce was
a good place to start because they were very active in the
city but still had external control, which meant a measure
of neutrality. A clerk with a thin face and a weary appearance took up the coin that Jack showed him and asked if it
was genuine.

The clerk turned it over a few times. He rapped it on the
counter, nodded and said, "Seems genuine enough." He
looked askance at Jack. "Why do you think it isn't?"

"A friend of mine tried to pass a dollar coin the other day
and the bank said it was forged. I don't want to find out that
mine's a forgery too."

The clerk examined it again. "It's perfectly good, but if

you want to be absolutely sure, take it to the Crocker Bank."

The name of Crocker always struck a nerve in Jack. It was due, he knew, to Ambrose Bierce's fanatical enmity toward the Big Three, one of whom was Fred Crocker, the despotic millionaire owner of the bank.

"Why the Crocker?" asked Jack.

The clerk turned the coin over and pointed at a small letter at the side of President McKinley's head. "See that letter *J* there? It means that the coin was struck at the mint here in San Francisco. There are five mints in the state of California, and the others have different letters. All of the coins from the San Francisco mint are distributed through the Crocker Bank."

"Thanks," said Jack. He had examined the coins in detail and knew that all carried the same letter *J* on them.

Jack was turning to go when the clerk added, "Their nearest branch is on Leavenworth."

"The branch on Leavenworth"—the phrase that Jack had heard between Stanley Hogben, Lem Tullamore and the unknown third man during the reception at the Presidio! It was a meeting place or an exchange of some kind. And it was the Crocker Bank.

Jack thanked the clerk again and left, his mind whirling.

Outside, the Crocker Bank on Leavenworth was a solid-looking building with large columns flanking a short flight of steps up to the main entrance. Inside, wooden cubicles took up most of the space, and cages along the other side reflected a strong feel of security. The low ceiling helped to fill the large area with the buzz of voices. Jack approached a window grille staffed by the most elderly man he could see, who he hoped would be the most knowledgeable. He repeated his story of being nervous about having a counterfeit coin.

The teller was in his sixties, gray-haired and stooped. He

studied the coin, bounced it on a marble slab and looked at it again. "It's genuine," he said authoritatively.

"You're sure?" asked Jack. When the teller opened his mouth to snap back a reply, Jack added quickly, "It's all I've got. I don't want to take a chance."

The teller looked at the young man before him, mellowed. "It's one of ours. The letter here . . . see this?" He pointed to the *J* and gave Jack the same explanation that he had received from the Canadian Bank. "This one's new, probably the shipment that came in from the mint about two weeks ago," the teller concluded.

Jack thanked the older man and walked away, considering his next move. He noticed that another large room adjoined, with enclosed offices down both sides of a corridor. These were presumably for managers; the Crocker Bank was a vast organization with many activities.

He was walking past the area when he heard two voices. Jack stopped in midstride. One voice was familiar—but whose was it? It was a voice he had heard many times. Of course, it was the voice of Police Captain John Morley! What could he be doing there?

The other voice did not bring instant recognition, for it was not that of someone he knew. But he had heard it, and though he racked his brain, he could not identify it.

Jack saw them now. Captain Morley was in deep conversation with a tall, spare man in a black business suit. He had a large head and thinning gray hair. The two stood some distance outside the first office in the corridor that led away from the main area. Jack's keen memory was already bringing up the name as he edged closer to look at the brass sign on the door of the office. It read, "ROBERT WINDHAM— VICE PRESIDENT." Jack remembered too that Bierce had left him to talk to Windham in the hope of getting material for a column.

The bank was beginning to get busy and both staff and customers were filling the place. Jack maneuvered himself into a less visible position. The two men had evidently just come out of Windham's office, leaving the door open. They began to stroll slowly in the direction of the main entrance, still talking intently. Jack did not hesitate. He walked confidently to Windham's office, went in and closed the door.

It was the most luxurious office Jack had ever seen. Wood-paneled walls, heavy wood furniture, brass lamps, a wall of shelves stacked with leather-bound books and a thick carpet gave it an opulent atmosphere. A large desk, with a padded chair behind it, held papers and a big black telephone. Farther behind the desk, a mahogany table was covered with a large map.

Aware of the risk he was taking, Jack moved fast. He went to the desk first, but the papers referred to bank matters, which meant little to him. About to look at the large map, his attention was caught by a large photograph on the wall. "YALE, CLASS OF 1876" was the caption, and a white circle picked out a younger but unmistakable Robert Windham.

Something about the face of the graduate on Windham's right looked familiar, and Jack scrutinized the face but could not identify it. He looked at the bottom of the photo but there were no names. Knowing he did not have much time, he went quickly to the map.

It was a large-scale map, part of a U.S. Army Ordnance Division survey map of San Francisco. In one direction, it ran from Battery Street to Stockton, and in the other direction from Bush to Vallejo. A red ring had been drawn near the end of Dupont Street.

A grid of lines had been drawn running across the streets, not following them but intersecting and crossing at irregular angles.

Dupont Street. That was where How Chew Fat had his headquarters—more than one of them, apparently. Was the Chinaman involved in this too?

A quick double knock on the door startled Jack, and before he could move the door opened and a youth of about fourteen came in, with a large stack of letters in his hands.

Behind him in the corridor was a wicker basket on wheels. It too was piled high with letters.

The youth had a pale face and corn-colored hair. He stared at Jack uncertainly, but Jack was just enough years older than him to discourage questioning. "For Mr. Windham?" he said in a lofty voice. "I'll take them." He grabbed them out of the youth's hands before he could protest, but as he did, another figure pushed into the office.

"What's going on here?" Windham demanded.

Jack deposited the stack of letters onto the tray on Windham's desk. "Your mail, Mr. Windham." He smiled and added, "Just learning the ropes." He put a fatherly hand on the youth's shoulder and guided him out of the office.

Chapter 32

Jack walked quickly to the Produce District and Noah's fish market. The big, bearded man was extolling the quality of a huge swordfish hanging from a hook, dripping water. A merchant with muttonchop whiskers was examining the fish as if determined to find something wrong with it.

"You don't want it," said Noah, "I can sell it in five minutes. A beautiful fish, this one." Jack had to agree. From his own years of experience as a fisherman, he knew that it was a fine specimen. The merchant shook his head. "I don't know."

"He doesn't want it, I'll take it," Jack said. "How much are you asking?"

"Hey, wait a minute," protested the merchant, "I was here first."

Noah and the merchant concluded their transaction and two of Noah's men trundled the big fish out to the merchant's cart. Noah grinned at Jack. "Maybe I should offer you a job here."

When the merchant had gone, Jack described his urgent need to talk to Morley. He realized it might be difficult—Morley had only left the Crocker Bank on Leavenworth minutes before he himself had. Jack tried to find out from Noah what Morley's likely next stop would be without success. He also asked about the network of agents and how word was passed around, but nothing came out of that effort either. Noah was clearly a cautious man—evidently why he had survived in his perilous position.

"Better the captain knows where you are," suggested Noah, and Jack had to be content with that. "One other thing," Jack said. "Can you let me have a sheet of paper and a pen?" When they were brought, he wrote a short note, folded the sheet and wrote an address on it. "Can you have this delivered?" he asked.

Noah's bushy eyebrows went up as he looked at the address. "It's unusual."

"It's important," said Jack, and Noah nodded. "I'll be at the Midway Plaisance," Jack told the bearded man.

"You're early," was the greeting he received when he walked into the auditorium of the big music hall. Two of the chorus girls were sitting at a table, evidently resting between rehearsals, and one of them, a long-legged blonde, was a friend of Flo and knew Jack.

"Looks like you're working already," Jack replied.

"You know how Flo is," said the blonde. "Never satisfied till you have it perfect. Is she that way with you?" She gave him a saucy look and the other girl tittered.

"All right, girls! Let's try it again!" Flo said in a commanding voice. She walked onstage and the lights came up in the darkened auditorium. Several other girls drifted on from the dressing rooms. Flo clapped her hands and the girls moved into positions. She noticed Jack and gave him a wave. He waved back. The piano player struck up a few introductory chords.

It was a new number they were rehearsing, presumably for the next show. The appetite of the audiences for entertainment on the Barbary Coast was voracious, and even good shows lasted only two or three weeks. This consumed a huge amount of material and the crowd would promptly start booing if scenery or a song or a dance was repeated. The comedians suffered particularly severely, and only the top performers, like Weber and Fields, Eddie Foy and George Evans, could afford the writers to provide them with constantly renewed material.

Jack sat and watched but his mind was not wholly on the stage. He was trying to work out the meaning of the map on the desk of Robert Windham at the Crocker Bank and the significance of the Yale class photograph on the wall. He was also concerned about the explosives expert, Soapy Groves. Morley's raid had not pulled him in, so where was he?

Jack had the gnawing feeling that events were moving swiftly to a climax and all these factors were tied together. It galled him to be inactive, just sitting there.

The main door opened with a crash and a noisy party entered. It was Belle Conquest with her manager, her two bodyguards and two other men Jack did not recognize. They were all in a jovial mood and Jack would have supposed they had all been drinking but for Belle's abhorrence of liquor.

"Hello, sweetie!" the star greeted him. "You're here waiting for me! That's nice. You can help me dress."

"Hush," Jack urged, putting a finger to his lips. "The girls are rehearsing."

Belle looked derisively at the stage and Jack expected some critical comment, but she blithely continued on her way to the dressing rooms accompanied by her entourage.

At the bar, Andy was waving to Jack. "Message for you. Somebody just left it."

It was a simple note, unsigned. It said only, "WALK OUTSIDE." Jack stared at it, then crumpled it and put it into his pocket before he followed the instruction.

A hansom cab stood there, the horse snorting impatiently. The door opened. Jack peered forward dubiously. Morley was inside. He beckoned quickly for Jack to join him and rapped on the roof for the cab to start. "Hogben keeps yelling for a lawyer," he said without any preamble, "but we're keeping the lawyers out of it so far. The deputy warden of San Quentin is coming to identify Kandel. He is anxious to have him back so he can return him to death row for killing a guard."

"And Thurston?"

"That's why I want you. You said Sergeant Healey struggled with Kandel when you tried to grab them at the docks. You fought with Thurston. I want you to identify him."

"I can do that," Jack said. "We were face-to-face a few times during that struggle. I can recognize him right enough. What about the other one? The explosives expert?"

"Groves? We haven't got him yet, but we have all his possessions and we're looking through them for clues."

The cab was bouncing over the uneven street. Jack waited for Morley to tell him of his visit to the Crocker Bank but he did not. Jack felt a resurgence of his earlier doubts and hesitated over whether he should speak of his own visit there. He decided to take the bold approach.

"I saw you at the Crocker Bank," he said.

Morley turned to him. "You were there?"

"Yes." Jack told him of the silver dollars that he had taken from the *boo how doy* and what he had learned at the bank.

Morley looked out the window of the cab. "I had one of our accountants at police headquarters look into certain of the Virginia Bank accounts."

"The Virginia Bank?"

"They are owned by Crocker."

"The police have accountants?"

Morley smiled. "You'd be surprised at some of the experts we have. Oh, we can't get into many of the bank's more closely guarded accounts, but there are a few they have to make semipublic. I've had my eye on Robert Windham for some time. You recall that occasion at the reception at the Presidio? When I walked past you with Windham's wife? He has a mistress and his wife knows about her. I was hoping that his wife would be angry enough about it to drop a few hints about his other activities."

Jack nodded. He was more interested in something else. "What did you find in Windham's office?"

"I wasn't in his office," Morley said. "He took me into a small conference room."

Jack felt deflated. His exuberance for the chase had led him to a faulty judgment. His suspicions of Morley seemed to ebb and flow.

"I was in his office," Jack said. Morley glanced at him sharply but waited for him to continue. Jack went on to tell him of the map on the table and the class photograph. Morley asked a string of questions about the map and Jack answered the best he could.

Morley looked out the window again. They were going along Filbert Street and Russian Hill reared up on the right. He was deep in thought. Jack allowed him a brief silence, then asked, "Why did you go to see Windham?"

"Your theories about inciting riotous behavior were probably right. The funding of the Eureka and the Tower music halls so that they could stage two such deadly rivals as the Paradino woman and Houdini right across the street from one another was one of the things I had the accountants look at. They found another thing—someone has been trying to buy up music halls."

"That happens all the time, doesn't it?" asked Jack. "They get bought and sold."

"This is different. Someone seems to be trying to buy a number of them, perhaps wanting to become the most powerful person in the entertainment field in this city."

"And it's Windham?"

"There's nothing else against him. He said he had been making inquiries on behalf of one of the bank's clients."

"How many clients do they have with that kind of money?" asked Jack skeptically.

"Not many. That's why I believe that it is Windham who has been trying to buy out the music halls and be the kingpin in that business. This map? What exactly did it show?"

Jack described it again. Morley shook his head. "Doesn't

mean much that I can tell. Maybe a proposed new building site."

"It's the strange crisscrossed lines that I don't understand," Jack said. The cab stopped, they alighted and Jack saw that they were at the precinct police station on Jones Street. "Our strongest cells are here," Morley said with a slight smile.

Thurston was in one of the cells. Jack looked at him through a small peephole and had no difficulty recognizing him. "You have Hogben here too?" he asked.

"Yes," said Morley, "and we're still keeping his lawyer away from him—a pretty high-powered one too. The people behind Hogben must be powerful."

"I'm sure they are," agreed Jack. As they walked through an adjoining area, Morley pointed to a small table with a number of open boxes. "These are the items we took from Kandel, Thurston and Hogben, as well as all Groves's possessions."

They stopped and looked at them. Obviously personal items made up most of the contents. Jack picked up a slip of yellow paper from the box marked "Groves."

Morley eyed him as he did so. "It's a delivery note for lamp oil. Does it have some meaning?"

"Not as far as I know," Jack said.

"The address is a storage depot for a lighting company."

Jack frowned, then sniffed the paper. "Doesn't smell like lamp oil. Have you checked on the company that shipped this stuff?"

"Yes, nothing known about them."

Jack turned the paper to and fro. "It's too creased and dirty to read the address where it was delivered."

"I had it examined under a microscope. With side lighting, we could read the address. It's Jefferson Street."

"Jefferson Street? I thought I knew every street in the city."

"It's only gone under that name recently," Morley said.

"It was previously named after one of our more prominent local politicians, but he was caught with his hand in the city coffers so it had to be changed."

"Ah, yes, now I remember," said Jack. "It's off—"

"It's off Dupont Street."

"Which is exactly where those strange markings were on that map in Windham's office," Jack said triumphantly.

There was a brief silence. Then Morley rapped out, "Come with me."

A nearby office had a large map of San Francisco on one wall. Morley's finger tapped on a tiny street running off Dupont Street. "It's there."

"Have you sent a man there to look at it?"

"No, I haven't."

"Why not?" asked Jack. "Wouldn't it seem a link to Groves?"

"You see where it's located?"

Jack looked at the map again. "Yes, what about it?"

"It's on the edge of Chinatown. There are sensitive political implications there. We seldom interfere. We have to be very careful about making inquiries in Chinatown, especially when a known criminal is involved. Oh, I've asked for a warrant, but the judges are slow and it hasn't come through yet."

"I have a nasty feeling," said Jack, "that we ought not to wait. We should go there right away."

Morley hesitated, then made up his mind. "The cab's still outside. Let's go." He paused. "Do you have a gun?"

"No." They went into an office with a wall cupboard, which Morley unlocked. It was filled with weapons of all kinds. "Any preference?" Morley asked.

Jack selected a Belgian-made pistol, which was compact and short-barreled but a big enough caliber to be deadly. Morley took a .32 Navy Colt. They loaded both guns and took a handful of extra rounds each.

"I'll alert a couple of constables to be in the neighborhood," said Morley, "but maybe we should take someone with us . . . like Stanley Hogben."

The remark took Jack by surprise, but then he chuckled. "Just the man we need. A representative of the government of our great city."

Chapter 33

Stanley Hogben was a surly companion on the ride to Dupont Street. His sojourn in jail had not reduced the color of his complexion and prison food had not yet affected his well-padded frame. He had blustered and complained about being brought out to the cab in handcuffs and given Jack a look, first astonished, then sneering. He had demanded to know where he was being taken, but on receiving no reply lapsed into sullen silence.

The address just around the corner from Dupont Street on Jefferson was fronted by a pair of double doors that were large enough to admit a wagon. Morley found a small door farther down. He knocked very gently but there was no response. He turned to Hogben. "You will be able to confirm that I sought admittance to the premises before entering." He took out a small tool, pressed it in by the lock and twisted. There was a crunch and the door opened.

Morley went in first, then Hogben, then Jack. It was a storage room with a number of empty crates. The area had two exits, a large doorway into another similar chamber and a wooden stairway that led down steeply. "We'll take the stairway," Morley said. Jack looked at Hogben and tried to discern from his face something about Morley's choice, but only the sour expression was there.

The room below was the same. They went through more rooms, finally reaching one that had a number of empty barrels. Jack sniffed at them. "Lamp oil." It was the standard fuel in Chinese lamps and lanterns, both indoor and outdoor, and they consumed large quantities of the stuff. Another staircase led down.

Jack detected a change in Hogben's expression as they descended the rickety wooden stairs. He looked apprehensive. What was he afraid of? Jack wondered. At the next level down, they stopped. Iron bars were fitted into the walls, evidently racks for storage, although tools hung from them now and a workbench was strewn with more of them. The most notable feature, though, was the more than a dozen wooden oil barrels, clustered together. Morley pushed one. It did not move because it was full.

"Do you recall from the map you saw just where we are?" Morley asked Jack quietly.

"I'm pretty sure we are right inside all those crisscrossing lines on the map that I couldn't understand," Jack said. "We're under Chinatown now."

Jack sniffed at one of the barrels, then took the yellow delivery slip from his pocket. "I thought this didn't smell of lamp oil. These are the barrels that were delivered. They don't smell of lamp oil either."

Morley took out the same tool he had used to gain entry and rapped the wooden bung in the top of the barrel. When he had loosened it, he pulled it free. An acrid smell billowed out.

"It's wood alcohol," Jack said.

He and Morley turned to Hogben, who shook his head violently. "I know nothing about this!" he protested.

"I can't imagine what industry in Chinatown would use this amount of alcohol," Morley said.

Jack beckoned him aside. "A Chinese I know and trust asked me recently if I had heard rumors about burning down Chinatown," he said in a low voice because Hogben stood by the barrels, trying to overhear. "This must be where it's planned," Jack went on. "All these wooden structures underground would burn fast from a fire started from all this wood alcohol. The blaze could spread through all Chinatown. Forty thousand Chinese live and work here, in the span of only a few blocks in each direction. Thousands would be trapped underground, with smoke spreading. . . ."

Morley's face was stern. "And look over here." On the bench stood lengths of copper tube and bottles of yellow liquid. "Incendiary detonators. This is Groves's work. He's an expert in arson as well as explosives. It makes sense—one last desperate throw now that the riots didn't work. Spread the word that whites had started a fire to burn Chinatown. It would set Chinese against whites—it would be like a small civil war. This time the governor would be forced to declare martial law and call in the militia."

A door slammed somewhere in the rabbit warren of chambers and stairways. The sound echoed through the stillness. They froze. Jack kept an eye on Hogben but he showed nothing.

After a few moments, Morley murmured, "There must be someone here." The words were no sooner out of his mouth than there came the creak of stairs. Someone was coming up from the lower level.

Morley's pistol covered Hogben. "Don't make a sound!" he warned and herded him into the shadow of the nearest stack of barrels, where Jack joined them.

A figure emerged from the stairway. A burly man with close-cropped hair and a hard face came toward them. In his hands he held coils of some kind. As he came closer, Jack could see what they were. During his experiences prospecting for gold in the Yukon, he had occasion to learn how to use dynamite. The coils were for fuses.

The man was obviously Soapy Groves. He dropped the coils onto the bench with the other materials and was about to go when Hogben made a coughing sound. It was not loud but Groves heard it. One hand still on the coils of fuse wire, he turned his head.

Morley promptly moved out into the open and covered Groves with his pistol. "Put your hands up!" he ordered.

The explosives man hesitated for only the briefest part of a second, then grabbed the coils and flung them at Morley.

They caught him in the face and he staggered back. Groves made a dash for the stairs he had just climbed and Jack, who had not pulled out his gun, flung himself across the room.

He caught Groves around the waist just as he reached the top of the stairway. Groves was heavier by more than twenty pounds, and prison had given him plenty of practice in fighting. He tore loose and lunged again for the stairs. He was four or five steps down when Jack reached down and seized him by the neck, falling to his knees as he did so.

Groves struggled to tear Jack's hands away, taking a couple more steps down, but Jack fell full-length, still holding tight. He was vaguely aware of Morley appearing by his side, trying to swing his pistol at Groves's head, but the explosives expert gave a violent jerk. It tore him free from Jack's grip and Groves went down the stairs, half falling, half stumbling.

Morley reached down and with one hand heaved Jack to his feet. Morley sought to aim the pistol in his other hand but Groves was out of sight already and he hesitated to shoot surrounded by so much wood alcohol.

Jack dusted himself off, then stopped and pointed. "There goes Hogben!"

The councilman was disappearing up the other stairway. Morley shrugged. "Let him go. It's more important to get out of here."

A voice called from below.

"Quickly!" Morley said, and the stairway creaked. Another man was coming up. He stopped halfway and called Groves's name again. Jack pulled out the Belgian pistol and released the safety catch. He and Morley waited. Groves's name was called yet again. Then after a pause of only seconds, footsteps sounded on the stairs and silence followed.

Morley and Jack stood rigid. "He's gone back," Morley said. "I wonder how many others there are." They waited but no sound came. "We need to have more men here,"

Morley said peremptorily. "A full-scale raid is what we need—and fast."

He led the way to the staircase going back up to the next floor when they heard footsteps approaching. The stairs creaked and two men suddenly appeared. Both held pistols. They stopped a few steps down. Jack glanced at the other staircase going down, judging the distance and weighing his chances.

"Don't!" snapped one of the men on the stairs and moved his pistol menacingly.

Morley and Jack still had their weapons in their hands. A gunfight would be a dangerous proposition, thought Jack, and he did not doubt that the same idea was in Morley's mind. Any such notion was quickly dispelled as additional footsteps told them that more men were coming up the other staircase. They were trapped.

With one man ahead of them and a second behind them, Morley and Jack went down the staircase, covered by two pistols after their own weapons had been taken away. Morley had given Jack a slight shake of the head and Jack had to agree reluctantly that discretion was better than a gunfight. The next level down was empty but the next after that was crudely furnished with Spanish-style wooden furniture and rugs on the floor to stem the cold.

Stanley Hogben stood there, a satisfied smile on his face. Jack thought he looked more authoritative, more determined—and more dangerous. Perhaps he had underestimated the councilman. Jack heard Morley's sharp intake of breath, but it was not at the sight of Hogben.

Another man was there, tied to one of the heavy wooden chairs and gagged. It was Windham. He looked grim and pale. A wooden door squeaked and Groves entered. He grinned unpleasantly.

"You've got our prowlers, eh? Well, we all know the penalty for that, don't we?"

"We don't have a lot of time," cut in Hogben, his voice

crisp and commanding. "Have you got those fuses rigged yet?"

"No, I was—"

"Then get them in place and ready to light."

Jack exchanged a glance with Morley. This was sooner than they had expected.

There was noise from one of the stairways; then a man with a Western swagger came down. "Got those two cops from outside." He was obviously one of the Riders of the Rim; they appeared to take care of all the physical aspects of the plan. Jack looked at Morley. He showed no reaction, but Jack knew it must be a blow.

"Tie them up next to the barrels," ordered Hogben. "And make a good job of it," he added, his voice hard. "Then you can come here and put these others with them."

Groves left to do as he was bidden. The two Riders of the Rim remained, guns held loosely. Hogben showed his teeth in a threatening grin. Jack noticed that Windham was moving one arm and struggling to break loose while Hogben's attention was diverted.

"You don't have to do this," Jack told him, wanting to keep Hogben talking. "You can—"

Hogben strode up to him and hit him across the face with the back of his hand. "You young upstart! Think you're going to run for mayor of Oakland, do you?"

"So that's what bothers you," said Jack, his face stinging with pain. "I know—you have your eye on that position, haven't you? Why, I could beat you in an election without even trying."

Hogben raised his hand for another blow, then lowered it. "You won't run in any election," he jeered. " 'Local Writer Dies in Chinatown Fire'—how's that for a headline in the *Chronicle*? Too bad it won't appear. There'll be nothing left—you'll just be one of those missing." A crafty look passed over his features. "You know, we might even arrange it so that it looks as if you started the fire!" With a final glare at Jack, he waved a hand to the two Riders of the Rim and pointed at Windham. "Take him first."

Jack glanced at Windham again. He had hardly had time to figure out what the businessman was doing here. Meanwhile, the businessman was still twisting one arm and might be almost loose.

Jack could see Morley looking at Windham. He might well be having similar thoughts. He strove to think of some way to stall, to delay. He did not want to think about being down here when a dozen barrels of alcohol started a fire that would engulf all of Chinatown.

Chapter 34

Hogben went off into an adjoining chamber, then came back a few minutes later, just as the Rider was returning. "Now take him—make sure the ropes are good and tight!" He grinned wickedly at Jack.

Upstairs, Jack found Windham and the two constables securely tied to the iron bars, a few feet away from the wooden barrels. One constable was barely conscious and sagged against the wall, eyes closed, breathing heavily. The other watched as Jack was tied to another bar, just far enough away that neither could help the other.

When the Rider had left, the constable asked curiously, "What's in the barrels?"

"Alcohol," Jack said. The constable was red-faced and bulbous-nosed. His eyes lit up at Jack's answer and he eyed the barrels with a new respect.

The ropes tying Jack's wrists to the iron rail were new, thin but strong. He struggled against them but it was useless. They were tied by experts, one arm well away from the other and his ankles were bound tightly too. Harry Houdini, Jack thought, where are you now that I really need you?

How would the master escapologist get out of this? he wondered. He wished that he had been able to be backstage when one of the master's escape tricks had been performed. He might have learned something that could save his life. But speculation like that was purposeless, and there seemed no way of escape from the bonds.

"Did they give you a rough time?" asked Jack.

Windham nodded. "They wanted to know if I had come here alone. I told them I had come with one of our clerks but I had sent him back. They didn't believe me at first." He winced as he tried to move. "Did you and Morley come with these two constables?"

"Yes," Jack said.

"He has more men outside, I suppose. I hope so—we don't have long. Do they know when to move in?"

"Morley didn't tell me about any others," said Jack. "I hope you're right, though—when that fuse is lit, we're finished." He felt a tremor at the sound of his own words. He had faced death before and hadn't enjoyed it. Most of the times he had had a fighting chance. This was galling, being tied like this. He struggled against the ropes with a furious burst of determination. "What kind of treatment do you suppose Morley is getting?" he gasped.

Sounds came from the stairs and Groves moved into sight. He carried a coil of fuse wire and an incendiary detonator. A leather sack full of tools was over his shoulder. He gave Jack another glare, but his professionalism had apparently taken command and he concentrated on his task of setting his diabolical tools in place. The semiconscious police constable groaned and stirred but did not open his eyes. Groves did not even look at him.

He was still intent on his work when Hogben came in. The first thing he did was inspect Jack's ropes and make sure they were still secure. He walked over to Groves, said something to him, and Groves nodded. Hogben watched as Groves completed setting the fuses and the detonator. The two of them looked critically at their handiwork and Groves checked the contacts of the detonator one more time. He nodded, satisfied.

"Shall I light it?" Groves asked.

"Not yet," Hogben said. He had a self-satisfied smirk on his face. He went to the staircase, leaned out and called, "Bring him up."

A pistol-carrying Rider came up with Morley ahead of him. The police captain had a smear of blood on his cheek and he carried himself stiffly, though his face was impassive. The Rider tied him securely to another of the cast-iron bars in the wall. Hogben watched attentively, then tested the bonds. He nodded and he and the Rider went back down the stairs.

When they had gone, Jack asked Morley, "Are you all right?"

Morley nodded, but even that motion seemed to cause him distress. "One of those fellows is an expert in inflicting pain without leaving any marks," he said hoarsely. He moved cautiously and winced. "I may have a broken rib or two but nothing serious. How about you two?"

"I don't think I have any broken bones," Windham said. "But I'm sore all over."

"I guess they don't think I know anything worth torturing to get," said Jack.

"What Hogben mainly wanted to know from me," said Morley, "was whether the two constables were all we had brought. I said yes but I told him I didn't know if others might have been alerted."

"I shouldn't even be here." Windham sounded annoyed with himself. "Some questions came up about suspicious activity in bank-owned property here. I made inquiries but could learn nothing. I foolishly came here myself with a clerk, but I sent him away. One of these Riders of the Rim caught me and dragged me through this rabbit warren. I was amazed to see Hogben here. Funny," he went on, "Hogben seems to have changed—he's become more forceful, more dominating."

"I had that impression too," said Jack.

"So did I," Morley contributed. "I even wondered—well, I wondered if Hogben might be Glass."

"I doubt if he's capable," Windham dissented.

In our position, it doesn't matter, Jack felt like saying. Much more important was to get out of there before the fuses were lit, and he went back to trying to loosen the ropes binding his wrists.

One of them seemed to give slightly, but when Jack renewed his efforts, the rope merely tightened further. "I can't make any progress on these ropes," Jack admitted. "The constable looks like a strong fellow. I wonder if he can."

The policeman struggled until his red complexion turned fiery, and he finally gave up, out of breath. "Can't do it," he gasped. "They don't give an inch."

"Keep trying!" Morley said grimly. "We've all got to keep trying!"

It was hard to keep track of time but Jack supposed that barely fifteen minutes had gone by when Hogben and Groves came back. Groves had some large industrial matches in his hand and Jack recognized them as the kind used in mining—waterproof and inextinguishable once they were lit. Groves struck one and lit the fuse. He and Hogben stood watching it—Hogben with ghoulish glee, Groves with a professionally critical gaze to make sure it was burning properly. Satisfied, they stepped back.

"For God's sake, Morley!" Windham cried out. "Where are your men?"

The one constable was still unconscious. The other had been following the scene with increasing disbelief. He yelled out, "They're going to burn us! Somebody do something!"

Morley turned his head to look at him, then at Windham. His expression infinitely sad, he just shook his head.

"All right, Groves," Stanley Hogben said. "Cut him loose." Groves nodded, took out a large pocketknife and slashed through the ropes at Windham's wrists and ankles.

Jack and Morley stared in amazement.

Windham massaged his wrists as he stepped free. "Maybe this charade wasn't necessary," he said, "but I didn't want to take the chance of a bunch of policemen bursting in here. There are no others, only these two." He motioned to the fuse, which was burning steadily. "We'll leave you with this."

"So my original guess was right," Morley said in a resigned voice. "You are Glass."

"I was surprised when you said, 'One of these Riders of the Rim caught me,'" Jack said conversationally. "I wondered how you knew that's what he was. It's not a thing you'd expect a bank officer to know."

"Bad company for bank people to keep," Morley added.

"And then there's that photograph in your office," Jack said slowly. "It's coming back to me now. . . ."

Windham's face was darkening. "Prowling around my office!" He stopped, aware that threats were pointless with that fuse burning steadily. "You've been a constant annoyance, nosing into affairs that don't concern you. Burning Chinatown was a last move that I didn't expect to have to resort to—and I wouldn't have had to if you and those girls and Houdini hadn't interfered."

"That smokescreen you put up about buying up music halls had me fooled," Morley said sadly. "Until then I was getting increasingly suspicious of you, but that persuaded me I was mistaken."

Intent on his own thoughts, Jack was hardly listening. "I knew that face next to you in the photograph was familiar," he went on, with nothing to lose. "The new governor . . . of course!"

"Photograph?" Morley called out.

"Yes," Jack said. "Windham and the new governor, classmates from Yale. Would you suppose that will make it easier to get the militia called out and martial law declared?"

Morley fought against his bonds in furious reaction, having no other means of recourse. Exhausted, he stopped, realizing the futility.

Hogben was eyeing the sizzling fuse with barely concealed alarm. "We'd better go," he said, urgency in his voice. Windham still looked about to unleash his fury on Jack, but he thought better of it and controlled himself. He turned and walked to the staircase, anger still in his motions. Hogben hurried after him and the sound of their footsteps on the wooden stairs died away.

All was silence—except the sputtering fuse.

"How long do you think that fuse is set for?" Morley's question cut into the silence.

"I'd guess twenty minutes," Jack said. "About five of them have gone."

The men fought against their ropes, and gasps and grunts were all that could be heard. One by one, they stopped, gulping for breath.

"It's no good," said Morley bitterly. "I can't budge mine."

"They know how to tie ropes," panted the constable.

"This floor's dusty," said Morley suddenly, "and our feet are only tied together. We can still move them. Can we kick up enough dust to put out the spark?"

It was the remotest of chances, Jack knew. A good-quality fuse could not be extinguished that easily, but he was not about to discount any idea. They all began to kick their bound feet, trying to raise a dust cloud.

A few minutes convinced them it was hopeless. They sagged against their bonds. Jack tried to resist looking at the fuse but it was impossible. He guessed that they had ten minutes or less left. The silence was total. Everyone must have vacated the building.

A hoarse chuckle sounded. The captives stared at one another. Where had it come from? It came again, an almost unearthly sound, not quite human, not exactly amused.

Chapter 35

They looked at each other. Jack thought that madness was creeping in from the unendurable stress of knowing they were only minutes away from certain death.

The chuckle came again. Then all three of them saw the source at the same time. A figure had appeared near the top of the upper staircase.

It wore robes of light green and white. They were not ceremonial, but more like those seen on the streets of Chinatown, worn by well-to-do Chinese on a social or family occasion. A high collar partly obscured the face, which was fat and blubbery with protruding eyes. A yellow hand dabbed a lace handkerchief at the eyes. Thick lips bulged pink and Jack recognized How Chew Fat as he had first seen him.

Jack felt relief flooding over him. The note that he had had Noah deliver to How Chew Fat had found its destination. It had confirmed that the Chinaman's suspicions regarding the burning of Chinatown were correct.

Jack saw that Morley and the constable were looking at this apparition with uncertainty. He wanted to call out and reassure them but thought better of it and held his tongue.

"Stop that damned fuse burning and cut us loose!" shouted Morley.

"It is not Chinese custom to interfere in white man's activities," said the high-pitched voice with that chopped cadence.

"Custom be damned!" Morley yelled. "This is a Chinese

activity now. If that fuse isn't cut, all Chinatown will go up
in flames!"

A few seconds passed and the figure of the Chinaman did
not move. Then he came slowly down the stairs and walked
toward them.

"Stop there!" called another voice. "Not another step or
I'll shoot!" The authoritative voice of Robert Windham
came from the top of the stairs. He appeared with a pistol in
his hand.

His face was gray with anger. "I had a feeling about you.
You people always know more than is good for you. I had
to come back and make sure at the last minute that no one
was interfering in my plans." He aimed the pistol at How
Chew Fat.

The Chinaman's reaction was strange. How Chew Fat
raised his right hand slowly in front of him. Windham's pistol jerked, and How Chew Fat opened his fingers to show
that his hand was empty. The hand rose higher, past waist
level, and continued to rise. When it was at shoulder height,
the fingers and the thumb contracted. Only the forefinger
remained, and it was pointed directly at Windham.

Windham's finger tightened on the trigger. There was a
dull thump. The silent tableau made a bizarre scene in the
dusty chamber. Jack, Morley and the constable gazed in astonishment.

Windham's head seemed to tilt. Then his knees bent
slowly and his whole body sagged. His arm fell, still holding the pistol, and the banker sprawled full-length on the
floor.

The thin black handle of a throwing knife protruded from
his back and Morley gasped. Jack followed his gaze and
saw at the top of the stairs a young man dressed in somber
gray Chinese clothing and with a short pigtail. His right
hand disappeared inside his robes.

How Chew Fat said something in Chinese and the young
man went to the fuse, studied it for an agonizingly long moment, then took out another knife. He carefully chopped the

fuse wire, pulled the cut ends well apart and stamped on the fuse till it had not only stopped burning but stopped smoking too.

He used the knife to cut the trio free. While they were rubbing their limbs and the constable was trying to revive his colleague, the Chinaman ran lithely up the stairs and out of sight. It was only then that Jack noticed How Chew Fat had disappeared.

Chapter 36

At the Midway Plaisance, the last show was just concluding. Jack could hardly believe that so much had happened in fewer than twenty-four hours. He knew he should feel tired, but weariness was pushed aside at the elation of having avoided certain death with such a small margin of time.

He had left Morley with the task of assembling a crew to dispose of the deadly barrels, sending the constable for help and getting attention for his still-unconscious colleague. A hunt for Hogben and Groves would be under way, and with two of their hideouts closed, Morley was confident of tracking them down quickly.

The audience was as wildly enthusiastic as ever and Belle was called back for encore after encore. Jack found Flo watching from a corner table, and she jumped up to drag him over as soon as she saw him. "No room for another chair," she said over the applause. "Take mine. I'll sit on your knee." She did so, and with one hand on his cheek, surveyed his face. "No marks, I see. Good, you've been staying out of trouble."

"More or less," Jack said. "It's all over, Flo."

Her face lit up. The roar of the crowd surged high as Belle swept back onto the stage yet again. "No more attempts to steal Belle's ruby?" Flo asked.

"No. It's all over."

* * *

Later, in Belle's dressing room, champagne was flowing despite the Broadway star's determination to stick to seltzer water. After shedding her costume, Belle donned a silk gown decorated with scenes that perhaps only Jack and Flo recognized as being from the Kama Sutra.

The crowd in the room overflowed into the corridor. Newcomers struggled to get in; others struggled to get out. Eventually, Jack found himself face-to-face with Belle. It was, in fact, more breast-to-chest and Belle was doing nothing to reduce that contact.

"You missed my show tonight," Belle said accusingly.

"I've been busy," Jack said, aware that every movement by either of them was more arousing.

"Doing what?"

"Well, writing, among other things."

"Writing!" Belle exploded.

"I'm working on a novel," Jack explained. "I wanted a heroine who was strong yet tender, dominant yet passionate, practical yet sensual."

"Anyone I know?" Belle asked, snuggling even closer.

"I call her Frona Welse in the book."

"Will everybody who reads it know it's really me?"

"Not everybody," Jack said. "You have to be seen to be believed."

"Mmm," Belle purred, liking that idea. "What else have you been doing for me?"

"Protecting your ruby. That's what I was hired for, isn't it?"

"That—and other things," Belle said, her sultry eyes not leaving his.

"Well, I've protected it. The danger's over. You don't have to worry anymore—not in San Francisco anyway."

Her eyes widened mockingly. "You mean you want to come with me to St. Louis and protect me there?"

"St. Louis?" Jack said contemptuously. "They don't know anything about crime in St. Louis. You won't have a thing to worry about there. You'll be as safe as in a cathedral."

"Me?" said Belle, batting her long lashes. "What about my ruby?"

"You never did tell me where you keep it," Jack said.

"You never tried to find it," Belle pouted.

"But it's safe?"

"Why don't we go somewhere and find out?"

"Somewhere? Where? Anyway, didn't you say they were all phonies?" Jack persisted.

"Maybe they are but I'm not," Belle said provocatively.

At that moment, a voice could just be heard slicing through the din of conversation. "Mr. Jack London! Mr. Jack London! You're urgently needed! Official business!"

Jack's eyes met Belle's. "Something important," Jack murmured. "I have to go."

"I'll still be here," said Belle softly.

Jack forced his way through the crowd. As he expected, he encountered Flo near the door. She grabbed his hand and pulled him outside. "Did I sound convincing?"

"You said it was urgent, the need."

"It certainly is," said Flo, who tried opening doors until she found an empty room.

The brass fixtures around Luna's bar gleamed from their daily polishing, the dark wood panels shone and the potted plants looked healthy as Jack walked in the next day.

Ambrose Bierce was already at one end of the bar, Sazerac in hand. Two men were down at the opposite end, deep in conversation.

Bierce preened his luxuriant mustache. "Well, young man, I got your message. You have a story for me, eh?"

"I don't know how much of it you will want to print," Jack said, ordering a schooner of beer.

"I'll probably need more than one column if even half of the stories I hear trickling in are true," said Bierce.

Jack took a handful of pickled oysters and some fried

shrimp as Bierce eyed him expectantly. When the bartender brought the beer, Jack took a long swallow. Setting the schooner down on the bar, Jack said, "Here's what happened. . . ."

He would have made a good reporter. His memory was sharp and he kept his account factual but vivid. Bierce interrupted briefly to clarify a point here and there but he listened attentively until Jack had finished.

"This Chinaman? Who was he?"

"He didn't introduce himself," Jack said carefully.

"Do you think he was already aware that some skullduggery was going on in that place?"

"Evidently," Jack said.

"He didn't stay to explain, you say."

"No."

"So we may never know who he was."

Jack was drinking beer but he managed a slight shake of the head. Bierce looked at him shrewdly, then took a sip of Sazerac.

"The police picked up that explosives man, Groves, at the railroad station," Bierce said conversationally. "He was wearing a false beard but they spotted him."

"What about Hogben?"

Bierce shrugged. "They haven't got him yet, but it's only a matter of time."

"It was a near thing," Jack said. "When the riots caused by the factions supporting Houdini and Paradino petered out, the attempt to burn Chinatown so that furious Chinese would be up in arms against white San Francisco nearly succeeded. What do you think would have happened then, Ambrose?"

"Martial law would have been declared, as you suggested. Oh, breaking the strike would have been the first consequence of that, no doubt about it. And that would have been a major achievement for the Big Three."

"You're convinced they're behind this?"

"Of course. They never expose themselves—they never

descend from their lofty thrones on Mount Olympus. They are strictly string-pullers."

Jack agreed, but he liked to provoke Bierce as far as possible. He always learned more that way. "Surely they've pulled enough strings already to have given them control over the port of San Francisco, most of the vessels going in and out of it, the waterways leading to it and even the railroads. What more can they want?"

"Since they failed in their attempt to have a canal built across Nicaragua, and as there are no more railroads to be built, the Big Three want to tighten their grip on our city. Acquiring the music halls through Windham—they always work through some intermediary—would be a first small step. Using Lem Tullamore as a blind was smart too. It was a convenient front for Windham's real activities, but perhaps it was more than that. It could have been the first phase of a real attempt to acquire those places. With the city under martial law, the opportunities would be immense. San Francisco is a bonanza of which they still have only a part. They are greedy beyond belief. They want all of it."

"But what would they actually do?"

"They could control tariffs and taxes. They could reassess property values. They could increase interest rates. They could set embargoes and trade barriers. They could cancel contracts and award others. They could refinance their own debts. Jack, they would get their fingers into every pie in the city."

"That wouldn't last though," Jack argued. "The president would eventually lift martial law."

"Poof!" Bierce exclaimed. "That would take time, and by then the Big Three would have gained virtual control of the city. Authority would revert to Sacramento, where most of the state government is in the pay of the Big Three already."

"You may be right," Jack conceded.

"Remember Rudyard Kipling spent a lot of time and ef-

fort investigating their activities for the *New York Sun* and
the *London Times*? He concluded that these are the three
most powerful men in the world. Remember his words in
the *Times*? He wrote, 'This is plunder on a scale not seen
since the Middle Ages.' "

Bierce turned to wave to someone over Jack's shoulder.
"Ah, here he is. I invited him to come and say good-bye to
you. He doesn't drink but we can find a sarsaparilla for
him."

It was Harry Houdini. Once again, he wore a suit with a
certain unease, and Jack thought he would only feel comfortable when wearing the costume of a stage magician. He
shook hands with Bierce and Jack.

"So you're leaving us already," Bierce chided him. "You
don't like our fair city!"

"It is a dangerous place," Houdini said with a slight
shudder.

Bierce laughed along with Jack. "You have yourself
blindfolded and handcuffed, sealed into a steel casket, then
lowered beneath the waves," said Bierce, "and you call San
Francisco dangerous!"

Houdini joined them in the laughter, but his was less than
halfhearted. He seldom demonstrated much of a sense of
humor, Jack noted, but he liked the man nevertheless.

"Did you hear, Ambrose," Jack asked, "about the time
Harry and I were locked in a completely dark cellar with an
escape-proof lock on the door?"

Bierce looked from one to the other. "What kind of an
act was that?"

"No act. It was serious," Jack assured him. "I'll let Harry
explain it. I don't know how he did it anyway. Besides, I
have to go. I have an appointment with a lady. We have
front-table seats for Belle Conquest—one of her final performances."

"Yes." Bierce nodded. "I hear she is leaving town too."

"Madam Paradino has already gone," Houdini said with
a satisfied smirk.

"So we'll never know what the dear departed have in store for us," said Bierce with a sniff.

"You will never know that from Madam Paradino," Houdini said derisively.

"Time for my exit," Jack said, finishing his beer and shaking hands with both of them. "Harry, you'll soon be the most famous escapologist in the world. Forget the madam and concentrate on that. Ambrose, keep up your quixotic attack on the windmills—you are probably the only man in the world those three really fear."

Both watched him leave. "An extraordinary young man," said Bierce. "He is destined to be a greater writer than I ever could be—thanks to my help, of course. Now, Harry, what do you want me to say about Eulalia Paradino in my column tomorrow? How does she fake that trick, the one where . . ."

Author's Note

Jack London was a real person. Ambrose Bierce, Little Egypt, Martin Beck, Carrie Nation, James McParland, Richard Harding Davis, Charles Crocker, Bret Harte, and Stephen Crane were all real too and Jack London knew them or was acquainted with them.

Harry Houdini was such a close friend of Jack London that, when London died, Houdini hurried from New York to California to be present in order to read the eulogy at the funeral. Belle Conquest and Eulalia Paradino are based on two prominent women who may be recognizable but whose names have been changed for various reasons.

All of the bars, saloons, and music halls mentioned were active at that time. The plot is fictional and a few minor chronological adjustments have been made in order to improve continuity. No dates are used though the time setting is clearly at the turn of the last century.

Don't miss Jack London's
next action-packed and adventurous mystery
by Peter King

"Jack London is perfect for the role of sleuth
because of the great author's lifestyle, which is
cleverly intertwined into the plot."
—*Midwest Book Review*

Coming Soon from Signet Mystery!

PETER KING

First in a "Dazzling"*
New Series

THE JEWEL OF
THE NORTH

This ingenious new series features Jack London, the legendary author of *The Call of the Wild*, in a mystery as thrilling as his fiction.

"A tale of high adventure and mystery worthy of Jack London himself." —Stuart M. Kaminsky*

"Historical mysteries don't come any better than this."
—John Lutz

0-451-20386-6

To order call: 1-800-788-6262

S434/King